Harutu Woman

Harutu Woman

Paloma Zozaya Gorostiza

Victorina Press
www.victorinapress.com

Translated by Juan Julian Caicedo from the novel in Spanish,
Redención, by Paloma Zozaya Gorostiza.
The right of Paloma Zozaya Gorostiza to be identified as
author of this work has been asserted by her in accordance
with the Copyright, Designs and Patents Act 1988.

Typesetting and Layout: Jorge Vasquez
Cover Design: Triona Walsh

Cover image: Los Caballos, 1938 by María Izquierdo
By kind permission of Dr. Alberto Carmona, representative
of Sucesión de María Izquierdo.

British Library Cataloguing in Publication Data
A catalogue record for this book is available from the
British Library.
ISBN: 978-1-8380360-8-9

Typeset in 12pt Garamond
Printed and bound in Great Britain by 4edge Ltd.

For Antonio

For the children of Central America,
that they may no longer have to abandon their
motherlands in search of a better life.

And
for Olvin Cloter, In Memoriam

There's a right-side-up and an upside-down to everything

Hati

La Blanca

"What's gotten into you now, thinking just the two of us can bury the mare on our own?" he asked.

"Why not," his woman answered. "Or else, are you up to go kicking this flood all the way into town just to look for help? Besides, with a deluge like this one there's nobody gonna want to come out here to The Bush. Let's go bury her. You and me, we'll bury La Blanca!"

Felipe looked at Selene with a mixture of admiration and mockery before he took off to get his shovel.

The rainstorm had finally stopped the previous evening. It lasted for four days, started with a shower of thick, fitful drops that grew in strength till it turned into a merciless barrage of shrapnel hitting the roof sheathings and, after a few hours, ended up numbing their senses. Felipe, as it would happen every time it rained, fell prey to an irrepressible urge to wander under the cloudburst, from The Bush to the beach, from the beach to The Bush and back again every day the same: he'd put on his hooded poncho, the rubber boots, and on walking through the kitchen grab a bite to eat. He'd return in the evening and without getting undressed, cocoon himself in a sheet and sleep motionless, until the next day.

Side by side with Ariel – Felipe's child who was

1

around seven years old by then – Selene went about removing furniture from the kitchen, all in all keeping the house clean and tidy. It was something that gave her the illusion of having at least a bit of control, even when the water reached their knees come the floods, as it did without fail every year. On that ocassion she made sure to take out pots, skillets, little wooden boats, tools, figurines made with coconut shells and tiny mahogany vessels – Felipe's early attempts at woodcarving. She was once and again amazed at the capacity of objects to reproduce and move about with a will of their own. "Like termites in the rafters, or like thoughts," she told herself now, while scrubbbing the shelves one by one with a disinfectant concoction of her own making, a blend of linseed oil, rosemary and camphor extracts. Once done with that, she polished with a rag and rearranged each and every one of the things that the kid kept handing her.

Even though he was by habit a quiet child whose Spanish was not the best, Ariel cut through the silence. With an aged feeling that turned his sweet face into that of an old man, the little one gathered some courage and told his stepmother with an urgent tone: "Selene, I've been here a long while already, it's about time now for me to go and join my cousins. Over there we used to sleep all of us together in one bed, we were really together."

She felt something like the crackling body of a huge dark moth fluttering above her heart as she realized how, during the four years since Ariel arrived in the little farm, the boy hadn't stopped mourning the separation from his cousins, all of them girls; and how his sorrow was now probably deepened by the absence of all the other children who hadn't been able to reach The Bush because of the rainstorm. Dismayed by the solitude she sensed in Ariel, Selene got up from the tiny stool where she'd been seated, wiping things, putting them away, over and over, and she grabbed the kid by his armpits. From where he was, settled on the floor, Ariel unfurled himself and climbed up the woman's body using legs and arms as though climbing a coconut tree, until he could dive into the lavender fragrance that flowed from her neck. She rested her head on his tight, smooth curls for a moment and, after laying a long kiss on his cheek, let him rest again on his little feet. With her hands on his shoulders, she looked into his eyes, two black cherries crowning high cheekbones, just like his father's – though Ariel had mahogany skin while Felipe's was more like ebony – and she promised him that she would talk to his dad, even though she wasn't sure she could convince him.

Whichever way Selene tried to explain to Ariel why it was better for him to stay – "You've got your own room here, your horses, your land" – it was all in vain.

In an attempt perhaps to stress how important it was for him to return to his mother's village, while transfiguring himself with striking gestures the child started telling her of a dream, making it all feel as though some premonition should be read in its symbols: "Selene, last night I dreamed there was a little monkey perched on a fence..." and he mimed the monkey's character, stretched torso, tiny hands crossed on his chest. "He was dressed in red and blue. I was sitting next to him and I knew that he was dangerous. Papa was wandering

3

around The Bush with his machete, but he couldn't see me."

At that very moment, the kitchen door swung wide open and Felipe stormed in with his soaked mane smelling of rain and sand. Battered by boundlessness and winds, his eyes turned a darker shade of black as his pupils got dilated while his sight adjusted to the dimness of the room. Ariel was startled and immediately went quiet. Selene fixed her almond-shaped eyes on Felipe, reading him, gauging his disquietude – the collective fantasy of the inhabitants of Redención: a discovery of some foam-covered, plastic-wrapped bale of cocaine abandoned to the waves by dealers fleeing the authorities, and hurled on the shore by the sea – something that would transform their lives, blessing or curse. She closed her eyes for a moment then, thinking, "God help us," and she went back to dusting knick-knacks. Felipe went straight to the stove, uncovered the big pot that was quietly bubbling over the fire; poured a ladle of beans into a small platter and sat on the hammock to eat, though with not much of an appetite. The whining voice of the hammock's ropes fixed on the rafters kept the silence at bay; but they went quiet after a few spoonfuls. Felipe got back on his feet, laid his half-eaten food on the table and covered it with another dish; then he took off his poncho and boots and disappeared behind the living room door.

Selene and the kid spent four days making up chores so as not to succumb to the hypnotic power of the rain, which nonetheless would end up mutedly sapping their energy. When it stopped raining, the house let out a sigh. Its residents stretched their bodies and started picking stuff off the floors; that because, when the rain stops, well that's when, noiseless and gloomy, the flood turns up. The three of them presently sat on the stoop under the porch just to see it make its appearance. It was just then they realized that La Blanca hadn't gone with the rest of the horses that Felipe had set free to go look for higher, dry grounds. She was standing nearly still, crestfallen under the mango tree, avoiding her little colt in need of suckling. Her dismay seemed disproportionate to the small wound woozing on her forehead – the result of her foal's hoof striking her. The little colt, Gavilán, had been born not long before the bad weather hit. Ariel and Selene had just come back from the village one evening at sunset, when amber lights brightened the pink plumes of the grasses, and came upon the newly born bay foal, by now emancipated from gravity, drifting and wafting around his mother. La Blanca was grazing, contented. "How can so little time change everything," Selene wondered.

"You take Gavilán to the village, all he's doing here is messing nonstop with his mom," Felipe ordered his child. "And take these here dry coconuts to your grandma," he capped off the order, pursing his lips to point at a bunch of coconuts on the floor.

"Yes pa," the little one responded, already jumping off to go get the rope; then, with the supple rhythm of his budding little body, but with an old man's knowhow, he lassoed Gavilán and turned back to offer a formal gooodbye:

"*Ayó*, pa. *Ayó*, Selene." And without missing a beat he threw the coconuts over his shoulder, spinned on his heel and hit the road.

"Hurry up, son, and don't you stop, even if your pals catch up with you; it'll be getting dark in a couple of hours," Father hollered when the kid was just about to start crossing the bridge.

As Ariel walked away pulling the colt, that was by now so much taller than him, Selene kept her eyes on the boy, her gaze carrying the hug she hadn't been able to give him. Gavilán's distressed, strident neighs, as he was being torn away from his mother, pierced her heart like darts and went on digging through her bosom even after the distance had silenced him. A deep vertical crease materialized in a flash between Felipe's eyebrows and he got lost in his own thoughts.

"I can tell by now what it is you're loooking for, Felipe, but ... what would you do if you found it?" she said after a while, having finally plucked up courage to let out the apprehension that had kept her nailed for days already. Felipe cleared his throat as though he was about to say something, but he remained silent and the furrow between his eyebrows got deeper, like a cliff, a trench between him and the world. His silence fell iron-like upon Selene's chest. "Think of all the people you know who've died because they got involved with that crap; the latest one, Coral – she, that was so close to us. How are you gonna start believing now ... ah, how can anybody live with anything like that? What happened shoulda been enough to make you see that one just doesn't play around with the devil."

Felipe was taken aback as Coral's presence broke into his memory – but not in the same way that Selene expected: he still could not shake off the intense and mixed feelings he'd had for that woman and, just over

6

a year after the tragedy, those had not stopped growing. With Coral he'd felt loving warmth and jealousy at once; oh well – to call a spade a spade – he liked her a lot, and then the more he got to like her, the more jealous he became of Selene and Coral's closeness; it twisted his innards to see that they shared a space where he, as a man, was not allowed to enter. From the moment she had died, Coral had become an unnamable phantom in the house out in The Bush. That was the reason why Selene mentioned her on that occassion: to drill into Felipe's brain the gravity of the venture he was taking on. But all she'd achieved was to spur his anger: "It's just like you to think you have the right to get involved in any of my business, to go check out all of your man's moves," he barked, hardened, bent on stopping whatever his woman said from entering his head. "Who ever said the woman has to have her hands in every single thing?" And he kept berating her: "Besides, what makes you think that you can read my mind, that you know more than anyone? Oh, but here you're *wrong*," he wrapped it up, sowing the seeds of doubt.

Selene believed him more often than not, and at times she would even end up reproaching herself for having been a stupid fool when Felipe, with his magician's touch, rearranged reality and molded it as a potter shapes clay. But this once her heart wouldn't calm down; she got up, entered the house, looked for the little case where they kept the grass, and fixed herself a little something to smoke. Doing that would always shave the edge off her, take the sting out and dry the weeping that now swirled in her throat. She returned to the porch, sat next to Felipe and offered him the little cigarette, the matches. For just a moment he looked at that perfectly rolled joint with an annoyed gaze but finally put a light to the thing and took a couple of deep drags before handing it back to her. They polished it off real quick, that reefer stick. Then it was Felipe's turn: without a word, as always, he got up, rushed into the house, reappeared in the porch, sat down, lit up, inhaled, and turned the doobie over to Selene in a ritual they both knew by heart already. They didn't exchange gazes nor a single word during the time it took them to be done with the second spliff.

Selene felt her body loosen and her mind entered a realm of peace. Everything around her took on a vibrant hue and the sky shimmered like polished steel. She noticed the absence of the golden orioles' mad song – a cry that's heard when they return in flocks to their nests; not so much animal talk but rather something close to brassy, with an initial snap followed by ringing streamers – and that lack of noise filled her with amazement, yes, nothing could be heard but silence that afternoon. Then Felipe threw another dart, snappy: "So you really think it's day-to-day normal for me to be sitting here with me lady smoking weed?" he said. "We're right screwed, you 'n me, woman."

At that, Selene felt the sting of rage but held back, letting her chin rest on her hands, her hands on her knees, and her gaze fixed on La Blanca out there; still she kept check of her mate from the corner of one eye. More than once she was just about to start talking – words rounding up over her tongue, arranging themselves, gathering strength – but right away her heart would get the shivers, like a leaf, and she'd fall back

8

into muteness. It was then that, wayward yet punctual, the water began to well through the swamped ground just like sweat out of one's pores. It came on fast and swirling, covered the roots of the nance tree and soon enough touched the foot of the cohune palm next to the kitchen. At that, Selene and Felipe had to obbey the signals, so they took up to the roof the few things that still remained scattered on the floor of the house. When that task was completed it was beginning to get dark, so, once again speechless they went to bed. They wrapped themselves in separate sheets and spent a fitful night, immersed in something like a twilight sleep.

A Fate-Bound Place

When Selene returned to Redención, now as a teacher, the century was coming to its end. It was the third time that circumstance would bring her back to that hamlet. Her first visit had been on a Summer vacation, when she spotted some tour agency in the small seaside town of Puerto and went for the one available activity that day: a kayak ride down Río Manzanares, the same river that – too implausible for her to even imagine then – would end up being her home's neighbor in a future day. On that occassion she had gone through Redención in the cabin of the small van that belonged to the Caribeña Tours guide. For her second stay she had gone as a last-minute volunteer enrollee in an education project. Only this third and last visit had been the upshot of her own volition, a mapped-out action.

In the arrivals hall, crammed with anxious gazes perched on outstretched necks, flower bouquets and embraces, awaiting her and holding a signboard, Señorita Selene, there was the man *Paciencia*, his face as kind as his name – Patience – and his curly hair gone totally white.

"Allow me please," he said, picking up her suitcase, and at once leading her to his car, an ancient yet shimmery Ford. Selene took the back seat; she wanted a quiet ride. The strawberry scent from the figurine hanging off the rearview mirror jabbed her nose, and she oppened the window with a mechanical gesture.

"Does it bother you?" she asked Paciencia. "It's just that I'd like to enjoy the warm air; where I come from it's been really cold," she justified herself. "See, the summer's warm in Guatemala City, but by year's end, like now, the cold starts getting to you." It came to her that she was speaking a bit too much, starting a conversation she didn't wish to have. So, with that said, she rested her head on the back of the chair and closed her eyes. Paciencia's voice sounded distant now: "Not at all Ms. Selene, whatever you wish ..."

Selene sensed her body slackening as her skin and hair soaked up the steamy air. She saw herself as an air plant, a swelling orchid traveling in space, its roots afloat in the wind, heading for a new tree. An intense emotion moistened her eyes, made her skin tingle. Then for a good while she just revelled in the simple pleasure of abandoning her body's weight to the coziness of the chair, while the breeze – as it crossed the window with the same beats it sweeps the sky – was getting rid of everything she had left behind: her city with its apocalyptic violence laid out in concrete squares; the anguish borne of a hopeless relationship; her unavailing job in a private school, attempting to educate kids for whom the only thing that mattered was being up to date with the latest fashions and gadgets, of which they had more than enough. Back there, in her hometown, Selene had come to feel an actual identity, a oneness with the plants that struggled to survive in the balcony planters of her apartment, in the dusty and gang-infested Zona Uno. Her mother made a scene when she moved to that neighborhood, to which Selene responded that she'd chosen to live a life free of hypocrisy. She was indeed trying to make sense of her life when an awful hurricane devastated the neighboring country, which straddled that narrow land strip between the Atlantic and the Pacific.

"My homeland is all of this Maya world, borders are bogus, we're all one single people," she announced when she picked up and started on her way across the border. To those friends who questioned her plan she'd answer, "It's to make myself useful, to turn my life around."

Then there was her distraught mother's plea: "Why is it every time there is a cataclysm you've got to run toward the brouhaha, just when everybody's running away from it?" But Selene had made up her mind; she was already over forty and felt an overriding need to find a new direction. Not even for an instant did she reconsider her decision to depart, a decision that some of her friends, the least of them, qualified as courageous, while the majority saw it as plain foolish.

The way the car hopped over the potholes that the recent hurricane had left on the pavement felt to her like nothing but a pleasant swaying. As she opened her eyes, she saw Paciencia's own reflected on the mirror, fixed on the highway – a thin asphalt band divided down its center by a yellow line. By now they were leaving the cane-field zone that surrounded the airport. They kept going for miles upon miles of rotund-green slopes, always crowned by dark though rainless clouds – because shower-bearing clouds rise out of the sea only. They went past villages smelling of smoke and tortillas on woodfire, houses humble and yet opulent in color and bouganvilleas, children with worm-ridden, distended bellies playing in dirt roads, emaciated dogs prowling the greasy fritanga stands set up on both sides of the highway. They came to a sudden stop behind a long row of cars held up before a great placard announcing: "Provisional bridge. Heavy-load vehicles must go through one at a time."

"That's because the hurricane swept this bridge away," Paciencia explained.

"Some God awful thing, that must have been, oh man," Selene replied. "And your house, your family, is everything alright?

"Yes, by the grace of God, señorita Selene, we're all fine. The people that suffered the most were the ones that lived by the riverbanks. You wouldn't believe your own eyes, how them darned currents were yanking and dragging houses, trees, crags and whole cliffs, everything that stood in their way! Nothing much happened in Redención, though; it just got swamped the way it always does. Even crocodiles were out there swimming by the main square and in the soccer field – things too ugly for your eyes to see! But if you ask me about people dying, no one did. There was roofs flying all over, truth be told, but not much more."

The row of cars moved along at a snail's pace, until only two pickup trucks remained in line before them: one loaded with watermelons and the other carrying timber; the drivers must have figured theirs weren't "heavy-loads," because both of them rushed in concert headlong into the iron bridge, which rocked and rumbled as if it was about to collapse, something dreadful. Selene held her breath when it was their turn to go across and the bridge started creaking under the weight of Paciencia's Ford. She kept her eyes shut tight until they reached the other side, visualizing the headline: *Middle-aged foreign lady perishes as bridge collapses on the Northern shore…*

Finally, there they were, the oil palm plantations that ushered in the approaching shore. Endless ranks of majestic trunks laid alleys dimmed by the fronds of their crowns. As she always did every time she came that way, Selene once again imagined herself running, dancing and even flying amid those plantations that, just for her, conjured up the grand stage for a ballet drama. On a par with that impromptu fantasy that emerged from somewhere in the recesses of her childhood, she reflected on the significance of those plantations, which belonged to a retired colonel, as she'd been told in her previous trip. "These are the modern bananeras," Selene thought and got to daydreaming how in her lessons she would talk to the schoolchildren about the Fruit Company, how it was that a Russian magnate had become a millionaire just by bringing their bananas to the rest of the world. She would tell them about the Railroad Company, whose rusty rails traverse Puerto, the same ones that the people thoughtlessly cross day by day. "So much history!" she thought, and emotion moistened her eyes.

It was getting dark already when they finally left the concrete highway and entered the village's unpaved streets. In the twilight, one could still make out the great signboard with its hand-painted landscape – coconut trees, macaws and a sun, a work of art more than a signboard – which declared in red letters: *Bienvenido a Redención.*

Paciencia took her straight to the cottages of Profesor

Jacinto Cortés. The professor was a man in his fifties, tall, thickset and constantly smiling. To anything you said he'd answer, "Yes of course," but underneath the surface Selene sensed something that aroused wariness in her. The cottage she got left her more than pleased, though: an ample, square room with two double beds; a high thatched ceiling; an alcove where a pipe with cold water stood for a shower; a wash basin and a toilet. By then it was dark outside, but the sound of the waves left no doubt that she was right on the seashore. What else could one ask for? Exhausted, she took care of the basic stuff and fell asleep right away.

Once awake, she lifted a slat of the blind and saw that, on the horizon, ceasing to be one single dark mass, sky and sea were beginning to come apart, each one taking on its own shade of gray – the sky's a flaxen tint while the sea was turning a mauve hue. With a little girl's excitement at the breaking of the day, Selene got up and opened her door, then tore the sheet off the bed, wrapped herself in it and sat on the stoop. She stayed there for quite a while, watching the sky as it unfolded its fan, which started bringing out all the colors of the rainbow, until the sun finally climbed to heaven, the sea released its turquoise-blue streaks, and an aquamarine strip materialized on the shoreline. Just as the very first time, and every other time she'd faced it, the Caribbean amazed her. "There's no picture, no remembrance, no story that could set you up for this," she thought. Her memory felt emptied out then, with nothing to forget, to forgive or to resolve – as though she was being born that very moment. Her nostrils were overtaken by a smell of firewood starting to burn in a kitchen somewhere, and her eyes looked out for smoke. She was hungry: having arrived worn out the night before, she'd fallen sleep without having dinner. The sun was starting to cast upon the sand the long shadows of palm trees. Now turned to steam, the night dew quavered over the broad, heart-shaped leaves that thrived in the flower beds outside the cabin. Everything was calm and Selene's mind felt clear as a mirror for the morning. She put on her bathing suit and over it a long-sleeve, denim shirt, then went out for a walk on the beach, to see if – with the hamlet still in slumbers – she could spot some place to have a bite, but most of all a cup of coffee. The smell of smoke from a mud stove coming alive must have ridden the breeze from a place far off, because there were no signs of life around her. There was only the crowing of roosters, straining to wake up the dogs still curled under door lintels, the women in bed with their children, and the nightcrawlers nursing hangovers in their hammocks. "Cock-a-doodle-doo! Wake up you lazy fools!" but nobody paid any attention.

Not a living soul was seen anywhere; there were no canoes on the beach, so the fishermen must have been gone before dawn. The farther from the village's central zone that Selene got, the more apparent it was how the storm had caused havoc: the small houses lined up on the beach were all disheveled; there were shredded leaves of macaw palm barely hanging from the remaining roofs, and rusted tin roof sheets were still slipping into the ground. Every few steps, once lofty palms now bereft of their aristocratic stature lay upside down on the sand with their roots looking skyward. Yet, thanks to the lapping of the waves, the strand did remain clean and bright. But a little farther up, between the beach and the villlage there was a trench of poles chiseled by the tide, branches, copper colored algae, empty containers, bits of plastic in every shape and color, ripped up nets and fallen huts – the famous champas: so many tiny trees sacrificed every year just to rent out three square yards of shade to the tourists that poured in from the Capital in extended caravanas of yellow buses – people that were just a little more afluent than the poorest in the land, because they worked in the maquiladoras and, to keep them motivated, their bosses arranged cheap employee tours to the shore on Summer weekends. There they were, the mestizos with their portable stoves, their baskets, their inflatable rings and their lust. Coming in as well, the confederates of diverse Mara gangs with their garish tatoos; but there was no reason to fear their presence, because the maras came to Redención just to cool off, have a good time; you could see them, all inked up, with their spindly legs splashing the edge of the surf, not looking at all like the hardened killers they were. Those were the kind of tourists that, after haggling over prices everywhere, packed their bags leaving behind nothing but trash and the occassional drowning casualty.

Selene walked along the shore picking up tiny seashells, coral scraps, conches and bits of sea glass, till she reached the foot of the jungle-covered hill – home to monkeys, jaguars and vipers – that marked the end of the bay. That's where she stopped and, after inspecting her trove piece by piece, she started returning it to the sea: clam shells purple and orange like the sky at dawn; spiral conches; pieces of coral resembling cauliflowers;

polished glass that came across as cristalized remnants of the sea. .... As she was busy doing that, a song entered her head which, from that day on, she'd repeat every morning as she walked gathering things of wonder only to hurl them back into the sea: *I seen a darkling heron doing battle with a river, that's how your heart falls in love, falls in love with my own heart, falls in love with my own heart...*

When the song was over and her hands were empty, she stood still, looked at the sea and walked toward the waves that rushed to greet her. The water yielded to her steps, wrapping her feet, her ankles, calves and thighs, welcoming her with the unflagging fluidity of its arms. Selene plunged into the tide and started chasing sardines under clouds of seagulls that sounded battle cries as they circled their prey. She swam to the point of panting and only then let herself float, belly up, feeling deliciously alive. It dawned on her just then that she was starving, so she came up from the water and walked back letting the sun dry her out. Arriving back at the bungalows – five little white boxes with high thatched roofs – she saw the blinds were open in the blue rotunda with the Pepsi sign that served as the hotel's restaurant, and picked up the scent of freshly made tortillas and beans.

"Good morning," Selene called out, almost in a scream to be heard above the voice of an announcer that was loudly reciting the news on Radio Reloj.

"Good morning, good morning!" answered the professor, bowed over the stove. There was no need for him to yell, as his resounding voice stood out naturally over the racket of the radio.

"What can we offer you? Cuppa coffe? Right

away we'll get the kettle boiling, take just twenty minutes, give or take ..."

Such is Life

From that day on, Selene's life followed a placid groove: going from the cottage to the schoolhouse and back to the cottage again. She only had to leave the hallowed space of the beach when she went across the street for her meals in Santa's house – Santa, the woman who cared for her just like a nanny. The second time she visited Redención, that's when Selene had met Santa, a striking, willowy, regal-looking person with a face marked by sharp angles, as though chiseled on ebony. She had passed by with a small fish hanging from each of her long, long hands; those she'd gotten for free in return for helping the incoming fishermen to drag their canoes out of the waves onto the beach, as was the custom there; so, grateful and contented, Santa was on her way to cook some fish for her family. She stopped for a moment to greet the education brigade guys and introduced herself as Redención's social worker.

"I have eleven children and five grandchildren, I'm going home to make a stew," she declared and, showing off the fish, let out a hoarse guffaw. The struggles she'd gone through to raise her family hadn't left any apparent dent in the little girl's soul that gushed from her eyes and her thunderous laughter.

It was because Selene had never forgotten that first meeting with Santa that she reached out to her for help when she went back to live in Redención. They'd go out on occasion, Santa and Selene, to dance and have a beer. They would join novena wakes as much as hit the disco – a great field shed of bamboo reeds and palm leaves. At such times, Selene would lose herself in dance, dissolved in the sea of bodies on the dancing floor, or in the rounds if it was a wake she was attending. Following the drumbeat, the swaying of hips and the ripple of shoulders came to her naturally; it was as if those stirrings had been there always, awaiting for the blessed moment of rejoining one's tribe – or, at least, that's how she felt it all.

"When I get outta here, you come with me," Santa would tell Selene, and they always left together when the night was over. Their path took them through the beach and, in some covert nook amidst the coconut groves, they would squat to get rid of all that beer while chatting away underneath the stars. During those days Selene moved about like some enlightened being; she felt light, like someone who'd gone around with a weight in tow and had suddenly let go of it.

Because she always had time for anyone that approached her to tell their stories, and she helped in whichever way she could, the people of the hamlet started growing fond of her. "How nicely she carries herself, that lady! And she dances up a storm! It's almost like she always belonged here", that's how they spoke of her. She had to get used as well to reading and doing her work under the ever-present gazes of so many children that fluttered around her nonstop. The lack of privacy – which would later come to upset her so much – did not bother her in the least at the beginning, because nothing bothered her by then.

Once, when – using the tiny white sugary pellets she always had with her – she cured a woman who'd come back from hospital without hope of recovery from severe dysentery, word got around that Selene was a healer, or even a sorceress. That because, after a couple doses of her pellets, the woman, who'd been till then crawling and groaning in pain and enervation, was completely recovered. The next day, when Selene went by to ask after the patient, there was no way she could tell it was actually the woman who received her, seated now before a great bowl of seafood soup. "You're talking to her," the woman said, smiling.

People started coming by her house asking for help, but recovery couldn't be as conclusive with all patients as it had been with the first one, because some cases simply had no cure. Santa's niece, Tinina, was one of those, and Selene did her best to alleviate the headaches that made her whimper and groan when the pain turned into seizures. But there was little that Selene could do for her, because the unmentionable epidemic scourge that was decimating the villagers had also infected Tinina, and it wasn't long before she passed away, leaving two little orphans behind.

One evening after dinner, Selene went back to her cottage to prepare her children's classes for the next day. She worked till around midnight, as usual, and was already about to fall asleep when, tearing the veils of her slumber, as if coming from afar she heard Santa's distressed voice; then fist blows on her door chased away whatever sleep she still had in her, and now the voice was right there: "Tinina is dead, she's dead, Tinina," Santa kept repeating on and on, standing by the doorway until Selene stepped out. "Come over to our house," the woman said with her face all contorted; then, without another word, she turned around and walked away, becoming one with palm-tree shadows. Selene had barely said, "Let me get dressed," when Santa's figure had already disappeared.

Seated on a wooden bench right outside the house, three men with greying hair were singing a sad song in muted voices. One of them played a guitar while, in tiny plastic cups, they shared a quart of rum which they poured from a flask full of herbs and twigs. Selene walked into the house, a square space of unpainted concrete blocks with wooden rafters that supported a zinc rooftop. Resting on a table in the middle of the room, there was Tinina in the coffin that the family had bought a few days before as they awaited the end. Selene set her gaze on Tinina's face, assuaged for the first time now: it was an empty mask drawn on fluid angles. Her bony hands rested upon an emaciated bosom; way before dying, the poor woman was already on the verge of becoming a skeleton. A shiver running through her veins drove Selene back into the patio, where the men were still singing. Santa's mother, grandmother to the deceased, was preparing a thin gruel of cornmeal – atole – on a big stove made of flattened metal atop some stones. The two newly orphaned kids, a girl about eight years old and a boy a bit older than her, were helping their great grandma. Attentive to his elder's instructions – standing tall and looking neat in a long sleeved dress shirt – the boy stretched out his delicate neck and tilted his ear to the old woman; he promptly turned toward the shack that stood for a kitchen and came back with clean cups on a tray, which he placed on a table under a loquat tree right outside. Then, as he saw how – squatting by the fire with her face flushed by the heat – his sister was blowing and fanning the flames to keep them alive, he took two shells out of a pile of coconut remnants and placed them squarely on the sputtering bonfire, which burst now into orange and blue flares.

As Selene tried to read the expressions in the children's faces, all she could detect was their absolute concentration on the task at hand; a staid dignity in the way they appeared to be bearing the blow of their mother's death; the stoicism with which they confronted the shame and the stigma that they were subject to in town because their mother had succumbed to AIDS. When the little ones sensed Selene's sentiment-laden gaze upon them, they offered in return two smiles that flared like searchlights in the darkness of the night.

Dawn was approaching and one could already feel the freshness of the twilight dew. The heat from grandma's stove and the children's smiles made Selene's blood run warm. The old woman started pouring atole into cups with a ladle, while the trio of musicians, now grown into a sextet, kept the muted songs going. The yard was getting increasingly crowded. Then there was a sudden cry that dovetailed into weeping and, in the blink of an eye, there was Santa rushing out of the house with her hands clasping her head.

"I closed her eyes meself, I promise you I closed her eyes," she cried out to Selene, grabbing and shaking her by the shoulders. Never before had Santa been this distressed, not as long as Selene knew her. "Tinina opened her eyes!" she was howling now. Everyone stopped doing whatever they were doing and came running into the house; grandma, the orphans, Santa drenched in tears holding on to Selene, the singers and the rest of the gathering.

Then again, Tinina was so poor, not worth the time of day to anyone in the hamlet and, moreover, she had died of a shameful illness; so, on that account there were not many people present at her funeral, and everyone of them looked scared out of their wits.

"It must have been a physiological reflex, her eyes opening," Selene tried to put them at ease, "things like that do happen." But nobody believed or even understood what she was saying. They started leaving the house ploddingly, convinced that the deceased had opened her eyes only because she was anxious about the fate of her children. Tinina's eyes remained open in the end because no one had the gumption to go close them for her again.

Santa got settled down presently with a shot of rum, and started singing along with the musicians that had gotten back together. Her voice was the strongest, and the more so when – her eyes closed out of zeal – she broke out into one wistful song that told of how the souls of the deceased return to the island of their ancestors, where la Raza came to be – *Yurumein tageirabei wayuna. Yurumein tageirabei wagutu* – Yurumein, that is the land of our ancestors, Yurumein the land of our grandmother. Still, when hitting the high notes, that voice of hers would crack; but no matter though, spectators as well as interpreters couldn't help but be moved by her singing.

Then with their poise, their simple gestures,

both kids too honored Tinina's memory throughout her humble wake: they went about serving cups with atole from big wooden trays. Downright serious in their stance, so elegant and graceful, they would lightly bow their heads in a show of gratitude every time someone took a cup from them.

Selene went back to her cabin as the roosters crowed and, sprouting from behind the hills, a sharp edge of clarity was beginning to insinuate itself. She turned the light off and lay on her back, looking up. In Santa's house the drum had taken over from the songs; she stayed still while listening to the sluggish, syncopated beats. While, on the thatched roof, fireflies took the place of stars, she drifted off to sleep under that canopy of heaven; it felt as if the sky had found its way into her cabin. Her heartbeats became one with the drum, with the motion of the waves, with the twinkles of fireflies.

Sharks and Doves

It was one out of so many early evenings when, as had become a habit, Selene rinsed the saltwater off her body and wrapped herself in a sarong before sitting down to watch the sunset. Now – as all along the beach a thick smoke rising from bonfires started covering everything with a red veil – she turned her head and saw a silhouette moving along the water's edge and growing larger till it reached the higher ground where she was seated. It stopped cold, turned about drawing a well-marked angle and headed straight toward her. What had been till then a silhouette emerged into an actual presence: two feet astonishing in size, slender legs that bore narrow hips, drawn-out arms dangling loosely from broad shoulders, a beret that tucked away a thick mane; and all the while on his face a smile puncturing the smoky haze: two rows of snow-white teeth with jutting canines, which made that mouth particularly appealing – at once attractive and scary.

"Hello there, I saw you swimming a while ago. You must watch out for sharks here, you know?" he told her, dead serious, his voice deep and slightly hoarse.

"Sharks, really?" Selene replied, guileless, just as she was thinking, "what a beautiful voice."

"Yes, there is *one shark* that hangs 'round this beach, his name is Felipe, yours to command," the newcomer jived, though with a blank face. Selene let out a chuckle, embarrassed by her naiveté. The two of them laughed.

"So, what's with the campfires?" she asked, to change the subject. Felipe seized the opportunity to sit on the bench next to her.

"Some of the fishermen haven't gotten back yet and, seeing as to how it's getting dark already, people make bonfires to show them the way home," he explained.

That's how it started, the fondness that since then Felipe sprinkled like a garden, with the bicycle rides – Selene perched sidewise on the crossbar like a backcountry bride; with the orange slices he'd try to put right on her lips and she'd take with her fingers, put off by the liberties he was taking; with hikes in The Bush and canoe trips down the river. He played her emotional chords too, with the story of his hardship-laden life: the mother of his children had gone up North taking the kids with her, all but the youngest who stayed with his aunt in a hamlet far away. He went about bringing down her defences and step by step bewitching her with his always wonder-filled eyes, which wouldn't stop prying into hers, looking at her in amazement and making her feel like a woman who'd just landed there from another planet. And, without meaning to, Selene fanned the fires, putting up as much resistance as she could – which was actually quite a bit – because, by the same token, she didn't want to miss out on the peace she'd just chanced upon. That's why Felipe went crazy for her. He so liked the way she'd swing her braid over her shoulders with a smart stroke of her head as she turned and then walked away with sure steps, skipping lightly on the sand, so at ease inside her own skin. It also delighted him to see her sharing the rewards of dinner with the cat that had moved into her place: "I never seen nothing like this, a person and a cat communicating in such ways."

And yet, Selene sensed fear in him, fused with the admiration that made his eyes shimmer. But it was her reticence, really, that turned his head to mush. Once she heard him say, "What a woman, she's the kind you could kill for!"

He went as far as to ask her to meet his parents, and so she did. Theirs was a tiny house built with royal palm, where tidiness and order struggled to cloak poverty. A dining-room set with a mahogany table and chairs, some ceramic tableware, and a large collection of pots, so clean they looked like new – all of those stood as testimony to their owner's painstaking care and to a more buoyant past. In the corners, through holes in the wall lined with compressed cardboard, electric wires peeped out like bare bowels. A sofa and two armchairs couldn't cover glimpses of their foam-rubber innards where leather had yielded to decades of rubbing by elbows and hands. Felipe's mother, Doña Chola, was in her sixties – a thin, sinewy woman with carved cheekbones and the sharp gaze of those who've gone through many battles. She was seated sideways with her feet resting on the sofa, an elbow on the armrest and her chin propped on her hand; that's how she welcomed her son and the foreign woman: motionless, visibly exhausted by the day's long haul. Don Joaquín, his father, who was noticeably older than his wife, sat quite upright on one of the armchairs, with both his hands set on a wooden walking cane; it was as if by way of pure, intense attention that he made

31

amends for his missing foot. Skipping any preambles and, by way of introduction, he set out to explain it all to Selene:

"It was an accident – happened way back when I was a labourer loading the railcars. But before that, when I was still altogether in one piece, every time I had time off, me and the old lady here we'd go up to The Bush: we had a good many cassava fields over there…"

Now Felipe cut in on his father: "I'm gonna marry her!" Straight out, he said just that. Selene laughed, thinking, "He's crazy." But she went back to her cottage that night with her head up in the clouds, bewildered to the bone. Nonetheless, she kept dodging Felipe's lures; her reluctance went so far that, for a few days, he stopped going after her, and she started missing him. That was until one night – as she came back home with rum and beers she'd bought in the corner store for a fiesta the *gringos* were having by the cottages – she ran into him in a darkened spot. He was going by on his bicycle, done for the day with his job as a bricklayer.

"What a coincidence!" he cried out, lowering one foot to the ground to bring the bike to a stop. "I was just going home to change clothes and come visit ya."

"Is that so? And here I was, really, hoping to see you, can you believe?" she responded, inhaling his sweat-and-plaster scent, a smell of hard work that touched her. The hair in her arms bristled like silk threads responding to the magnetic pull of amber.

Felipe saw no need to change his clothes. Pushing the bicycle, he walked side by side with Selene to the cottages, where the party was already underway at the professor's blue Pepsi gazebo. Selene had prepared a sea bass she'd gotten from one of the canoes that morning; the outsiders had come up with various salads; and Santa brought a pot of rice and beans cooked in coconut milk.

Throughout what came to be a full-fledged banquet, Selene and Felipe had eyes and ears for no one but themselves. Among many other things, he told her he had this plan to rent his land parcel to a man from the city for an African palm plantation.

"Wouldn't you rather start a nature reserve?" she put in her two cents and, at that, Felipe's eyes sparkled. "Well now, that would be *really* great!" he marvelled at the thought. His pupils dilated and the twinkling of his eyes reflected in hers, which had gone from brown to black.

"Sure, I bet you could make it into a real paradise, raise horses, bring in tourists. You could even have your own restaurant," Selene went on as he listened to her, attentive, spellbound. And they took flight together, conjuring up white-faced capuchin monkeys cavorting among the trees, great macaws landing like firebolts just to eat from people's hands. Marching now inside Selene's mind there was a parade of elephants and giraffes, lions and butterflies.

When dinner came to an end in the small gazebo, everybody went into a salon that stood on the beach not too far off, and there they got the groove going. Right away Felipe ushered Selene into the dance floor; he wrapped his arms around her waist, long fingers pressing hips; they remained entwined through song after song, swaying, barely following the beat, and when there were calls for switching partners, they found it hard to let go their embrace. The dancing went into a sudden crescendo as the native Punta rhythms burst out of an old jukebox, and it kept going till there was nobody standing still; it ended up a full blown shindig, with brown and white skins melding on the dance floor.

It was close to midnight when Santa came around with the now proverbial sign: "Let's get going, Selene." But Selene, breaking the established order, shot back: "You go ahead, I'm staying."

That night, sitting in a canoe on the beach, she and Felipe shared a kiss for the first time. That was the night he lost his hat and Selene lost her compass.

Felipe left before sunrise to go fishing, and Selene couldn't get back to sleep – feeling as though she'd spent the night swimming at sea, and the salt-laden waters had undone every gnarl there'd been in her body. Her freshly cleansed mind was unable to come up with one single thought, so she stayed in bed waiting for the sounds of dawn. It wasn't long before she heard the cooing of doves, sweet and familiar. Then, in the coconut grove next to her cabin, golden orioles ushered in the morning with their metallic voices. Selene stretched out a hand and lifted a slat of the wooden blinds. A faint lucidness was hovering through the dark cloud layer that concealed the sky. She listened to the waves breaking forcefully, relentless, and with that, Felipe came into her head: "What could make him go out fishing on a day like this," she wondered, fretting. And as she thought of him, a sweet warmth filled her body: it was the refuge of sheltering wings; the skin heat hiding in flesh creases; the fever that flowed subsurface through the prodigal arteries in Felipe's groin. Like the wind hitting a ship's sail, a seagull's sudden squawk swelled up her heart and prompted her to get off bed. She splashed water on her face, smoothed her tangled mane with her still-wet hands, threw on a dress, and went over to Santa's place. She wanted to apologize for having refused to leave with her the night before but, more than anything, what she needed was grounding.

She slow-stepped her way across the still deserted main street. Redención consisted of three parallel promenades: la Pícara – the scoundrel's way – named for being the darkest one, closest to the beach and thus frequented by those who wanted to go unnoticed; la Principal – Main Street – which was the widest; and la del Monte, a vaguely meandering row that disappeared now and then amidst thickets or gardens. Countless little streets cut across those three sand-covered pathways before reaching the beach. La Principal was barren and dusty, because one by one its trees had been cut down for firewood, or simply to stop having to sweep dead leaves or pick off the ground fruit left to rot under the tangerine, lemon and orange trees, which bore so much of it that the town couldn't consume it all.

Santa lived across la Principal. Selene came upon the woman – tucked into a nylon nightgown that came down to her feet and made her look rangier than usual – as she was bent over her mud stove, blowing on embers that had started lighting up amid the logs. Wood-scented smoke flooded the kitchen, mingling with the timid light that was sneaking in between the bamboo sticks of the wall.

"*Buenos días.* You did come early today!" Santa said, unfolding her reedy figure. Then, after studying Selene's face for a moment, "And you look twenty years younger," she noted with a toothless smile: she had not yet put on her dentures. Selene blushed and looked at her feet. When she looked up again her eyes were brimming with water. "Ay Santa, ay Santi, Santi!" she cried out, trying hard to curb the voice blast that was streaming through her throat and breaking her breath.

"You go sit down," Santa ordered. "Just let me get dressed and I'll make you breakfast." She offered a tiny smile, intimate and cheeky, before concluding, "Take a break."

Selene went and sat on a deck chair in the porch. She let her body slide down to the bottom of that ample seat and rested her head on the backrest. Instead of breaking open, the sky had turned duskier, as if meaning to come down in a cloudburst. The stillness of the street was disturbed when two men riding bicycles, and carrying their backpacks and machetes on the bike racks, went by talking loudly so as to hear each other bike to bike. Another biker came after them, and then another till the street became a river of bicycles, of dialogues and early-morning greetings fluttering around bird-like – with just about everybody going in the same direction. On the corner next to the well, five women, each carrying a bucket, had started some hoop-de-do with their trumpeting voices. In Santa's kitchen, beans crackled as they fell on sizzling coconut oil. The aroma of freshly made tortillas and coffee embraced Selene.

"What if Felipe were to come around here just now?" Her heart started beating hard when that thought rushed into her mind; it felt as though a drove of horses had entered her chest. She closed her eyes and saw Felipe laughing at their navels – hers so tiny and his a flat, round thing; saw him stretching his arm to turn the light on so he could shamelessly inspect her, then let his eyes, so very black, rest upon hers. There was Felipe lifting her up airborne, testing the two beds and finally dropping her down on the sand-covered rush mat. She saw his fuzz-covered chest, remembered how, even as it inspired a certain fear in her, she had not resisted the temptation to run her fingers through it.

When Santa walked out into the porch with breakfast and caught her smiling, she let out a coarse cackle that startled Selene into opening her eyes at last.

Having placed the coffee mug and the dishful of food on her little table, the hostess settled in the deck chair facing Selene, who was now struggling to bring under control the twitching tiny muscles in her face, to stop herself from coming unstitched with mirth. Santa was not one to beat around the bush, however; she spoke in earnest, to the point:

"He's a good man, Felipe is. He works hard. You don't see him fooling 'round with women. And then, the way he talks is real nice too; he does have a way with words, that man. Mind you, the neighborhood he comes from, that's a place of real workers, not like the ones who hang out here just sitting idle waiting for them remittances, you know? Over there you find fellows who's always ready to go fishing, willing to do whatever job they get; yes ma'am, good men they are!"

Santa's sharp-edged face softened as she spoke. She delivered her final words in less of a hurry, with a kindness that was tangible. Then she just stared at the ceiling, deep in her own thoughts. Selene, in silence, spread refried beans on a tortilla wafer and ate it haltingly, more like a mere supplement to her coffee with milk, since, truth be told, she didn't have much of an appetite.

Aside from swelling up her heart, Santa's words had made her realize as well why it was that every evening, after they'd had dinner, her friend dumped her flip flops, put on real sandals, aimed her long, arrow-like feet toward the neighborhood with the *good men* and got cracking without saying *adiós*, just humming and crooning with her arms swaying in tandem as though oars helping her reach her destiny in short order. Once at the corner, still walking she would turn her head and, letting go one of those little-girl smiles of hers, wave goodbye before turning into the Pícara street.

In Redención romance was always cloaked in mystery – as though it should be something to be kept secret in a hamlet with no secrets. Lovers didn't go together on strolls, and stoked their zest spying on each other at a distance in parties and wakes – a delight akin to savouring chili peppers. And that's the way Selene was feeling, chili-stung, her insides taken by dancing flames that wouldn't let her keep still.

"Santa, keep this food for me, I'll come back to finish it later, I'm not used to eating this early, it's not even eight in the morning yet." That was her bare response to the knowledge Santa had just shared. She let her legs take the lead. "I'm going to walk awhile and then I'll take a rest at home, see you around lunchtime." Getting up she felt vertigo, felt as if her head were a helium-filled balloon.

While waiting for the bicycle traffic to stop before crossing the street, there were moments when she thought she saw Felipe amongst the bikers that rolled by raising dust clouds. When she was about to reach her place, she saw him standing there by the cabin's door. With his red-yellow-green, swarthy presence, Felipe brightened whatever stood in darkness that day. He was spiking a silver fish, not much bigger than his hand: threading the tip of a palm leaf through a gill and pulling it out through the mouth. Then he took another fish from his bag, pierced it the same way, and knotted the leaf's end to string the two together firmly. Once done, he stood by the corner of the cottage, turning his head from side to side, scanning the beach, waiting for Selene to show up.

Watching him as she came closer, a burst of joy like a fireball overtook her body and her eyes somehow got moist. She couldn't even tell when it was that she ran to him, as though carried in a twinkling by invisible arms.

"I've been here waiting a good while already," said Felipe before giving her a kiss that took her mouth whole. "Gotta go now, though. You see, I promised the old man I'd help 'im fix the fence in his yard." Selene felt a vacuum, a rising nausea, in the pit of her stomach and she went weak at the knees. Felipe's chest was pulling her in like a magnet. She felt a need to take refuge and cry like a baby right there. But he remained composed and, projecting a colossal self-assurance, gathered her waist in one hand without taking his eyes off of hers. "Tell Santa to fry them for your lunch," he said, letting go to hand her the stringed fish. Selene – who had felt so strong, so at ease, so self-possessed the day before – wanted nothing but to hold him in her arms, felt that she was dying, that she could exist attached to him and to him only. "I'll come by in the evening," he said, and, using velvety tones: "Get real dolled up for me." Then he turned on his heel and walked down the beach away from her.

She just stood there speechless, holding her present in one hand while watching him move off till he was just a tiny dot against the grimy skyline. With her lips still wet from his kiss, it dawned on her that all the while she hadn't been able to come up with one single word.

Not even realizing how she'd gotten there, she found herself back in Santa's place. "*Santita*, look, got this for our lunch," she chirped, turning over the entwined fish. Santa's face lit up. She received the fish and, fumbling the words as the thought of it made her mouth water, "Do we want them fried," she asked, "or stewed in coconut milk?"

"Let's have them fried, *Santita*, it'll be less trouble," Selene answered; then for the next two minutes weighed whether to tell or keep it to herself, but anyhow the words came rolling out: "He's going to come later today! Ay, Santa, What am I to do?" she warbled, delighted as one who has gladly decided beforehand to let fortune drag her where it may.

After bolting the door when she got back to her cottage, she opened the blind on the window that faced the beach next to her bed, laid down covering her feet with the still tangled sheet, and for a while stared admiringly at the image before her as though it were a painting on he wall: the cobalt blue of the professor's gazebo stood out against the greyness of the sea in the background; it looked like one of those black-and-white photos that someone had later colorized.

In her dream she was a tiny caterpillar poking around from underneath a pile of dead leaves and, as it found its way towards the surface, the flesh-colored little guy kept growing till it was as big as a finger, while a crackling of shattered dry leaves grew more and more staggering. She half-opened her eyes and it took her more than a few seconds to make out the sound of the torrential rain that had just started coming down. The window-framed landscape had disappeared behind a curtain of water. The clock by her bed said it was noon, but the cabin was in twilight. Her modest lair looked splendid to her.

She barely heard knocks on her door and then Santa's voice calling: "I've got everything ready, frying is all that's left to do now. Are you coming any time soon?" she asked when she was let in.

"Ay, Santa, I totally forgot," said Selene, seeing how the clock pointed to well past one. "Would you believe I've lost my appetite? I can't see myself eating anything right now. Go ahead, do fry the fish, yours, and keep mine for later, will you?" But she had to think twice as Santa's look gave away her disappointment. "OK, I'll be there as soon as I get myself together."

Santa grabbed her umbrella, which had left a puddle on the corner behind the door, and rushed out but not without reminding the foreigner that she had barely touched breakfast and needed to eat for real. She vanished behind thick sheets of rain with her umbrella fluttering about like a bat behind her. Selene broke into song underneath the spout that played the role of a shower, "I seen a darkling heron doing battle with a river, that's how your heart falls in love, falls in love with my own heart …" She picked up the one bar of sandalwood soap she'd brought with her, which was lying on a small ledge in the bathroom, still wrapped in sky-blue rice paper – the one she smelled every time she passed by, without ever daring to use it: she'd nose the round tablet in its paper wrapping, sniffing it briskly with eyes closed, her senses inebriated by the sandal fragrance, only to place it back on the ledge. Now, taking good care not to rip the blue wrapper, she unglued the golden seal, took the soap out, brought it to her nose and inhaled the sweet resin-and-musk perfume. She started by giving herself a foam headdress; then slid the bar down the smooth shoulders; the achy muscles of her arms and thighs confounded her; and yet, coming near the pubis she moved quick and lightly, barely touching. It felt as though an outlandish creature, some sort of sea anemone, had come to life between her legs during the night. She couldn't recognize her vulva as it appeared now: open, alive, fertile. It was then that, as though of their own accord, streams of salt water started pouring from her eyes and running down her body along with the water from the spout above. "If only I'd had a child, perhaps my life wouldn't be one of searching for things that can't be seen," she thought.

Many times Selene had been to the Maya temples sprinkled throughout that strip of land she felt so much her own, not as a tourist but rather as one who returns to the seed, looking for the soul of things.

"But it's here that I've come to find that soul; in the everyday dramas of this place; at Tinina's wake; in the dignity of her orphaned kids; in the heat and the fragrance of firewood crackling in stoves; in the beating of drums; in the hands and backs of women who – leaning over carved-stone laundry sinks – day after day wash the clothes of ten others; in the plantains growing through trash piles by the cabins; in this ambience pregnant with the scent of coconut and sea tides. It is here, in this place that is so distant from all I'd known before, while at the same time it feels so comfortingly familiar. A return – that's what this is. I've stopped searching for the soul of things: I found it here, alloyed and in synergy with the flesh, with the soil, just as yeast is essential to the raise of bread. It's present in Felipe's velvet skin – oh God, in Felipe's flesh!" Her body wouldn't stop shedding tears. Russian nesting dolls came to her mind. "It is what it is, all of it," she told herself: "Me, crying under a waterjet under the tears of a weeping sky. Me, a meagre grain of sand, yet a reflection of the entire universe."

By and by, she finished scrubbing herself till her burnished skin and hair squeaked. Having wiped her body dry, she threw on a robe. Then, as she pulled a towel off a chair's backrest to dry her hair, coiled between its folds she found a golden scorpion. Gingerly she managed to bring the four corners of the towel together into a sort of bag, held the bundle in one hand, opened the door and shook the towel over the flower bed, setting the scorpion free. While rubbing her hair dry with the same towel, she drew a mental picture: what would have happened if she hadn't seen that animal –

the stinger sinking into her jaw, or her cheek or, even worse, her neck, chocking the life out of her...

When she used the ruffled sheet to swoop the bed clean, myriad sand grains fell like whitewater on the rush mat. She did her best to fluff up the corners of the two pillows where the jute filling had gone lumpy; next she shook out the sheet which, swollen by a gust of wind that entered the cabin, flew into the ceiling; only on all fours could she finally stretch it smooth over the bed. Done with that, she lifted the mat off the concrete floor and swept the room; a multitude of little voices whispered as the sand landed on a newspaper sheet.

All set! Now we go see Santa. She checked the time: four o'clock, and yet the light was so dim that it looked like nightfall was approaching. She grabbed the olive green hooded poncho and rolled her Capri pants up above her knees. The hood fell over her eyes and so, unable to see beyond her feet, she stepped out and locked the cottage. The rain pressed the cold plastic poncho against her body, gave her a shiver. Wrapping her arms about her ribs, she ran over to Santa's place.

"Santa, *Santita*, let this needy body have some food, feed your sister, feed me," Selene chirped as she stood on a puddle before reaching the porch. Taking the poncho off, she rushed into the room where Santa sat on a sofa watching a soap opera with her daughter, her two grandchildren and her grandma, who was fast asleep flopped in an armchair. Seeing her come in, Santa sprang readily to her feet and headed for the kitchen, but Selene took her hand in hers and put her other hand around her waist: "Let's dance, *señorita bonita*..." As the two kids and their mother bent over laughing, she lifted the youngest one into her arms and danced with him while the little one let out delighted cascades of baby cackles; she then returned him to his mother's arms and danced with his older brother, who barely reached her shoulders in height. All that ruckus awoke the old lady, who started cursing in her own language and that made everyone laugh even harder.

Laughing too, Selene went and kissed grandma on both cheeks. At that, "Good Lord, what bug flew up your chimney, girl?" the old one barked, making Santa guffaw in turn from where she stood working the Kerosene stove she used when bad weather made it hard to cross the yard into the real kitchen.

Selene barely managed to finish the small fish that Santa made for her, one single slice of fried plantain was too much to take, and even the salad was out of the question. "I'm sorry, Santita, I'm so sorry," she apologized, "but I think I better go, it must be close to five already and Felipe will be coming any minute now. *Ayó*, Santita, *ayó*, see you tomorrow." She dove right into her poncho and took off splashing warm water puddles on her way back home, as the olive shades of the poncho made her blend in with the greenish atmosphere.

Night was falling and the storm eased up, turning into a lullaby-like gurgle. Selene switched off the lamp that hung over the bed and turned on the bathroom light, not to be left in total darkness. While her ears probed the silence, she went and sat on the chair pretending not to see the clock that was pointing at seven already. It was a while before she heard the whirring sound of a bicycle split the night air as it drew near. Its wheels crushed the sand when it went past the cabin; Selene sensed a flapping of wings, a stirring, an arrested heartbeat, until silence swallowed the bicycle as well as her anticipation – her hopes in flight chasing after those two wheels. Then she wished that it would rain as hard as it had rained not long before; she wished for the sky to break open and let its sheltering mantle land on her; for a gale to bring the hamlet to a dead stop, so that bicycles would no longer roam about; for a squall that would allay her now aged wound, which was smarting anew – a torrential downpour to erase all and everything like words written on sand. But the sky, merciless, refused to break, and now one could barely hear raindrops dripping off the palm-tree leaves, the shrubs and the macaw palm by the roof. A few women walked by and then a group of boys, stinging her with their laughs. Selene heard the professor's resounding voice as he arrived with a labourer to see how things were looking in his gazebo; the two men went in, placed all wooden benches on top of the tables, fiddled noisily with the shutters trying to fasten them, padlocked the place and walked away. After that break in the storm – which people took advantage of to go hither and thither, returning to their houses, securing their properties – once again the downpour took possession of the night, easing the burden of Selene's expectation. Taking it for a fact that no one could possibly come now, she wrapped herself in the sheet and fell asleep.

When the doves started cooing softly and stirring in their nest on the roof, Selene opened her eyes half way, feeling vaguely unsettled, close to nauseous. The rain kept coming down as if driven by inertia, falling for its own sake, despondent. The blanket felt heavy and she tossed it away, then got up and tried to start the electric teapot, but the electricity had been cut off. She went to the washbasin now, opened the faucet and no water came out: the pump had stopped working. She filled a gourd from the five-gallon water jug and used that to freshen her face, taking care not to meet her image on the mirror. A stomach cramp made her bend in pain: it was her empty stomach; even though she wasn't hungry, she felt weak. Sitting on the bed, she made an effort to clear her mind. "I've got to have something to eat; must let Santa know that I'm taking a leave from this hamlet – that's it, I'll get myself over to Puerto, rent a hotel room there, air-conditioned, with hot water, room service, TV…"

Having a plan lifted her spirits just a bit. Yet, she had a moment of doubt thinking about the children in the school, but managed to reassure herself: "It'll be just a couple of days; besides, it's a weekend." She threw the poncho over the wrinkled clothes she had slept in, drew her feet into the flip-flops and left for Santa's house. A rooster crowed as though nothing was off; the rain had stopped. There was fresh moss spreading over the concrete walls of the still silent shacks.

"¡Santa! ¡Santa!" Selene called out next to her window. There was a long silence before she finally heard a drowsy voice saying something unintelligible; but soon enough there were clicks coming from the door latch and the chain on the railing in the porch, and Santa came up with her mouth pleated over toothless gums. "What's happening?" she asked, pulling on the towel that covered her shoulders and, seeing how Selene just stood there under the rain, "Come on, girl, come in," she said in earnest.

"Felipe didn't show up," Selene moaned, aching. No matter how she tried to explain it to herself, she couldn't understand why she felt so lost in facing the absence of a man she had just met and without whom she'd lived at peace until just two days ago. Why in heavens did she feel so hurt? It was as though Felipe had found an old wound and then, with strict accuracy, had implanted his goad right there.

A few sips of the coffee that Santa offered her – heavy on the sugar and piping hot, the way she liked it; got to be mouth-burning, she'd always say – those made her see at least a tiny opening in her horizon. She took a deep breath and let go the weight of her body into the deck chair. As soon as she started sharing her plan with Santa she had felt stronger. Santa brought her two slices of toasted bread, margarine and honey. Even if somewhat forced at the beginning, a single bite was enough to undo the knot she had in her stomach and to get her appetite going. She ate the two slices in a flash and asked for a second coffee.

"Look it here, finally I see you eating with gusto," Santa observed, and right away got back to the main point: "But do tell me, what am I to do when Felipe comes here asking for you?"

"I can't see why you're so sure he's coming," Selene protested, sulky. She just hadn't thought about that. And yet, Santa's words had offered some solace. Then again, the idea that Felipe would go looking for her and find her cottage locked gave her just a touch of a pleasant feeling.

"Tell him – tell him whatever you want," that was her answer.

It Never Hurts to Have a Choice of Refuge

Selene took the bus and shared the twenty-minute ride with the women that, uncowed by the bad weather, were going to sell their wares and produce in the small neighboring town of Puerto: coconut bread, pulpy green coconuts, oranges so yummy. These women with such commanding presence, so cheerful and at ease in their own skin made her feel in turn so very small, so out of place that she couldn't help but envy those who had their homes, their children, their mothers, their roots so firmly present there.

Once in town and when it came to choose where to stay, on the beach or up in the heights, she chose the latter: a hotel built on a terrace atop the hill, standing between gigantic palm and mango trees, with massive steel columns buttressing its red-and-cherry ramparts. As Selene climbed up a very long stone stairway, she left behind the main street – a strip strewn with small bars and dining rooms with loudspeakers outcrying each other – *ranchera* here, *bachata* there, *cumbia* over there – and swarmed with people schlepping parcels, packs of mangy if not mangled dogs carrying on here and there, preachers and beggars with their own hawking songs. She took a breather for a moment and looked down: the stands displaying knickknacks on all sidewalks cooped the people up into a human river that flowed down the street ducking and dodging cars, trucks and buses that kept blasting their horns while spewing clouds of black smoke. It was a good five minutes of climbing before she finally got to the red fortress that towered over the downtown chaos. On the ground floor, facing the reception counter, an overhanging terrace that floated between two huge mango trees served as a restaurant.

It was mid-morning on a September day – well off the tourist season – and the hotel looked empty. Selene took a seat at one of the restaurant's tables, to fill out the guest-register form while sipping from a glass of chia limewater, a welcome treat for new arrivals. Looking west, she could see a vast patchwork of rusted tin roofs nested on the slopes of a strip of hills that embraced the tiny port. Toward the north, there were the marketplace and the bus station, which was in fact no more than a wasteland that served as the depot for the yellow buses that went back and forth between the hamlets and Puerto, gobbling up and spitting out loads of humans, parcels and baskets. Just a few yards away, as sombre as the sky on that day, there was the sea. Then, a bit toward the left, and facing the dilapidated wharf like a great toothless marimba, stood the building that had once housed the Railroad Company. A long row of bow windows stared at the horizon from its upper level like vacant eye sockets; and, seen from so far away, the company's title, carved above the entrance arch, appeared as barely a stain striking across some defensive walls that had once been white. To the east one could see the cliff that marked the end of the bay and kept Redención apart from Puerto; on its ridge you could clearly make out the canopy of corozo palms that crowned the thick jungle. Somehow it came to Selene that she could just extend her hand to touch it and she sensed wings beating inside her chest.

"If you'd please follow me, I can show you to your room," chimed the voice of the woman who had received her. Only then, revived by the short break and the chia water, did Selene take note of her beauty: she seemed to be fully wrapped in an amber light, her tightly curled black hair falling in a braid over an embroidered *huipil*, the traditional handmade tunic; she had great black eyes, a striking aquiline nose, and her face gleamed when a candid smile displayed teeth as pristine as early-harvested corn. "She must be my age, or maybe a bit younger, just about going on forty," thought Selene, reckoning how the harshness of life in the tropics made people age too soon.

As if the climb up the hill hadn't been enough of a test for her, she ended up in a room on the top floor. The world below started shrinking as they made their way upstairs, and already from the third floor it looked like a diagram. Each new level was its own garden – white hibiscus, wax palms, purple-crowned parrot's plantains, orchids and cacti with impudent shapes standing out amongst a foliage of bromeliads and grugru palms, and all of that enclosed in the dusky framework of mango trees that shielded the sparse and rugged grounds.

Following the woman that quietly led the way up the concrete staircase, Selene felt embraced by the aura of that being who appeared to stand in ideal harmony with her surroundings. It was as if she and the site had been conceived by the same architect, as if she'd been

51

sculpted from one of the crags in the cliff, or impulsively sprung out of the ground as native plants do. Once on the fourth floor, the street rumble was left behind and only the tops of the mango trees could be seen. When the woman opened the door, the space inside released a fragrance of resins. They entered an ample room with high ceilings, all painted in soft tones of straw yellow, cream and sky blue. A wrought-iron curtain rod on the great picture window that took up an entire wall held thick cotton drapes printed with birds in the same smooth and lightsome tones of the walls. The furniture in aged woods looked like family heirlooms or happy findings in bazaars, and you could tell the pieces had been painstakingly restored and polished.

"Welcome to the house! My name is Viola. Anything you need, just dial zero," said the woman, spinning her words with the same fluid, graceful tilt that she spun her movements. Then, without further expositions, she handed over the key chain marked with the name of the room: IIK, and its Maya translation underneath – Air – pyrographed on the rudimentary mahogany handle. When Selene looked up, the woman had already turned around and was on her way out. "*Muchas gracias*," she barely managed to say as Viola started down the stairs.

She stepped out into the terrace, leaned on the railing and fixed her eyes on Viola going down the steps with the same parsimony as when she'd come up. Her mind took off on its own, playing with the word *viola*: voilà, Olivia, oil vial, by Allah … then she entertained the image that, if she were a musical instrument, her hostess would be a viola. The core of that woman's rotund, compact body seemed to harbor a power that would make her able to go through walls, a power that animated every one of her slinking movements.

Amidst a persistent penumbra, one could almost smell the water that storm clouds hanging from the sky held in their bellies. Lines from a Sandra Cisneros poem turned up in her mind now: *I'm a bell without a clapper. A woman with one foot in this world and one foot in that. A woman straddling both...* It was then that Selene realized she hadn't had one single thought about Felipe since her arrival in Puerto. She went through everything that had gone down in the last two days, and cringed at the way she'd come apart on account of, well, nothing much. "What a fool I am," she thought, feeling the pinch of shame. "What was I expecting? For God's sake, what a sorry figure I've been cutting! Lucky me that close to no one saw what happened." Then, "Oh, but come on, I see what's going on and that's enough! I see I'm not contented, I see how costly that night with Felipe has been, how it's not something worth repeating." And yet she couldn't help but imagine how nice it would be to have him there with her, how his little kid's eyes would sparkle as that delightful place was unveiled for him.

"Look Felipe, look at those flowers; see how they've built all of this in just a few flattened square yards; look it here Felipe, how by traveling on a vertical one can reach a different world, with its own mountain weather even, and right smack in the centre of town, right here in Puerto..." But daydreaming only plunged her back into the blues. She thanked the day for being dusky: the disparity between a radiant sun and her mood would have been unbearable. She took shelter in the room when the first coarse droplets splattered the ground giving way to the cloudburst.

The clock on the bureau said it was noon. She lay down on the bed, pulled on the woven quilt, covered herself and curled up, listening to the rain as it started blanketing everything. She wouldn't know how long she stayed like that; it was only a pang of hunger that made her move to call room service and order a sandwich and a passion fruit juice.

The girl that brought her supper looked like Viola: same tight glistening curls, same cinnamon skin, same straight-edged nose. "Ms. Viola said to tell you if you should need anything, just dial her, no problem at all," she intoned; then, empty tray in one hand and just about to leave, on her own account she asked, "Is there anything else you might need?" and, now sounding concerned: "Are you all right, *señora?*"

"Oh yes, yes. But ... is it bad, the way I look?" Selene answered, in doubt herself.

"No, it's just that, well," the girl said frowning, uneasy: "you haven't been out of your room the whole day."

"Ah, no need to worry now. You tell your mom I'm really thankful, though."

"She's not my mother," the girl shot back, laughing. "My sister and me, we come from the same village as *la señora* Viola, and when her husband passed away we came here to work with her." Even though Selene felt a sharp sting of curiosity, she refrained from questioning any further and just pulled a bill out of her wallet, gave it to the girl for a tip and thanked her.

The sandwich was no run-of-the-mill concoction:

molten farmer-style cheese, avocado and alfalfa sprouts nestled in a loaf of whole-wheat-with-seeds homemade bread. And then, the passion fruit juice worked as a sedative; so, when done eating she did a little thanksgiving prayer for the food, before snuggling in the broad ottoman facing the picture window, where she once again fell asleep cocooned in the crocheted quilt.

She dreamt about Viola. Roots were sprouting from the soles of her feet, plunging into the ground and sinking into paths of darkness that led them to the core of the bluff, while her arms and hair were spreading over the treetops and winding up as two blooms: the blushing palms of her hands. Waking up she felt disoriented – must have been asleep for over twelve hours; it took her a moment to figure out where she was and what it meant that the sun was already up. She got up, washed her face and hands, and finally changed the clothes she'd been wearing for the last two days, then left the room, went down the stairs, walked by the reception and the restaurant, both deserted, and kept going down all the way to the gate which was unlocked.

Minding practical stuff would bring some order into her head. Her bank account was something tangible, something with her name printed on it, attesting to facts like who she was, where she was and what she owned. She could go check her balance and pull out some cash.

The air was getting increasingly thick with every step she took down the stone stairway. It had stopped raining, just because it couldn't rain anymore: there was no water left in the sky, even if clouds were still hanging like wet rags over the soaked grounds. Having finally reached sea level, she turned toward the main square. One could hear brooms beating left and right, as they shoved water off the sidewalks. Here and there an iron shutter roared as it got lifted, and some radio station cried out the eight o'clock news. Gathered in one corner, a pack of dogs were stretching sleepy bones. Selene walked into the first establishment that looked like it was ready to serve customers and ordered coffee, just to make time as she waited for the bank to open. The first cup was so tasty that she had to go for a second one.

Across the street, with a building's ample entrance hall as his shelter, there was a barefoot young guy sleeping with his head resting on one arm; he was sucking on the thumb of his free hand. The childlike features of his face stood at odds with his corpulence; a sizable belly popped out between his grimy T-shirt and his pants, barely held together on his hips with a hemp string. He was oblivious to the people that went in and out of the building sidestepping him as if he were some sack of junk. Between sips from her second coffee, Selene tried to picture places such as that, where life can lead you – how can someone lose everything, or be born to nothing – but it was too dark a thought, something untold, too steep, so she thought it better to focus on finding a way to get that young man some breakfast. But he wouldn't wake up, even when two women set up shop right next to him, arranging little pyramids of vegetables, tomatoes, beets, chayote squash on cardboard pieces on the floor.

Selene asked the waitress if she knew him, "Do you think he's OK?"

"He's a madman that's always hanging out

around here," answered the waitress and, detecting concern in Selene' face, put her at ease: "Don't you worry, the people here take care of him."

It was not rush hour yet; only now and then would a car or a bus pass by stumbling over waterlogged potholes. A white police pickup truck poked its snout into a junction; then, as it turned to join the flow of the main street, its grim body came into view. There were two soldiers standing on the truck's bed and leaning on the cabin, each holding a rifle – those were the sort that go about in camouflage gear, "cobras," they called them. Two more stood at the rear of the bed. As the pickup with the national emblem stamped on its door rolled in front of her, Selene saw two black men squatted between the four soldiers; one was covering his face with his hands, the other was sternly looking ahead, and his defiant face seemed familiar. Then she saw a group of people following the pickup truck, and those she did recognize: they were all from Redención. Seeing those faces she knew moving closer to where she sat, the whole thing felt as though it was a dream she'd fallen into. There must have been about fifty of them; some shouted, others joined in songs; most kept stabbing the air with their fists. Two women held a banner: *¡Libertad! Ours is the land*, and the crowd kept shouting out, singing actually: *"Nuestra tierra, Libertad* – Freedom, it's our land..." Selene, distressed, ransacked her canvas bag looking for her wallet, got it, pulled out a bunch of coins, left them on the table and waved to the waitress. It was imperative that she follow that group.

As she was putting the wallet back inside her bag, she heard a masculine voice calling from the crowd: "Where have you been holed up?" It was clearly addressing her. When she looked up, for a second she thought she saw Felipe and her blood sank to her feet. But it was Joba, Santa's brother, coming up to her with his mane stuffed in a green, yellow, black and red woven hat. Seen from afar, he could have passed for her Felipe – something close to his doppelganger, though not as handsome as her lover. "Me and my man Felipe," Joba went on, "we spent the whole day looking for you yesterday!"

Taken aback, she felt the peculiar searing surge of chili fumes going up her nose, so intense that it almost made her sneeze; her cheeks lit up and her eyes teared up. Now speechless in surprise, she held back and let Joba rattle on: "We went over every hotel on the beach back there, we looked at every guest list. It was like you'd been erased off the face of this earth, come now," he let her have it. "Cousin's going out of his mind, I tell you! There he was crisscrossing the village on his bike under the rain, crying out for you and how you'd disappeared, so, 'let's go look for her in Puerto,' is what I tells 'im. But we couldn't find you here either and he went back a mess. Lucky for 'im, I'd have to say, dat I came back today and found you at last."

On hearing that, Selene got this urge to run off and hail a taxi, rush over to the hamlet to look for him, find him. Suddenly, full to the rim that heart of hers, which she'd been carrying around as though it were a hole in her chest, was raging to take flight, madly wanting to devour the distance. But no, once again she held back, took a deep breath, sat back on the chair and, without much forethought, pulled out a small notebook and pencil from her bag and started drawing a map. Feeling as though someone else was guiding her pencil strokes, she set down reference points as crosses: the bus station, the marketplace; then, within a circle with a more prominent cross: the hotel. She linked the crosses with arrows signalling the route from A to B, that is, from the bus stop to the hotel. Finally, she wrote at the bottom, "This is where I am, come." She ripped the sheet off the notebook and folded it in two.

"Give this to him, would you please?"

"Just lemme go to the courthouse with them brothers now, but right after that's done I'll take care of this for you," said Joba, putting the note in his pants pocket. Selene, somehow relieved now, turned her attention to the situation going on right there and then. "Yes, the courthouse, let's go, you and me," she joined in. "But listen, tell me Joba, what happened?"

"What happened is two leaders of the Land Defence Committee got busted," Joba shot back, sounding crossed. "And what are they're being charged for? Land invasion. Now you tell me, who's been invading who 'round here?"

"Well, come on, let's go. We should start by looking for a lawyer," Selene put in her two cents with a pressing tone. They rushed off together to catch up with the group that was already turning into the main square.

In the square, rubbish, flower beds and weeds vied for space; empty wrappers in sharp metallic colors wrangled with the hibiscus that grew like miracles amongst the trash and refuse. At the bandstand in the middle of the square, a group of children in gala uniforms were starting to set up enormous tin drums. On all four corners, hawkers and peddlers were busy arranging goodies in the vending stands they'd hauled in with their bicycles. The courthouse building stuck out like an ominous shadow, a grey menace on one full side of the square. The police pickup had come to a stop in front of the tribunal's entrance and the soldiers were shoving the two handcuffed men off the truck and down to the sidewalk. Looking like they resented not being able to unleash their spite, prison guards at the gate shot apprehensive glances at the crowd that had gathered around them. Selene knew neither of the prisoners by name. One of them was bare-chested – his shirt had been ripped off – and one side of his face was swollen, throbbing red; the other one had blood dripping down the front of his white shirt. The crowd's voices kept growing louder – "Ours is the land, ours is the land!" – till the chant turned into something like wounded howls. At that, even the soldiers seemed to flinch and cringe. Yet, when the gate closed behind the two men and their captors, the clamour subsided and the people just loitered about talking heatedly.

"Wait for me right here a moment, Miss," Joba told Selene. She stood still at a short distance from the hubbub, checking the urge to go talk to someone in the crowd, and grudgingly so, because Joba's stern attitude was clearly signalling that she had no dog in that fight. Anyhow, she resented his insistence in addressing her so formally – saw it as a way to make her stand apart, an outsider.

"Let's go find a lawyer," Selene stuck to her guns as soon as Joba got back.

"There's no need, Miss Selene, really, leave it be: our organization, the Fraternidad, we do have lawyers," he responded, edgy. "Now I better go take care of this errand of yours..." He promptly turned around and took off at a good pace – hands in pockets, stooped and leading with his forehead – on his way to the bus station. The initial chords of the national anthem rang away, as the spruced up kids on the bandstand began to make the guts of their tin barrels sing with rubber-tipped drumsticks. Selene went to join the queue to enter the bank.

The scene she had just witnessed stoked anger in her, a zeal for giving shape to something new, as well as an almost maternal, loving desire to protect, to defend, to give shelter to so many who suffer unending miscarriages of justice. But, truth be told, the battles she was waging lately had been just to keep her own spirits up. It wasn't certain whether much of anything could be achieved with the children in the school, who missed classes so often. Some parents had objected to her project for a small pageant on the history of the banana plantations: they argued that the kids didn't need to know such things; that doing it would only make their problems worse; that, all in all, the whole affair had ended terribly, with real bloody episodes to boot. But Selene was well aware of the true, the actual and raw narrative, which belied the official story. It wasn't what the kids were taught in school: that everything had been caused back around 1940 by a bunch of workers in a banana plantation who were misled by a gang of communist outsiders. No, Selene knew about the rivers of blood that ran that day when, following directions "from above," some general gave the order to indiscriminately shoot at a crowd of peasants that were gathered in a peaceful demonstration, just asking for safe working conditions and fair pay in the plantations. When that day came to its end, bodies by the dozen lay dead on the street; one hundred women and men were murdered that day. And now there were the parents, or the parents of parents who'd suffered those events first-hand, in their own flesh, and it was them who thought it better to keep the stories buried away. Then again, there were others who turned their backs on her project simply because they needed the children at home to help with the ever-pressing house chores. Others still, or perhaps all of them, mistrusted Selene because she was a fair skinned one – *una blanca*, a *harutu* woman, they would say – and moreover, it was beyond their comprehension that someone would work so hard without looking to profit from it, or that someone would be fine with living in a God-forsaken hamlet when they had other options to choose from.

Yet, as a new action plan arose in Selene's mind aside from all of that, she felt heartened and right away sensed her soul at last returning fully to her body: she'd have to go house to house speaking to the families. "Anything that can be done here counts," Selene told herself. "The Fraternidad just might end up standing with me, if I can earn their trust; I'll go introduce myself, talk with them. They should be interested in their people getting to know the story, knowing the ways that others have amassed fortunes through centuries mining what rightfully belongs to them here." She felt a brand new emotion rising up her body as she waited for her turn at the cashier.

When she was done with the bank, which took a bit over an hour – even if unable to think of anything she could be missing or had to buy – she headed for the street with all the shops. First stopping at a fruit stand, she bought some grapes and then, a few steps away, came across a stranded German fellow from whom she used to buy bread in her past forages through Puerto – not just to help him out from feelings of sympathy, but also because his bread was really good. This was a tall man with flabby flesh; what little hair remained on his head was a mix of red and grey; and, worn by the rigors of the sun, his sagging cheeks bespoke disillusion. He always carried a cardboard box pinned by a hand on one shoulder. On this occasion, he kept wiping the sweat from his brow over and over with a red bandana in his free hand, even though the morning was cool.

"How are you doing?" Selene asked the man, as he set his box on a bench and rummaged in it, looking for a loaf of bread.

"Today I've got seeded bread, Selene, the way you like it."

"Oh, that's great! ... And, how have you been?" once again she insisted.

"Well, as you can see," he answered with a sigh, "still here..." He was one of those foreigners that, driven by a youthful infatuation with the Caribbean, had burnt their ships only to end up stranded there in old age with nowhere else to go. His survival depended on the bread he sold, which he made following his Brandenburg grandmother's recipes.

Selene paid for the bread and wished him a good

day; the loaf went into her bag as she hit Comercio Street. On display in a shop window, there was a simply cut white dress made in a fine gossamer – looked perfect to mark the new beginning she sensed was coming into her life. Forcing herself to wipe off her mind what she'd seen just minutes before, the image of the prisoner's bloodied white shirt, she went in and bought the dress. Like an automaton and without much of an appetite, she entered the taquería she always visited when in town, barely managed to eat two tacos while standing up, asked for an *horchata*, drank half of it, paid the bill and rushed out of there. Once again she was walking on Comercio Street, hurriedly now even if slowing down her pace would have been more to her liking.

She arrived at the hotel gasping for air, her heart aflutter with the excitement she felt knowing she'd soon be seeing Felipe; and winded as well by the climb, having gone up the steps two by two. From the kitchen, next to the reception desk, along with the aroma of freshly baked bread there were women's voices and giggles flowing out. They spoke a different language, between cooing lullaby and murmur. Her first impulse was to go in and say hello but, realizing that Viola and her two girls hadn't seen her arrive as they chatted sprightly while hurrying to make the day's lunch, she chose instead to go straight to her room and rest a bit before Felipe came over.

Up on the fourth floor, the calls of birds supplanted the women's voices. She rushed into her room with her feet barely grazing the tiles on the floor. This time there was no doubt that Felipe would show up, of that she was plain certain. Since his friend Joba had drawn such a dramatic picture of the situation, there was no way he'd fail to come. Just as she was about to hit the shower, like in a *déjà vu*, she had a sense of having been there before, and then gave up on washing, getting dolled up. Coolly, she jumped into bed to take her rest, and to make believe she wasn't expecting anything. The phone stirred her up.

"*El señor* Felipe Flinn is asking for you," Viola's warm voice chirped through the line.

Felipe Flinn: that was the first time Selene heard his full name. She paused for an instant before answering: "Yes, yes of course, please Viola tell him to come up, and thank you."

She made a dash for the bathroom, checked herself on the mirror and ran her fingers through her hair. "What to do now," she wondered: "Leave the door open and just wait? Wait till I hear him knocking at the door?" In the end she just opened the door, and stood out on the terrace holding on to the railing with both hands. Looking down, she saw Felipe walking up the stairs with his backpack hanging from one shoulder. His face wasn't visible yet, only the knitted black beret. His dark outfit notwithstanding, he cut a luminous figure. Selene turned her eyes upward and scanned the treetops: a couple of crows were building their nest, him bringing twigs in his beak and her arranging them.

"Whoa! You couldn't have found a better place to hide," said Felipe, short of breath and following the angle of Selene's gaze. "Just look at you now, took yourself right up to where the crows come nestle, couldn't get any higher up, could you?"

Once within reach, not knowing where to park

their hands, they tugged and clutched each other while their mouths, bent on kissing, refused to come apart. Felipe paused to try an explanation: "I'm so sorry, please forgive me: I couldn't get to you, my neighbor's house got flooded and I had to stay and help her out…" Selene was in turn trying to push aside a wave of embarrassment and for that one moment she felt so very stupid; Cisneros' voice reappeared to whisper fleetingly in her ear: *you acting like a white girl… a white girl.* But soon enough her distress was assuaged by Felipe's presence so close now, and she kept kissing him – one by one kissing his upper and his lower lip, each like a silk-skinned fruit that was now black now crimson. Intertwined, quivering, stumbling, with drunk-like glassy eyes, still kissing they got back to the room and slumped down on the bed, with Felipe still lugging his knapsack on his back.

Come nightfall, starved, they went down to have dinner at the restaurant. A greyish streak of clarity still remained on the sky; the babel of the birds was gradually fading and crickets were beginning to chirp and sing. Under the faint, flickering light of gas lamps, the great terrace appeared to be swaying between the huge arms of the mango trees that stood around it. Almost every table was taken. Flowing from hidden speakers, the voice of Vinicius de Moraes blessed all those present. Wearing a fitted black dress, so unlike the morning's *huipil*, with her hair loose, her lips bright red and wreathed in jasmine fragrance, Viola walked over to welcome the couple and kissed Selene on the cheek, as if they were old friends. Felipe let out a barely audible growl in the presence of the handsome hostess, who gave them each a menu after getting them settled at one of the tables with a better view, on the edge of the terrace.

"I'll be right back to take your orders," she said and got back to tend to and chat with the other clients that – in view of the pleasant, extended-family feel of the ambience – seemed to be regulars in the place.

Selene and Felipe couldn't stop staring at each other; they didn't even look at the menu. Underneath the table, Felipe would lightly yank the hem of Selene's new dress, as though wanting to pull her toward him. She kept stretching her neck toward him, beaming.

It wasn't long before Viola returned. "What do you two feel like eating?" she asked. Unlike how it had been in the morning, her voice was high-pitched now; she was carefully articulating each word, so as to make herself understood amidst the buzz of the conversations at the tables and the bossa-nova that the speakers were spewing at enough volume to prevail over the cocktail of rhythms rising from the street below along with the incessant barking of dogs.

"Bring us anything you want, whatever is the day's special," said Selene.

"There is the baked fish in *achiote*," Viola announced. "It comes wrapped in plantain, leaves – real tasty – and it's served with tortillas, rice and beans. As for drinks, today we have our own house wine in two flavours: date palm and grapefruit." She was of course referring to the brew that the locals call wine, a kind of mead made with fermented fruit, muscovado and spices.

"Excellent!" Selene burst out, with an enthusiasm that seemed just a bit exaggerated; but it wasn't just the food that she was praising, it was everything that life had put on her lap at that moment. Even the weather was improving: the sky had cleared, letting the stars shine through, and she was beginning to feel a slightly sticky warmth on her skin. "What do you feel like drinking, Felipe?" she asked.

"Let's go for the wine but, really, we should try both flavors," he suggested, sounding like some gluttonous gourmand. "Oh, and a double order of tortillas." Then chuckling and, casting a loaded glance Selene's way, he concluded with a kind of warning: "one big eater, that's what I am."

Felipe's eyes gleamed, going from Selene's face to the grand natural pageant that was unfolding before them: beyond the lights of Puerto, a dazzling conflagration of stars above the darkened sea. Presently, their drinks arrived in tall frosted glasses. In just one gulp Felipe took in close to half of his wine.

"It's pretty strong, be careful,' he admonished Selene, who was taking tiny sips from a straw without lifting her glass off the table, with her eyes still fixed on him. She felt like a little girl on a date with daddy for ice cream in town.

"Ever noticed how there's no lighthouse? Felipe asked, pointing with pursed lips at the tip of the bay. "It's been a couple years since the lantern was stolen and they still haven't replaced it."

"Oh, but who could have stolen a thing like that without being seen in a port as tiny as this one?"

"Well, namely: word's out there that it was the son of one a them big kahunas in town – you know, of course, how it is that 'round here there's two or three retired generals and colonels who feel free to do as they please."

"Yes, yes I get it," Selene said, frowning and twitching her nose as one does when smelling something rotten. Right there and then she recalled – as a storm cloud returning to darken her horizon – the scene she'd witnessed not long before. She turned to him, in earnest: "Felipe, what happened in town this morning, those two men that were arrested ... what's going on?"

"Oh boy, the lady does get around, don't she?" he said, and then, calmly: "Joba told me you was there, and well, what's going on is they're two of the leaders of the Land Defence Committee and well, them being so upfront and all, it's them who get their heads bashed at first. But don't you worry yourself now, it ain't the first time things like that happen with us; I bet they'll let them go free tomorrow, and just because the government can't afford to carry more of the people's martyrs on its book of debts to pay. Thing is, though, one can't be sure that some other day they won't be murdered by some no-name killer-for-pay; that's what usually happens to people that dare make life complicated for the moneyed class, those with power and their own interests 'round here – stuff like growing African palm, so they can grow even richer selling palm oil. ... Well, lemme tell you, that's dangerous shit, Selene. I don't mess 'round wid stuff like that, oh fuck it!"

Selene found it awesome, how clearly Felipe expounded his arguments. He paused for a moment, shook his head and changed the subject: "Look over there, at the end, where there's them red lights." His lips curled, calling her attention to a great shadow towering over the beach. "Ah, the Railroad Company?" Selene wondered.

"Yeah – well, not really but – yes, that's actually where they had their offices; but anyway, see, next to that building, a bit further to the left ... right there, that was the train station."

"Oh yes, I see it now! There's that circle of red lights – must be where the trains used to turn around, eh?" Selene chimed in, as she could see perfectly from afar even though her eyesight was beginning to feel weak when reading.

"That's right, and then, my sisters and me used to go there to sell oranges, or the bread Ma used to bake. Sometimes, depending on how much stuff we had to offer, we'd ride the train both ways till it was all sold off. And that's how we made the dough to buy our notebooks for school."

"How old were you then?"

"Let's see, that was no more than two years... musta been when I was between eight 'n ten – that is, because around nineteen seventy five *La Yunai* – the Fruit Company – they had already moved some place else and their trains stopped coming this way."

Quickly putting two and two together, even if she didn't have much of a head for math, Selene realized: "I was already an adult when he was just a kid." She used to find it hard to wrap her mind around the fact, even if she'd often forget it, because Felipe looked older than his actual age – what with the grey that was starting to show on his sideburns, and the crease on his brow which got deeper whenever he was lost in thought.

"So, you went to school in Redención? The same one that's still there?" She tried picturing him in her mind: his presence in the place where she was working now, in those classrooms, in that playground, in those hallways with his uniform and his books, just like any of her own pupils who barely stood at her shoulders' level. Like a mosquito landing in her ear, that image, the notion nettled her for a moment. Thing is, starting from the first day they slept together, she had felt small next to him: a child coiled under his shadow as he had turned into a giant, an oak tree affording shelter.

To hold her ground and gather strength, Selene led the conversation to a subject she felt passionate about: "I'm teaching the kids all about the history of the railway and the fruit companies." That was the reason for her being there: the history of that place – how once and again the beauty and the richness of the land have bought ruin upon it.

"Yes, you've told me about that, when you showed me that book you have by a Nicaraguan priest, right?"

Selene, touched and impressed at how attentive he was to her stories, to everything she said, concurred: "You're right, Ernesto Cardenal."

"Hey, let's get this straight, what is he then, a priest or a cardinal?" They burst into sidesplitting cackles at the easy wittiness of his riposte.

When the mirth wore off, and back in a serious tone, she recited the first passage of the book that came to her mind:

They corrupt the prose and they corrupt the Congress ...
After all, that shitty railroad meant
no benefit to the nation

because it was a railway between two plantations,
not between two cities, Trujillo and Tegucigalpa.
Then the banana is left to rot in the plantations,
or to rot in wagons along the railway tracks,
or it's cut once ripe
so it can be rejected
when it gets to the piers, or gets dumped into the sea,
the bunches of bananas declared bruised or too skinny,
or withered or green, or deceased or overripe:
so there'll be no cheap bananas for us to buy,
yet for them bananas will come cheap.
Till there's hunger all along this Caribbean Coast,
as the farmers go to jail for not selling at 30 cents
while congressmen get invited to garden parties.
But the black worker has seven children
and what can you do? You've got to eat,
so you take whatever they offer to pay you:
24 cents a bunch ...

Once done, Selene kind of giggled as she realized the wine had got her tongue rolling and her mind all tangled.

Felipe was now looking at her as though spellbound. "Hold it there, I've got to know, there's so many things you've got to tell me…" He was moved, not knowing where to start, his words stumbling. "How is it possible that a great man in another country went and wrote the history of this lousy port, and then, how can he say so many things with so few words?" Selene was taken by the sharpness of his insight: this was a fisherman, gardener, plumber who had barely finished high school. "How much prejudice some of us carry around in spite of ourselves," she thought. "And why should book-wise people hold a monopoly on understanding? It's such hogwash, nonsense! Could be just as well the other way around."

She turned to him, "That is precisely the privilege of poetry: to share truths with just a few words." Now Selene's voice crackled and she got goose bumps, as it always happened when she spoke of such things. "That's why I chose this poet's book to have the children learn their history, and also, to try and make them see that whatever happens here really matters, that *they matter.*"

"There's something else I wanna know," he kept on probing, "and that is, woman, how the hell can you manage to learn so much stuff by heart?"

"Actually, it's not hard to memorize poetry: you only have to follow the rhythm of the words, just like in music. It's something that has come easy to me since I was a little girl."

The chat was cut short by the girl that brought them their meal. Then silence ruled as they paid homage to mister fish: a red snapper laying on its plantain leaf before them like a sacrificial victim bathed in a red sauce, neither too thick nor too runny – just perfect. They sprinkled it with the house wine, of which they'd had four glasses already. With every step of the meal, Selene's admiration for the hotelier kept growing: every single detail was an act of exemplary love – the glazed clay tableware; the woven basket for the tortillas; the blown glass drinking cups; the large napkins in thick cotton. Everything being so richly tasteful in its simplicity made Selene feel right at home. Yet, in her euphoria, it didn't cross her mind how alien all of that might seem to

Felipe – that is, even if, according to his account, he had covered a good chunk of the world during his industrial fishing trips, gone all the way to Caracas and San Andrés Island in Colombia, where he'd rubbed elbows with all kinds of folk and surely got to meet gorgeous women, as she could well imagine.

When nothing but fish bones was left on the plantain leaf, the hankering lovers went back to their room. No one nowhere had ever been so happy, not even them: it was the first time that they'd experienced such utter bliss – felt like some gaseous blessing was filling their insides.

The next morning, Selene took care of the bill and they said goodbye to Viola. As Felipe shook hands with the mistress of the house, "Congratulations on your wine," he told her with the seductive tone he could turn on at will. "Some day I'd like to have you taste the one I make. Now, if you don't mind, I'm gonna steal from you that allspice touch you put on that wine of yours, it works real good!"

And Selene: "Thanks so much, Viola, I'll see you soon. This place of yours is wonderful." She wouldn't know where to start the list of all the things that had delighted her so much. "The colors on your walls, I'd never seen those; where do you get them?" If she ever had a house her own, it would be painted just like that. So, Viola says, "I make my paints." That woman, whom Selene already saw as a heroine, was once again leaving her awe-struck. And Viola went on: "I make them with lime and pigments, glue, a bit of soap. Pigments, the ones people use for concrete floors, you find those in any hardware store."

Selene filed the information in her mind. "*Gracias* Viola," she said again, giving her a hug.

"You be careful," she thought she heard Viola tell her in a whisper.

They went back to the hamlet in a taxi, entered the place like a bride and groom on their wedding day, riding the back seat of the jalopy that hopped and skipped trying to avoid the ever-present potholes.

It wasn't long before Selene left her cottage and, together with Felipe, rented a little house a few blocks from the beach. Right away, she earnestly proceeded to paint all of her new casita, making the paint herself with Viola's formula. The new abode was far from perfect, but it felt like paradise to Selene and Felipe, with the added edge that it had a kitchen, which was a great advantage in the end because, the moment Santa saw things had taken a serious turn with them, she started turning grumpy and sluggish, till she plain refused to keep cooking Selene's meals.

There was the time, before the move to new grounds, when following Santa's dictum – "You gotta show up at the beach to receive him with a bowl big enough to carry the fish; it's yo' duty now" – they both went to greet Felipe when he returned from fishing. On that day the sea had yielded an abundant take of fish, so all the motorboats and canoes had gone out. Then at sunrise, one by one, two by two or in clusters, the vessels slowly started reaching shore, some of them submerged almost to the gunwale from being overloaded.

While the crowd of bowl-carrying women was waiting on the beach and Selene, covering her eyes with one hand, tried to spot the boat Felipe was in, Santa let her have it in plain words: "Now you have a husband," she said, "now you have to cook for your man."

Selene did her best to clear the air: "But why can't you just cook for both of us? I thought you liked him, Santa."

"I do, but that's not my place," Santa shot back, surly. "It's your job now, and lemme tell you, there's something I gotta warn you 'bout, you hear? Felipe's family, they're never gonna see you or accept you as one of their own."

Selene didn't pay much attention, thinking that perhaps Santa was just jealous; and yet, those words of hers would remain floating over her head like shadows. Just about then Felipe's boat came in; it was the most heavily loaded, so much that it looked like it was about to capsize. At first the two women made out only Felipe's outline standing on the bow with arms outstretched; then, as the boat got closer, they got to hear his voice: "*Eihaba! Eihaba!* Blessings family, blessings," he was shouting and laughing with that raspy voice of his.

When the boat hit land, the crowd darted over and, in a flock of hands, they pulled it all the way off the water. The yellowtail snappers, the mackerels and bonitos that boiled over the boat spread silver flashes under the morning sun, while the fishermen were giving the due share of one fish to each extended hand. As Felipe filled Selene and Santa's bowls, the latter laughed, excited, and the foreigner wondered if her friend weren't feeling regret for the words she had spouted just minutes ago; but then, amidst that fiesta of abundance, what had felt like an affront was forgotten. An hour later, when the communal sharing out was over, Felipe took off for

76

his parents' house with a sack over his shoulder. Going back home that day, Selene and Santa stopped at the professor's gazebo to have a beer – but those shared moments would gradually become more and more sparse, until the two friends parted ways for good.

La Blanca is Laid to Rest

The barn owl did not sing out, neither did the roosters, and all the birds outside were silent as well. When faint hairlines of light started seeping through the cracks in the window shutter, the barrels that supported the bed were already underwater. La Blanca died at dawn. The wound on her forehead had weakened the mare so much that she couldn't hold out against the foul weather, and when Selene opened the door that morning, there she was, dead under the mango tree: a tiny island, white as her name. Felipe shoved his sadness under a cloak of annoyance: "There was no fucking need for us to stay out here, cut off from everyone. You and me, we're living like damn fugitives, and now what: we're gonna have to find our own way outta this mess."

Selene nodded in agreement. Even as the neighbors who evacuated the day before had warned them – it was best to leave the grounds with their animals, they said – Selene and Felipe stuck to their guns, reckless, and stayed put. And then again, poor La Blanca wouldn't have had the strength to make the trip to the hamlet, so that was that.

"Brother, sista', listen here: this flood gonna be worse than it's been in years, 'cause the sandbar hasn't opened and the water can't find no way out," *el Búho* – Nightbird – had said, fixing his great canny eyes on Felipe and Selene to give wing to his argument. "Maybe if you two could act mo' sensible: just go over on your own 'n take a single gander at that river, so still 'n quiet now – like a lake it looks, it does. Ah, you may say, nothing like it was last year, when it took a bunch of houses. But we had no flood back then, mind you: today it's gonna be the other way 'round." And he kept going with that preacher's voice of his: "You both woulda been better off leaving with your son, Felipe mon; we just seen the kid going 'cross the sandbar with the colt."

El Búho was the leader of the group of men who – absent any kind of local official authority – had taken upon themselves the heavy load of looking after the physical and spiritual integrity of the children of the hamlet. He was a teetotaller. Selene always wondered if it wasn't in reparation for youthful excesses. While the man's pulchritude didn't allow even a glimpse of any past dissipation, he did run in his backyard a family business selling drinks, a place also well known because of his wife's culinary treats: stews made with turtle eggs, lizard meat and foodstuff from other tasty yet illicit endangered species.

"Mon, there's no better place to be than one's own home," Felipe shot back, "even if at times you end up having to wear rubber boots inside the house, even if your bed is set on top of barrels and you hang your stuff from the rafters on the roof."

Another fellow in the group went ahead and cleared the air: "Hoity toity, rubber boots inside 'n out, wooee! " he chimed in, and finished off the wisecrack with a whole lot of hip shaking. That was *Patatiesa* – stiff step, a nickname given him because he had a hobble, but they shortened it to Pata. This guy Pata, full-time illiterate, made his living from whatever he could forage: coconuts, firewood, wild little critters. Days on end he'd spend scavenging around like a blue arsed fly, his cart squeaking like so many birds chirping away. A great collective cackle echoed throughout the house at Pata's flashy quip; it flooded the yard, crossed the fields planted with cassava, glided off the mangroves and the palm trees, and came to rest down in the hamlet. Felipe's chuckles were the loudest then: that wild laughter of his could chase the birds off the maize fields and send kittens into hiding.

Selene didn't join in the whoopee though; she kept quiet, her face hardened. For one, Patatiesa's grungy disposition turned her off; but, most of all, because she knew a load of fearful guilt was the real reason Felipe avoided going to town.

Now, putting on his white cap with TEXACO in red letters across the top, el Búho broke in: "OK then, you two, so be it," and he stepped out of the house with the whole group following behind. "But make sure you guys be coming ova' to me place tomorrow," he went on, "y'all know we doin' the novena for me mother in law." And then there's Patatiesa, howling now from beyond the porch: "You can always swim yo' way over to el Búho's in your bikini, Felipe mon!" They took off, once again laughing till, a few bends on the road and a while gone by, their voices finally faded away.

The following morning, as though in the midst of a bad dream, Selene and Felipe had to face the hard-and-fast reality: La Blanca was dead. Sunrise had caught the poor mare lying still on her side with bluegreen flies fluttering around the gash in her forehead.

"She needs a resting place, but where?"

"Up there, above the forest, in the bend by the orchard with the mango trees," said Felipe. And then – for what felt like forever – with the water somehow easing off the task, between wafting and tugging they carried her over and along the flooded cassava fields. With his shovel under one arm, Felipe pulled on the front legs while Selene pushed the croup, carrying on her shoulders the blanket she'd chosen to shroud the mare. Her head got to churning as, with her gaze fixed on the rolling water, she struggled to keep the lifeless body moving. To hold back the urge to throw up, she stared ahead and set her eyes on Felipe's bent-over figure. As they made their way forward, following the beat of their breathing in tandem to dovetail the pushing and the pulling, she felt a chill climbing up her back all the way to the nape of her neck as minute fingers tugged at her hair. A zinging heat ran over her lips, her eyelids, her cheeks, her forehead, and right away she felt the presence of the ancestors – the same ones that by now she'd grown accustomed to live with. There they were, Felipe's deceased grandparents, and others who came before them: survivors from the wreck of a ship full of African slaves, who would come to find refuge in the sweet embrace of native *Arawak* women in some Caribbean island – the ones whose couplings begot the race that inhabits the Antillean shores of Central America. It was them, the spirits of the woodlands that – with voices almost imperceptible, with songs only a buzz – went along and stood by Selene and Felipe when La Blanca was laid to rest.

On and on they went, dead La Blanca, the man,

and the woman, till they reached a point where a patch of clear land loomed. Felipe stuck the shovel into the ground like a settler staking his claim with a flag. Right then, Selene saw in him the embodiment of the soldier that Horacio the wise healer had spoken of one day:

"You Felipe, in another life of yours, on that night o' the shipwreck with the slaves, you was one o' them folk who belonged with the white men; that's why you so at ease among them Indians 'n half-breeds; that's why your woman's white."

People in the hamlet feared Horacio. With his deep understanding of plants, persons and things, and the seasoned ways he had of dealing with them, he would manage to come up with cures that could be explained only on account of some supernatural power. And, since Selene knew as well how to cure with her tiny sugary pellets, the lovers ended up making good friends with the man. Whenever they needed help, they'd go see him, paying no heed to the entreatments of Felipe's mother, who never stopped warning them against that wizard's fiendish powers and kept recommending other healers, women mostly, that prescribed prayers, invocations and scented-potion baths.

Selene and Felipe drove over to his place when they took it for a fact that a curse had been cast on them. That was after a couple of dark occurrences went down: Felipe shot his best friend twice, and on the wake of that mad incident, the sweet woman Coral passed away. The shooting itself happened on Independence Day, September the fifteenth.

"I did warn you 'bout that, me brother," said Horacio once he'd heard them tell the story. "I told you that house you two went and leased, that place had to be cleansed, but you wouldn't listen to me."

As Felipe hung his head, Horacio laid down his advice: "First things first, my man: you gotta wash the house, all of it with sea water real good. After that, you gonna get me four chickens, no more no less. We'll have to get behind this for a couple weeks for things to come out right. Once we're done with the sacrifice, I'm gonna need to do some heavy work on you, with smoke, with *guaro* and all the rest," he spoke out loud, staring at Felipe. Selene made a list of all that was needed: sea water; four chickens; twenty quarts of sugar cane rum – Horacio's guaro; thirty cigars; candles…

They told Pata to hit the yard and get the four chickens that the warlock needed, and to pick the best ones too. Being an expert at such chores, since he was part of a gang that people called The Broth because they stole chickens to make soup, Patatiesa grabbed the chickens in a jiffy and brought them over all bundled up. Then, returning from school and seeing how the four birds were fated to be sacrificed, Ariel made a fuss: "No *hombre*, no way, it ain't fair we're getting rid of our fattest *pollos*!"

At the break of dawn the next day, Selene and her man got busy washing the whole house with tubs full of sea water they brought in the cart pulled by Rey, their prized stallion.

"Bind the woman's waist, gotta fasten her good," Horacio instructed. "Now, Selene, you go ahead 'n grab this chicken real tight."

With the natural plain sailing that she assumed in dealing with anything Felipe himself flung her way,

Selene knelt down and grabbed the chicken by the wings. Right away, Horacio chopped off the animal's head, waited as it jerked till motionless, and then poured the chicken's blood, thick and warm, over her head.

"It'll be all of five sacrifices we gotta have before the spell is broken. With them chickens it's been four, so there's one left for us to do," the healer told them and, as he was taking his leave: "Uh, but that's not all, before the fifth we still need to do a few smoke passes with you, my man Felipe, and for that you best be coming home to me."

Horacio lived out by the other end of the hamlet. His was a small house built of giant reeds in the middle of a garden strewn with wildflowers and medicinal herbs. Everything in the place suggested intelligence and gentleness. His homestead was surrounded by a dyke with willows laid throughout to soak up the water; in those backstreets the only patch that didn't get swamped with the floods was Horacio's. The healer was a sharp-sighted man of no discernible age; it was only his knowingness that made one see he had already passed the peak of life. Selene and Felipe often paid visits to his garden; they liked that he made them gifts of stem cuttings or roots of plants too rare for the tropics, though not so strange to her, since she came from a mild-weather place. Horacio too enjoyed sharing his garden with Selene and talking about the healing properties of dandelion, herb of grace and aloe.

When he came out next time around, with a dapper *guayabera* shirt and his recently shaven face exuding cologne fumes, they were both standing by his collection of sage plants and salvia shrubs. Felipe, absorbed, stared vacantly while pretending to listen to his woman's comments, as she spoke non-stop trying to make things feel normal. "Sage smoke works as a very good protection against envy..." she was saying when, as though by way of a greeting, Horacio's voice finished the sentence: "That is to say, for the evil eye," and, looking askance at Felipe now, he concluded with a heavy tone: "A much-needed kind of smoke in this village."

Then, politely, he led the way with his left hand, weighed with three heavy rings: three identical silver bands with small obsidian inlays. Felipe followed him into a small palm shelter in a corner of the garden and Selene went in after them. The light that came in through the door and the flame of a candle barely broke the dimness of the windowless interior. Horacio had Felipe sit on a chair in the centre of the space, and Selene made herself as tiny as she could on a bench by the side. Placed atop a small table and around the lit candle, there were three quarts of *guaro* and a few cigars.

"Take your shirt off, brother," the healer ordered as he uncorked one of the bottles. Then, after taking a swig, he lit up a cigar with the candle and started reciting prayers in a strange language, while emptying the *guaro* over Felipe's head and naked torso, all the time tapping the ground with his foot to stress his words. Now, wrapping him with a heavy cloud of smoke and – as if the smoke were the lines of some ancient book he was reading – Horacio uttered the sentence that stabbed Felipe's brow and struck his eyes with something like flashes of darkness:

"That night when the slave ship went down, you, Felipe, you was one of them white men."

"Right here, way up above our parcel, that's where we should of built our house in the first place..."

Selene heard Felipe's voice as if coming from afar and it startled her, abruptly pulling her reminiscing mind back to the present. She responded, and rashly so: "Oh yes, and I suppose this is the perfect time for you to start thinking things like that?" The words just shot out of her mouth and immediately she wished she'd swallowed them whole. It came as no surprise that, feeling put upon, he went back to the chippy track that they'd started on the day before: "Ah, you always be thinkin' you're the smart one everywhere, eh? ... Just 'cause you was born in a golden cradle, good 'n cosy, right?"

With every day that passed, there were more things about her that rubbed him the wrong way. When riding the car, more often than not they couldn't help but stumble into all kinds of quarrels that he'd get going out of the blue. "What are you, a truck driver?" he'd yell at her every time they left the hamlet with Selene driving uphill on first gear to make the turn that linked the dirt road and the paved highway – or when she'd reverse-park without the slightest hitch: "Yeah right, that just goes to show you was born already in the driver's seat."

As they took turns in digging, the shovel blows lent a rhythmic base to the chaotic concert of the forest, while butterflies joined the farewell ritual for La Blanca, filling the tin-gray air with brushstrokes of electric blue. They had barely gone three feet deep when the water started sipping through.

"These grounds, they're saturated, Selene. The

land being what it is out here, you never need to dig too much to get yourself a well," said Felipe, no longer with even a hint of animosity in his voice. Looking taken by how his woman was giving all she had to the task at hand, he spoke softly now, respectful, with tones she hadn't heard for a long time.

The only possible solution now was to lay La Blanca down as deep as they could and then cover her all the way by adding more and more soil to the tumulus. Selene stretched the blanket over the dead mare's body before beginning to throw dirt into the makeshift grave. It was then that, no matter how high she kept her guard, how much she looked up to heaven just to hold back the gush of grief, the tears started rolling down at last unchecked. Never again would she snuggle up to the warm body of her *compañera*. She did her best to fend off her memory that time when she had just fractured her knee and La Blanca showed up with her loins badly bitten – when she cured the mare with calendula extract and both of them went to lie down under a tree where they could lick their wounds in peace together.

La Blanca was sired by el Rey out of la Huraga. That equine family was thought to be a miracle because el Rey, a gorgeous white horse, had crossed with la Huraga, a molly mule; and then of course, as the spawn of a jennet and a horse, she was supposed to be barren. "Mules cannot bear foals; the Good Lord made it that way, so that the species wouldn't get all ruined." That was the explanation given by Hati, the woman who lived across the sandbar and knew *everything*.

As for La Blanca's dam, la Huraga: she was a thick-bodied, lush brunette with a big round rump that she swung about like it was mulatto hips in a dance hall. So el Rey, the town's stallion, was crazy about her. He didn't fancy any of the mares around; for him there was nothing compared to la Huraga. In his zeal for that mule he'd bust the toughest fettering ropes and go missing for days with everyone having to look for him all over the fields and out in the woodlands. There was even a time when he tore off the dark hide that covered his genitals when he jumped over a barbed-wire fence just to be near her. In the end, Selene and Felipe went and bought la Huraga from her owner, an old bachelor who, as some sharp tongues put it, was married to that mule.

And then el Rey, that horse was indeed the talk of the town. He was seen too as an extension of Felipe's spirit, since people said that, when he was born, the man's grandma had vested his hands with a supernatural force, for working, for fighting and for pleasuring women as well. El Rey himself went on to sire a good bunch of foals, all grown to be tough workers; but that must have been a virtue inherited from la Huraga – though, as it often happens, the credit and the praise end up falling on the *macho* side. La Blanca was the first of many offspring that the couple bore, refuting the notion that a cross of a mule and a horse always ends up being barren.

Selene and Felipe arranged her grave as best they could and returned home leaving behind a simple knoll of neatly swept soil. On the way back, he suddenly reached for her arm, held her back and close to him. As the man projected a rather imposing figure, he appeared to be taller than he was, but in height he was actually even with Selene; and so, once standing face to face, they couldn't but look into each other's eyes; now he exploded:

"*Hinsietibunu* Selene, I love you, you're one for the trenches and you're mine, *mi blanca* you are, my *harutu* woman!"

Selene's heart swelled up like a tortilla on a hot clay griddle as she sensed the rebirth of the loving fondness that they'd been carrying around like a moribund body for a good while already. At that moment the beat of a distant drum started filling the air: *tuc-tucu-tuc, tuc-tucu-tuc, tuc-tucu-tuc* ... Even from afar, the one-two-three measure of a *Punta* was clearly present: its funereal beats and cadences announcing the beginning of the novena at el Búho's house.

"Tonight you wear a real fine skirt, we got a wake to go to," Felipe whispered in Selene's ear, well aware that he was sparking a blaze with his breath. Like a spark flying off a bonfire, she released herself from his grasp and kept on walking ahead of him, feeling the sizzle of his gaze on her hips.

Rites

One at a time they bathed next to the well, even as the water had erased all borderlines and one could barely make out where it was that the well stood or how to get to the tilapia farming ponds. Felipe went first. All the time it took Selene to pick an outfit and lie the pieces on the bed – an embroidered-lace thong and its matching bra; the white, Egyptian-cotton blouse; the wide, red-and-green printed skirt to trigger the drums in the Punta dance – there was her man making a ruckus out in the yard while cascades slid down his body, water burst against skin and water splashed on water; she could hear his cackles turning into shouts, his shouting into guffaws, jus as it would happen whenever he was filled with glee. Water/laughter/roars/skin. She pictured him as a lion or some bird of prey, shaking his mane along with the family jewels, as was his wont. "If he were an animal, which one then? A horse would be just about right," she was thinking when Felipe's resonant voice streamed into the room: "Your turn, *preciosa*."

Selene hung her towel from a branch of the nance tree and right away felt tiny as she saw herself fully naked amidst such liquid vastness. With water up to her knees, she used a gourd to slowly and quietly wash the sweat and sludge away from her hair, her body. The cool water freshened her head, relieving the fever that had been boiling in her since early morning. With soapy hands she rubbed her right knee for a good while, as the pain had returned with the exertion she'd just put herself through. Above the bulge that remained as a deformity, the thigh – now concave where it had once been convex – was noticeably thinner than its left counterpart. To offset its disadvantage, the calf of the injured leg had turned more muscular than its matching limb. Bereft of vital force, that sorry leg of hers had become a magnet for mishaps of all sorts; if she laid on the grass, ticks would climb all over it; a cat's scratch on her right ankle put her at risk of gangrene; the barbed wire in fences would prick only that one leg. She finished her bath, once again wrapped herself in the towel and went back to the house; on tiptoes she did it like someone afraid of bursting a bubble, startling a wild animal, or being awaken from a dream. Once in the kitchen – something she wasn't prone to do – she took a couple of strong anti-inflammatory pills, the kind she'd been given in the hospital after the fracture.

The bedroom welcomed her, imbued with inviting essences; there was Felipe, polishing himself head to toes with amber and lavender oils, his body beaming in love. Having finished his ablutions, he put on his briefs and sat down on the rattan chair just to feast his eyes on his woman. Under his gaze, Selene ended up brushing off the pangs of her shriveled leg; she massaged oil into her body too, put on the thong, the bra, the blouse...

"What do you say we finish off getting dressed out there, before going across the river; that way we won't be a soaked mess arriving at the wake, uh?" he suggested.

"Hey, great idea, let's do just that!" she answered, already in giggles at the notion of them both wandering half naked up to the river. As she laughed, her eyes lit up mirroring Felipe's, which glimmered from the other end of the room like obsidian shards with his rising want, while Selene combed her still wet hair into a thick braid. As she caught on the rush in the man's face, her eyes travelled instinctively towards his groin. It was as though, coming awake, his sex were now an iron shaft and her eyes two magnets drawn to it. Yet she knew that, even if things could heat up in a jiffy, he wasn't going to touch her, not just yet:

"You'd have to be a God damn moron to go fooling 'round in the water when all your pores be wide open," he'd always say when he was done with work, or after making love. Add into the bargain, come to things like that his preferred way was to "let them urges pile up," so as to "build an appetite" – an art that Selene herself would get to master with time, even if at first holding back was an ordeal for her, the cause of bellyaches by the bunch.

As he stepped into the living room, Felipe went ahead and put on the T-shirt Selene had given him recently, arranged his hair and fixed his necklace – a snail shell nestled in macramé network. "Look it, Sombra's fallen asleep on the table," he said, and then: "Might as well leave her be, ain't no way she's gonna go swimming all the way to el Búho's, right? ... Tell it how it is, 'round here it's just you 'n me who take our pet bitch with us even when we're going disco. Just imagine what it'd be like if every folk in town took their dogs to every party, nah mon!" he concluded, securing the latch on the kitchen door before grabbing the keys and lock to batten down the main door.

Holding clothes and sandals in their hands – and laughing still about them being the only ones bringing their dogs along to dance at the discotheque – they left the house on their way to the wake. They did share many a laugh, Felipe and Selene, their ideas of what's funny being just about equally matched.

The percussions were doubling down as they approached the river: what had begun simply with a triple-time beat was now engaging many drums and weaving a hot, hot Punta. The water level kept going down as the path went up the hill. They stepped on dry land as they reached the riverbank, where they always had their boat moored. That's where they finally got fully dressed before pushing the vessel all the way into the water. The river looked like a swollen lake on the verge of breaching its own limits. Wary of messing up their outfits, they went across standing up, Felipe on the oars.

"Oh boy oh mon, just look at me brother here: him a'looking just like one o' them moo-bee stars today!" That was Patatiesa welcoming them, always the joker. Chomping on a cigarette, he pulled the boat off the water along with Felipe and then stretched his hand out to Selene, helping her get off into firm ground.

"Oh, and Selenita here, no offense but gottta reckon she lookin' extra cute fo' the get together, she is," he told Felipe. "Phew, go figure now how it is you two manage to get outta The Bush in the middle o' them floods 'n arrive here still looking like a million and a half; tell the truth, you guys kind of spook me, uh?"

"Come now Pata my mon, no way you really mean to tell us to our faces we're witchcraft makers, or phantom creatures, come on!" Felipe shot back, staring straight into his eyes, dead serious, only to burst out laughing with one of his proverbial cascading cackles as he saw bewilderment creeping up on Patatiesa's face. Pata, no longer the comedian, took off his knitted cap and scratched his head. The fact that Selene and Felipe chose to live in the hamlet's outskirts had always been fodder for rumours in the community: people would go to The Bush only during daylight time to mind their planting grounds; and then, since the couple had no fear of living out in the open, and they would walk all over at night, word in town had it that they were real close with the old spirits that made The Bush their home.

The novena honoring el Búho's dead mom in law was going strong in the yard. It had been a while already since la Doña started showing up in her son in law's dreams to demand the ritual; that was the reason why the man was forced to put away money to buy the cows and the guaro for her celebration – so that, as he paid mind to her calls she'd leave him alone at last. That's how Hati, who knew all and everything, told it to Selene.

Five drums and the same number of voices presided over the great circle of celebrants. The women flaunted green, pink or yellow cotton skirts, the traditional dress for the Punta. Watching over the dance, his image everywhere on the men's jerseys, there was Bob Marley, the prophet born in the neighbouring island. Caps knitted in the Rasta colors framed glimmering masculine faces. "Black is for the land, red for the blood of our martyrs, yellow for Africa's abundance, and green for the greatness of our plant kingdom," that's how one day Felipe had brought Selene up to speed on such matters. Just as in the world of birds, men stood here as the most ornate; it was them who wore the flashiest necklaces, bracelets and rings; others yet, the less affluent, sported the types of pullovers that OXFAM or UNICEF hand out by the thousands – all recipients in blissful ignorance of the messages those gifted rags displayed: *Get shit done; My pen/ is huge; Keep Calm; Jesus is our saviour; Glaxo Welcome.* It made Selene recall how once, when coming upon a pile of red flip-flops – all of them the same enormous size – men, women and children, obviously with feet of every measure, had pounced on them as though fighting for Manna; and how not much later, as the things started getting worn-out and unusable, the beach ended up covered with red-rubber carcasses looking like dead fish. That's how she got the idea of making a mural with the children, using the plastic remains that they could gather from the beach: small water-carrying bags, slippers, broken dishes, cups, dismembered dolls, empty containers, pieces of string. They would need a huge wall, maybe one from the Centro Comunal, why not; but the elders in the hamlet would have none of that. Always in the vanguard, the youngest of the kids did the recycling: they made small toy cars with empty juice containers and lemons for wheels; walky-talkies with plastic cups and string; dolls that came out looking somehow like Frankenstein monsters – one black leg, the other white, one arm longer than the other, a duck's head.

In the middle of the circle there was a couple doing the dance of life and death: they challenged and provoked each other with stinging stares, with undulating hips at once inviting and rejecting. When a second woman detached herself from the circle of spectators and joined in the dance to claim the main spot, the original dancer stopped her moves, exchanged charged looks with the drummers and concluded her turn with the properly piquant banter: "*Ah, ah, ah, uy mami, uy papi, así, ah, ah!*"

The same give-and-take took place with the man a moment later: another one came in dancing to take his place; and from then on all couples would take turns in recreating the ancestral dance that stands for the fleetingness of everything on earth.

One of the singers was Santa. Even though the two women hadn't seen each other for a long while, that night when Selene came to stand by the musicians' circle soon after arriving – as if a whiff of the past were sneaking into the present – Santa greeted her old friend with her bubbliest smile; then she went back to her singing. But soon enough and out of the blue, as playful as yesteryear, she wrapped one arm around the harutu's waist and thrust her right into the middle of the round, commanding in her ear: "Go out there, challenge Vidia, go ahead 'n take her place!"

Santa knew how good her friend the foreigner was when it came to dancing, but please, to challenge Vidia now in the dance ritual? The one and only matriarch of the hamlet, the singing voice of her people, that was Vidia; a woman, besides, that could grab the attention of a bunch of rowdy youngsters just by lowering the tone of her voice to a whisper, one who'd have the gang downright hypnotized as she fixed on them her eyes half-closed till they were but tiny slits flashing the essence of her woman power. It was Vidia who people went to when in need of judgment, and she would comply, talking quietly yet projecting absolute authority. She could pull on the community's every string just with her majestic stance, her singing voice and her wordless messages; and by the same token she could weave intrigues without soiling her hands. Even though she had at times joined Selene and Santa when they used to go partying, that woman instilled fear in her.

Quite a long time had gone by since Selene had last danced. Way back when she first arrived, her gift for dancing had made her everyone's sweetheart, and on that account she was even honored with the title "daughter of the village." However, after coming together with Felipe, she had gradually stopped going out. Her singing she had given up as well, and that because one day, without asking her first and just to mute her voice, Felipe lent her guitar to some friend of his – which was the same as giving it away. "There's nothing wrong in saying there are things worse than being unfaithful that a man will do to bring a woman down," Selene thought years later, when she was able to start thinking again.

But that night, as had been the case in better times, being challenged and drawn into a scene by Santa, she had no choice but to get her feet back in dance mode, jump in and attempt to take Vidia's man away from her. That was a young fellow with arms looking like the lathed branches of a mangrove tree, as he spread them out the way herons unfold their wings on the verge of taking flight; his feet seemed to gather the earth's energy, his legs drawing it up to his delighted hips and further up until it reached his shoulders where it burst into graceful rippling moves; the man's head shook from side to side in minute rhythmic motions as though he was signalling "no" while, arranged in ultra-thin braids, his hair shed radiant sweat beads.

Selene's hips started flowing into the groove of the drumbeats, and yet she wouldn't let herself go all the way, kept her eyes fixed on the floor lest her gaze end up entangled with that man's. But not even two minutes had gone by when something akin to a howl pierced the circle like a knife, and – one whip-swing of his hips to every three drum strokes – enter Felipe moving ever so slowly with arms wide open toward the centre of the floor. With his eyes fixed on his woman's, he had just jumped bull-like into the circle just as the long-armed young guy vanished as if his presence had been nothing but a mirage. Felipe and Selene were left as the main couple dancing in the middle of the circle, while drums and voices rose up to permeate the night and an aggregation of mirthful hips joined in the moves as a swarm of blinding-white teeth lit up the darkness like fireworks.

There came a moment then when almost all at once the voices dropped to a whisper and the drums followed suit. Selene, curious, turned her head and saw el Búho's daughter, *Caramelo*, approaching them with that awesome honey-and-cinnamon figure of hers. The cheeky brat was dancing with her signature sweet wiggles and nailing Felipe with her impudent cat's eyes. Caramelo, Caramelito: she'd spend hours sitting on the porch of her house fixing her hair and, since that house stood right on the sandbank in the path to the hamlet, her presence was part of the landscape in the couple's daily life. And, she had also become part of Selene's mental space since the day the girl went to their farm looking for tilapias and Felipe told her "we've got a deal" as he handed them to her, but Selene saw no money changing hands, only the sparkles of their colluding stares.

Even if Caramelo was as sweet as her own name, she always looked at Selene with a quizzical half-smile, acted like hers was the superior spot, as if she knew that, no matter how she worked her butt off on a par with Felipe, Selene would always be just another outsider. So she felt as if a wave was pulling the sand from underneath her feet when she saw Caramelo coming at them, all flashes and lifting her skirt with one hand to offer peeks of her amazon's thighs.

But that night Caramelito had to be contented with sucking her own sweet thumb: Felipe was in love with his woman.

"Let's go home," he said in a whisper, taking Selene's hand and giving her a tug to get them both out of there. They slipped through the shadows and went unseen when passing behind the arbour that el Búho had turned into a kitchen for the wake. The orange reflections of the fire that flared around the terracotta burners spotlighted the faces of women hard at work shaking, mixing and allotting steaming stews. Felipe pulled a small bottle of the homemade, healing *gifiti* liquor from his pocket and let go of Selene's hand to open it. "Take it, drink."

The first, fresh hit of the concoction was echoed by the bitter taste of the *palo de hombre* herb; then the chamomile and the anise filled her mouth with a sweet fragrance, while the clover and the allspice skipped around her insides making it feel now as if the glare of the fire had invaded her body and she even sensed a light coming off her cheeks. He took a couple of swigs himself, planted a rum-soaked kiss on her and proceeded to lead them to the place where they had moored the boat, not too far from the kitchen.

Set against the glow of the burners, darkness seemed thicker and deeper. Felipe struggled to untie the rope with one hand while still holding his prey with the other, as though wary that she might flee; his gestures were rushed, as if driven by despair. In next to no time he gave up his battle with the mooring, took Selene's head in both hands, messing up her hair while covering with his mouth one of the tiny pink ears he liked so much. "My wee tender snail, this tasty little clam o' mine," he liked to tease her when doing that; but he had no words this once, only blew in her ear and the entire ocean entered Selene's body with its wind-voice singing as it does when one brings a seashell to one's ear and listens to the sea that lives within it. Like tide-tossed bodies, they climbed on the boat with disjointed moves. Felipe got a hold of himself and straddled the thwart. Shaken as she was, Selene stumbled, but he propped her up with one hand, while the other was already climbing up sweat-soaked thighs, drawing silk folds aside, scrambling till it reached the lace boundaries of her thong, the pubis, where the skin is softest. Selene became at that moment a garden of sea anemones that opened and closed at every call of his fingertips. As though entering a forest, gingerly, gently, almost reverently – stretching out every second of delight – Felipe started sliding his dark, red, purplish, humid, sinuous, outrageously stiff phallus between Selene's labia; like a mouth, her sex clasped his as he finally entered.

A gasping sound arose unwitting from Felipe's throat, marked by the guttural U's of his language, so alike the sounds newborns make: "*Ugh…*" Selene tightened the muscles of her groin to welcome him, and as she did so an uncontainable surge of delicious waves was unleashed and permeated both their bodies, wrapping them in a shaft of light.

At that very moment a familiar voice tore through their private Eden: "*Compa* Felipe, me brother, I saw you leavin' so I tell meself I better catch up before they gone, get you guys some food to take home. The beef's real tasty, mon; me lady did the cooking …"

It was Patatiesa. The whites in his huge eyes shone bright; he had taken his cap off and his now lose tufts blended with the shadows and the bushes. He was holding the dishful of food in one hand and his machete in the other. Selene, delirious, froze with fear; her heartbeats overflowed her bosom and ended up knocking on Felipe's chest. "Was this man spying on us? Does he mean to kills us right here now with that food as bait? ¿Has the time come for me to meet my end? But what an end!" Selene's thoughts were crashing, running over each other, and her heart kept beating wild against Felipe's ribs. He placed a hand on the nape of her neck putting her at ease as one does a startled kitten. Then fear, anger and astonishment got tangled inside her as she felt the rigour of Felipe's erection anchoring her even more forcefully. It was as if the presence of Pata were turning him on and yet, fully self-contained, at the same time he gave instructions, pursing his lips to point at the thwart on the bow of the boat: "*Pata, compa, gracias*, thank you me brother; go ahead, mon, put the plate over there…"

Patatiesa did as he was told and walked away. Selene felt like crying. Relief was followed by shame at having let her imagination roam in such unfettered ways, at having misjudged poor Pata. Felipe started caressing her hair with firm, constant, deliberate touches, until the sobs boiling inside her came finally undone.

"That guy, Patatiesa, he scares me, Felipe," she said in a murmur, but her man kept stroking her head and looking into her eyes, kneading and softening her till once again they were immersed in a smouldering well sprinkled with tender sounds: *oogh…toog uh…noog ah…* Then, just like the flood, the mellowness began rising up their feet and calves until it built up into a boiling rush that blurred their vision and brought on a burst of multiple light beams. Selene must have let out a squeal, because when she regained consciousness and inhaled Felipe's piercing marine odour, he had his hand over her mouth. They kissed with diminished want now, and remained hugging a while, basking in the touch of the cool breeze on their heated skins.

Suddenly, "We're catching the night air, no good," said Felipe, fretting. He nudged his woman aside, arranged his clothes, untied the boat and, with Selene in it, got them into the river. Once on the opposite bank, they had to tug the thing over dry grounds to the point where the road was flooded, and there they climbed aboard again. Felipe rowed unhurried while Selene fed him little morsels from the stew with her fingers. There were instants then when questions would reach the tip of her tongue: "Felipe, how long was Pata looking at us? Did you know he was there?" But she chose not to spoil the moment. Besides, Felipe would tell the truth only when he darned well pleased, at the most unexpected times, and when there was no one asking him anything.

And then, the Undertow

Selene woke up to the cooing of doves near her window. Water reflections flickered on the walls. Having barely felt Felipe's absence in bed, she heard the groan of the hammock ropes in the living room. Her blood, now flurried from the gifiti she had drunk the night before, brought on the sensation of being aboard a ship in choppy waters. She closed her eyes once again. Heedful of Felipe's movements, and hearing him suck his teeth, she could tell the man had awakened in an ornery mood. Those curt little sounds, like the ones made by insects when crushed under a shoe, put her on guard. She sat on the edge of the bed and put on the rubber boots, then wrapped a sheet over her shoulders and, with water up to mid-calf, waded out to the front room. There he was, rocking in the hammock and staring at the roof, like a levitating figure suspended over the lake that had made its way into the house. He swung back and forth hitting the wall with a bare foot, harder and harder, as though anger were building up in his gut against that house which kept him trapped: that home whose walls Selene had painted yellow – a house with cotton lace curtains, hand-drawn designs on its doorframes, and even a mahogany dining set so similar to his mother's, Doña Chola. All those things that she had gotten and made to create a nest – for them to feel at home – those same things would make him feel resentful when anger took over. "There ain't nothing in this house that's mine," he'd say. He was putting off the moment when he'd walk out to the village, leave behind the main street and turn into some alleyway searching for a bar, or wherever it was that he went then. Even as he sensed Selene's presence, his eyes remained fixed on the roof. It felt as if someone had turned the lights off; the place got cloudy and Selene found it hard to breathe.

She went back to the bedroom, threw on the first dress to hand and stepped out into the sticky warmth of the small porch. With the sun beginning to pierce the dense cloud canopy, Selene's eyes turned to slits adjusting to the sudden glare. Channels of fresh, sparkling water had taken shape among the islands of palm, mahogany and corozo trees. The breeze entered her bosom with a long-drawn sigh.

"Felipe, what about we go look around the grounds on the boat," she said, with the numb and hoarse voice of one barely awake and yet attempting to project a reassuring, positive tone – something she was far from feeling at that moment.

A shadow flew over the house: a raven that came to rest on the nearest mango tree. Once there, the bird started going through his vocal repertoire, mad with glee, as in a fevered celebration of the rain's demise. A now familiar heat made its presence felt in Selene's head. Quivery gleams romping in the water passageways called out to her – an invitation to lose herself, to give in to the summons of that Bush of theirs now turned into a marshland. The occupying water had softened the landscape, making it at once mundane and magical, like a remembrance rising from a forgotten world.

Then Selene was shaken by the realization that being by herself was something she actually favored at the moment. Then again, she should have foreseen Felipe's sudden change. "We men, we're like coiled springs: if you stretch us to the edge, we gotta get ourselves coiled up again," that's what he often said, and the day before he had stretched himself to the very edge.

"What's left to find out is how them people are doing out there beyond the sandbar," he broke the lengthy pause, and went on: "The water stopped rising on our side already, but who knows how they're managing the flood in town..." And once again he fell back into muteness.

Selene wondered if those words had been directed at her, or, was Felipe only talking to himself? Was it perhaps that he hadn't even spoken and she had read his mind, which happened more often than not? She heard a buzzing sound coming from around the branches of the almond trees that lined the entryway to the house; it was two great orange-colored flies with green eyes bulging. She waited for them to move in closer, drawn by the heat waves of her fever and, when they got within reach, killed one by crushing it between her palms, as in a lone applause. The second one managed to sting one of her fingers before it disappeared, leaving its hurtful anaesthesia right on the knuckle. She had become adept at killing gadflies, since they were always buzzing around her, lured by the hot clouds borne of the fevers that afflicted her. That ability of hers didn't equal Felipe's expertise, though: he'd squash them between his index and his thumb, and then rip off their wings or burn them with a cigarette, killing their corpses again and again – well, things you do just because the hurt from their sting really does drive you into a wild rage.

"I'm gonna go take a walk, see how things is looking out there," Felipe growled, already on the defensive. He was hearing the siren call of minute speakeasies under whatever palm grove, in any of the village's hidden nooks where fishermen gathered to drink and jive when idle because of bad weather: a world with a language of sly whistles exchanged in dark corners, leading to doors that open and close to let shadows in and out; a fearsome world rife with secret deals where Felipe existed without her.

In her dreams Selene would often see her man disappearing behind mirrored doors with naked women. Whereas there had been a time when she'd feel she was being flayed alive just at the thought of Felipe sharing himself with another woman, now Selene didn't have the energy in her, didn't even feel the need to satisfy him. What went down the night before had been only the enacting of some sort of *déjà vu*, a pause in their estrangement, a truce. It was because of La Blanca having died that their buried affection was stirred and once again she had felt intertwined with him, melded, cut from the same cloth. That was the reason why, in anticipation of his leave-taking, a hint of dizziness muddled her head and she felt as though afloat, as if the floor had been pulled away from her feet. Yet she stilled herself, heard Felipe getting up, walking into the bedroom, rummaging the wardrobe, adjusting the Velcro in his sandals.

"Later, mami, we cool, right?" he said. "Be back

before night-time," and when he kissed her forehead, the man didn't even notice how the fever was consuming Selene. He went across the drenched bridge with the water up to his knees. Her soul returned to her body when she saw him close the front gate and disappear. She went into the house and sat in the hammock. "How did we end up where we are now?" she asked herself as she rocked, watching the trail drawn by her feet in the water.

When Paradise is in One's Hands

Selene got together with Felipe because the things they wished for were much the same: the presence of trees and plants; the company of birds and butterflies; living with animals, lots of animals. They left the hamlet, took to The Bush and, aided by a couple of friends, started clearing the ten acres that Felipe's parents had worked with zealous devotion till their bodies no longer responded. By now the place was close to unbreachable, as it had turned itself back to a jungle brimming with bitter cane reeds and palm trees covered with venomous thorns. When the men went in wielding their machetes, the way sculptors do when chiseling wood or carving stone, they were met by secret shapes that brought to light lemon and orange trees; coconut palms heavy with fruit; a copse of mango trees; and wild growing sugar cane, both black and white. Then, flanking the bridge that led from the path to the heart of the plot, there were apple trees that sprinkled the ground with their burning pink flowers, creating a carpet which mirrored the faces of the foliage.

They discovered a mangrove in the middle of a small lagoon in a recess of the field; so it was possible that if the wilderness were cleared all the way, by chopping off branches and throwing deadwood aside, the resulting opening would lead to some estuary branch that should take them to the Manzanares river. They'd come upon a canal in their property that ran parallel to the path, and found that, working on it just a bit, a watercourse could be created to afford them a passage from the house to the river in the canoe. A Garden of Eden, that's what they had within reach of their hands.

Since there was no way she'd ever learn how to handle a machete, Selene's job consisted of clearing roots off the ground with the hoe. Her body got used to the grind in no time at all, thanks to the strength she gathered from being Felipe's partner, and there was nothing could stop the two of them together.

"Just look at these hands a yours, and to think they was so smooth 'n tender when I first met you," he told her one day, taking her hands in his and kissing one by one the calluses on her palms, which she offered to him, chalice-like. "The heart of my universe, Selene, that's what you are," he owned up, and they drank kisses from her open hands, finding it hard to take in so much bliss.

They built a wattle-and-daub house – a bahareque abode – on the high grounds of the plot. Ebullient volunteers came in from the hamlet, and a huge cauldron of soup went on simmering over the wood fire during the two weeks that it took to finish the job. They all went at it, wattling and daubing while singing, laughing and blabbering away until, when it was all good and done, Felipe and Selene at last had a home of their own, one steeped in joy within high, undulant red walls.

Once the house was ready, the first thing Felipe did was to go fetch his son. "Now that I got me a woman, got me a home, I'm taking back me boy," he told the child's aunt who, even though outraged at the notion, couldn't stand in his way.

"This here is Ariel. She's Selene," he introduced them, and by way of a warning: "This kid a mine won't speak nothing but our Garifuna language; he does get Spanish alright, but won't talk none of it – ain't it so, little partner?" And the little one just responded by biting his lips as Selene fussed over him.

"Oh Ariel, I'm so happy to meet you. You're so very welcome, *mi amor*."

The child fixed a probing gaze on her but no words came out of his mouth. Ever so serious, standing barely at knee height next to Felipe, Ariel was a mirror image of his father. Felipe broke the pause, leading his son toward the house: "You hungry?"

Selene served him a dish of rice with fried chicken, and the boy made short work of the meal, eating everything with delighted eagerness, down to the cartilage till the thigh bone was left thoroughly clean, and not even a grain of rice remained on his plate.

"How old are you, Ariel?" Selene asked him, to break the ice, but he only stared at her, quiet as a mouse.

"Speak up, son," Felipe broke in and tried to encourage him: "*Urua*, three!" But Ariel stuck to his stubborn silence.

"Let's go wash your hands," Felipe told him then.

"*Tainki*, papa," Ariel thanked his dad as he got down from his chair.

"You gotta thank Selene too, for the food."

Embarrassed, the little one mumbled something that sounded like, "*Gacia, Tenene*."

Even as he refused to speak with his elders for the first two weeks, Ariel soon opened up to Chuy, Omar and Pichín, three children that were Felipe's most loyal followers and who loved to hang out in the homestead when not in school. Together with the new boy, they'd roam around grabbing themselves mangos, nances, passion fruits or whatever was in season; it was them that first laid eyes on the fruit that was barely starting to ripen on trees and bushes. They turned into elated, sweaty hunters after prey when, before the once-a-year rains, the huge hololo crabs came along with thunder and lightening. There were so many of those that you could see them climbing up the trees and they'd even jump into the gathering sacks by themselves. It was something to behold: The Bush looked like a fiesta then, with so many people out in the open pulling on sacks and chasing after the outsized creatures.

"Eihaba, look at that one!" you'd hear the kids cry out as they ran behind the fleeing critters that scampered about, always sideways and with their eyes sticking out like antennae, that is, until the little hunters caught up with them and used sticks to shove the prey into their sacks. And, everything went on to the beat of hands swiping and slapping, hands smacking selves as well as others, to kill off swarms of mosquitoes zeroing in to foreheads, necks, cheeks, arms and legs. Thing is, just as much as it brought them giant crabs, the season also brought a mosquito infestation

While the walls in the house changed color as they got covered with the flying pest, Selene spread around the cheapest and most hideous insect repellent – the only one that did its job – a noxious thing that reeked of gasoline; but not even then could they escape being tortured by the tiny beasts.

One of those days, Ariel finally spoke: "I been wondering, why did God have to go and make mosquitoes? Do you know why, Selene?" And that got her thinking. There was of course no reasonable explanation, but she went ahead and told him how in the Popol Vuh – the sacred book of the Maya – the two young heroes of the tale had called on mosquitoes to help them defeat the wicked Lords of Xibalba just by forcing them to reveal their true names. That was the only way she could at least attempt to convince Ariel, and herself too, that there was perchance a preordained reason for those minute bloodsuckers to exist, that their role in the world made sense.

The children would come back to the house with sacks full of crabs. There were times when they brought in so many that the concrete tub in the yard got filled to the brim, an then Selene stayed away from that tub for as long as it was full of critters desperately clawing at the walls and kicking each other as they attempted to escape captivity: the clanging of their shells scared her witless, and she turned a blind eye while Felipe and the kids sat under the mango tree killing and cleaning them. It was only when they brought her the clean crabs on trays that she would cook them with coconut or, if she didn't feel like grating the pulp to squeeze the milk out, they ate them straight.

Ariel was a huge fan of the ones with big claws. "Ain't it a pity that hololos come with no mo' than one single claw, they should come with two, or even three," he would complain. Then the deeper their color, the tastier they were; the purple and the blue ones were the best. Felipe liked them in a broth and not much else; he said they were salty on their own, so no need for extra seasoning.

In the beginning, their shared life was blessed by abundance. Everyone that came by the homestead ended up catching the feeling of gladness that permeated the air like a contagion. No one would go away with empty hands: every visitor left with a few coconuts, or plantains or cassava, eggs, oranges, or sweet cane to chew on. The couple's life was nothing but prosperity: Selene's work with the children in school was yielding undreamed-of results, while Felipe's crops and tilapia pools had made the little farm close to self-sufficient. Ariel, delighted to be in kindergarten went about singing non-stop: "*Voy pa' arriba, voy pa' arriba* – am on me way, flying high on me way."

She did receive mail from her friends, mostly concerned by her having chosen to go live *in the jungle*. "But, how do you spend your time while the watermelons ripen?" And she wouldn't write back, telling herself: "Intellectuals, how very little they know about life."

Well, that was until tropical cyclone Ramona came ashore. The hurricane changed their geography: it laid a brand-new river between the farm and the hamlet. During one single night a huge surge of muddy water came pouring down the slopes, uprooting every one of the houses that stood on its way. When it finally cleared up, neighbors left and right could do nothing but stand still and watch their crops running off, full-speed into the sea. The brunt of the blow caught Felipe, Ariel and Selene out in the village because, confronted by the rising fury of the storm, they'd left the farm behind the night before.

Once he saw the enormous damage that the hurricane had brought on, and quite likely evoking what had supposedly occurred eons before in Eden, Felipe cried out: "Look it here, see that now? Ramona done its thing. Mon, lemme tell ya, this shows how it's always them females that brings the messiest screw-ups on us."

Selene tuned out his comment, just as she had shrugged things off another day when, refusing to let her go along with him into the watermelon grove because she had her period, Felipe warned her: "A woman with dead blood coming outta her mustn't set foot on anything like a watermelon garden, things like that can only ruin the crop." She had then rushed away quietly to get some eggs for breakfast, knowing he'd immediately stop her from doing it, arguing that, in her condition, there was no way she could go near a nest without bringing harm to the eggs.

He would stay at a "safe" distance from Selene and didn't even let her cook whenever she was menstruating. But no matter what, she pretended not to be alarmed by such signs; certainly, as time went by he would straighten out and see the light: "It's just throwbacks to outdated crap that will surely fade away," she'd tell herself once and again.

The town folk started coming by in their canoes, or plain walking with water chest-high, just to take a gander at the weirdness: a come-out-of-the-blue river cutting through The Bush. The crowd grew as morning turned to noon, until a red haired, moustachioed *mestizo* man sporting a cowboy hat showed up riding a horse – a character that turned out to be the local candidate for the assembly of deputies.

"I'll get you all whatever's needed," the guy declared. And then, following the lead of El Búho the gathering of men got their selves busy drawing a plan. "Most of all, rope is what we need," was their conclusion, and so the wannabe deputy rode away to search for rope, to get it by the hundreds of yards as it was needed.

When he returned, mission accomplished, the men fixed one end of the rope to Felipe's canoe and pitched the other end to the far side of the newborn river, where another group anchored it on a tree. That rope arrangement was meant for safety, but one of the strongest guys went aboard the vessel to serve as guide and lead.

That was the birth of the ferry service. There was no lack of volunteers to keep it going as daylight turned to dusk. The boat would go back and forth loaded with passengers: fishermen with their nets; bundle-laden women taking supplies and food over to their homes in the glens and ravines by *la Punta del Manzanares*; there was also Pata and others like him, who earned their keep scavenging whatever The Bush left out for them to grab. One peso was the agreed upon charge per crossing; half of the earnings went to the handlers and the other was used for the maintenance of El Búho and Felipe's boats, which took turns providing service. Pickup trucks loaded with provisions came in from el Puerto. Selene organized the women so they could store the incoming stuff in Hati's house and distribute it from there to all who were in need.

Amidst that disaster that turned the neighborhood into one single body and brought out whatever was most noble in everyone, side by side with Felipe, Selene came to see the true meaning of life.

Paloma Zozaya Gorostiza

This Land, Whose is it?

The neighbors of the zone that was cut off by the hurricane – that is, Felipe and Selene's neck of the woods – they didn't think twice before grabbing their machetes and hoes to open up the new pathway that would make the world once again reachable to them. It was just over a dozen people who'd been left stranded between two waterways, as the track linking the two was now totally wiped out. Looking eastward, on the opposite end of the newly formed river, which they named Ramona, there stood a wooded hill that the Manzanares River enfolded before flowing into the sea, La Punta del Manzanares, it was called. Atop that hill was a retired colonel's walled-off and fortified mansion. Out there, the sand bar stood as a sort of clandestine harbor, a wharf for boats handling all types of cargo. Beams of light criss-crossed the sky at night-time, and during the day there were vans and station wagons with blacked-out windows going back and forth amidst thick clouds of dust, and carrying a different kind of dust: the pricey, white one.

"Things as they are right now, one would expect *el coronel* to lend us a hand in rebuilding the road, huh? Really, after all, his vans and pick-up trucks are the ones using it the most, wouldn't you say?" Selene told Felipe the first morning they picked up the machete and the hoe to go join the group and get to work.

"The colonel's wagons can reach his fancy place from the other side, it's just a couple of extra kilometers from the paved highway to his manor," he answered her. "Anyway, no matter what, the arsehole himself gets there by helicopter, so don't even waste your breath on 'im. Besides, ain't no one around would want the colonel's workmen with us down here – bunch 'a killas all 'a them, no shit, no way."

Felipe proposed that the group of neighbors be given a title; they should call themselves *Fágayu* – the paddle. "All of us together here, we're like one single oar rowing against the current," he explained, "that name, you see, it makes us strong."

Everybody went along with his idea. Selene alone kept to herself, staring at him with mouth agape as once again he'd given her an undeniable taste of his wisdom and his gift for lyrical images. Fágayu went about their work with a zestful spirit. As the first rays of light broke through mist behind the hills, men's and women's voices would start ringing out Good day, Good morning: "*Buity binafi…*" Straight away, the metallic rasp of sharpening files working on hoes and machetes would begin, at times turning the tools into ringing bells that awoke all sorts of songbirds: thrushes, cardinals, mockingbirds, you name it. Then, spreading across the field, unevenly at first, the strokes of those farming tools would gradually join together into a shared rhythm until they'd reach a chorus that echoed as a single cadence multiplied. After a few hours, when the cruel sun in its zenith flattened shapes and made colors fade away, the midday heat came down like a sizzling iron plate on the toilers' backs. Then the monotone screeching of crickets and cicadas replaced the birdsong, as the sweltering heat wave silenced the people's voices and their laughter. The only things left to be heard then were the sluggish pounding of machetes hitting cane reeds and slashing tall grasses, and the cackles of the kingfisher hidden in the bushes mocking humans, those creatures devoid of colorful plumage and doomed to a never ending tussle against the jungle. The children, machete masters already, were the only ones that didn't miss a beat, and not too often they'd take a short break to squeeze the juice out of an orange or sip water from a coconut underneath whatever shade they could find.

Even if he was much younger than Chuy, Omar and Pichín, Ariel took on the role of leader in that quartet. It was a commanding stance that he assumed as a natural entitlement just by reason of being his father's son and his great grandfather's great grandson. Sometimes he did things that went beyond his ability or the limits of his age, only to make an impression on his pals; just like one day when Selene, apprehensive, saw him struggling to break a coconut open: the kid, not yet five years old, was sitting on the floor hitting the coconut with his child-size machete. His three friends stood around him watching intently, licking their lips as they anxiously waited for the chance to quaff the sweet water. Ariel hit the hard shell, turning it around gingerly to give it more and more blows, but then suddenly the water started spilling out on the floor from underneath the wounded fruit.

"Stupid, stupid coconut!" he cried out, furious, and Selene had to swallow a cackle, not to make him look bad in front of his brave *compañeros*.

And then Chuy, he was the only slacker out of the whole group. The boy was approaching puberty and all his energy seemed to be spent in growing taller day by day. Listless but ever-present, he would kind of drag his lengthy frame always following behind Omar, Pichín and Ariel; and he'd drive Selene crazy with his endless requests for water: "*Musu duna.*"

"Help yourself, Chuy, come on, you well know where we keep the water and the glasses."

After a while it dawned on her that attention was all Chuy wanted, really. It was always a struggle for Felipe and Selene to make him go to school; every morning when they opened the door that looked out into the mango tree, there he was already. Selene would then take him back to the hamlet, with Ariel perched on the bicycle crossbar, Chuy on the rack behind.

Being notorious as the foulmouthed one, Pichín was always engaged in all sorts of squabbles. Out of the blue, "Eat my dick!" he once shouted at one of the women who were hoeing the field.

"You get yo-self ova' here, you good-fa-nothing brat," the woman yelled back at him, and once the kid was at arm's length, she pulled his pants down, laid him face up on her thighs, bent over him and clasped her toothless mouth hard on his dick. Omar – who never missed a thing, and looking worried now – kept his huge, inquisitive eyes fixed on the scene but said nothing at all. Pichín, in full shock, went back to work and kept his mouth shut tight during the rest of the day.

A few days after the works had started, when the once soaked ground had become again dry sand, women showed up carrying bundles and chairs, brightening the disheveled cassava fields with the vivid colors of their skirts and headkerchiefs. A band of young men with resounding drums and seashells formed the rear of the procession. It was the women's branch of the *Comité de Defensa de Tierras* – the Land Defence Committee. They were singing the nostalgic hymn shared in every celebration – *Yurumein tagurubey wayuna* – the song that tells the story of how the ancestors landed on those shores. The group marched forward in a slowly swinging flow, while the calls of the seashells seemed to be heralding a war-like tide. Arising one by one from the tall grass and the bushes, workers' faces started appearing with bandanas drying off the sweat; some joined in the chanting, others just stood and stared. A spontaneous revelry swiftly followed the conclusion of the song, and it kept going for as long as the Defensa members searched for and found shaded shelters to set up camp: off-color wordplay, jesting confrontations, flirting, competing witticisms and rib-tickling cackles fluttered over the fields. Then as everyone started getting back to work, the women unfolded banners that, once affixed to tree trunks, displayed their messages in vivid colors:

Ours is this land, … it's our life.
This land is ours… inherited by right.
Our ways and customs: Cultural Heritage of Humanity.
Land usurpers not welcome here.
Out with the enemies of their own people, ¡fuera!
¡Fuera el Coco Suazo!
Coco Suazo – black skin, white insides – betrays his people.

"Who's this Coco Suazo, sweetheart?" Selene asked Felipe, who – bent down to the ground going at the scrub and weeds with a vengeance – had paid no attention to the arriving women. He took the opportunity to stretch his body, looked over the near-by grove of mango trees, pulled his handkerchief from the back pocket of his pants and wiped dust and sweat off his face, cleared his throat, spat on the ground and stared at the landing spot till the sand fully absorbed his saliva. All that time it was as though he were making time to put things in order within his head before coming up with an answer. Finally he fixed his sight on the scene around him, squinting his eyes, struggling to make out the messages written on the banners in the distance.

Selene knew of course that he was much more near-sighted than her, and so helped him, reading out loud. "*Fuera el Coco Suazo…*"

Felipe sucked on his teeth to show his contempt for the man: "That Suazo mon, he just another black guy from here in Redención, no different from me, he is. But – why or how, no one knows – he went n' got 'imself involved in politics and, truth is, he got a real knack for gettin' jobs in government; no matter what party's in power, he always ends up standing on his two feet. He crooked, real sneaky da mon, that must be why." And now, as his bitterness, his grudges were fast kindled, he went on: "Some years back, before you came around, mon shows up in town telling people, 'you all here who refuse to sell your parcels, the government's gonna take 'em from you just the same, believe you me." He stood first with the town's board of managers – the *Patronato del Pueblo* – that was by then the playing ground

for a bunch 'a vultures just like 'im – called themselves
The Entrepreneurs' Association. Those the same old-
boys-club that went together to the one and only school
in town – professor Cortés, who owns the hotel where
you stayed, he too one 'a them – so they went and forced
the people to sell their plots facin' the beach for peanuts,
chicken feed. It was a pay-dirt sweet deal, a cool windfall
for them all. Then the *grupo de Defensa* took their case
to the Court of Human Rights and that shit's being in
litigation since who knows how many years. That's the
only reason why you see that millionaires' residential
development standing there abandoned halfway into
construction."

Felipe puckered his lips now pointing at the
luxury-residence compound with private swimming
pools that stood as an alien triangle of land forced upon
the space between the beach and the Río Ramona, carving
up the grounds into something like a slice off a birthday
cake. Domes and cupolas peeked over a concrete wall.
The ones that had been lucky to be painted were yellow,
pink or blue; all others still concrete-gray. Some were
crowned with surreal tiaras made of iron rods encrusted
with rust. It all looked like an aerial oyster farm, making
clear who was boss in that realm ruled by the tyranny of
humidity and time.

Always seated under an arbour jerry-built with
branches and palm leaves next to the entrance booth of
that ghostly, closed-off locale, there was Jeremiah the
Indian with his stony nose and half a face sticking out
from under a 10-gallon sombrero. Every time Selene
went by him on her way to and from the village, she
made sure to engage: "G'day." And, "g'day" he'd answer

127

back, his hands always busy filling little paper bags with the peanuts he bought wholesale to then re-sell in his baggies. And now, while Jeremiah's head bobbed under his hat, Felipe picked up the thread of the story: "Thing is, now there's others wanna do the same with the lands on this here side, not the ones on the beach but the ones that's good for growing African palm out here. And you see, our famous coronel, well, he's got his hands all over that." With those being his final words, once again Felipe grabbed his machete, which he'd left stuck in the sand. But now he thought some more and said, concluding: "That's why I don't get me-self involved in none of that crap, I'm just making a road so we can get through to the other side." And he went back to chopping off cane stems.

When they returned to work at sunrise the next morning, there was a pile of rocks blocking the segment of pathway they'd finished the day before. The campground of the *Defensa de Tierras* was still deserted and the banners still waved in the cool breeze. The workers looked everywhere but there was no one around. Those were hefty rocks, the smallest ones being the size of footballs. They asked each of the *compañeros*, as they kept arriving, if any of them had seen anything, but the general response was *nobody knew nothing* – which was strange in Redención, a hamlet with eyes in every nook and corner. They picked up the rocks and lined them up by the side of the road.

From that day on, every morning they had to remove new rocks that invisible hands laid on the road every night. On one occasion, in response perhaps to the tenacity of Fágayu, the rock layers left a message written in big red letters, one per stone:

P-r-i-v-a-t-e-P-r-o-p-e-r-t-y N-o-T-r-e-s-p-a-s-s-i-n-g

No longer bothered, no matter what, one more time they put the rocks aside and went on clearing the scrub. When they were finally able to bring carts into the gap they had opened, the thing became an actual road just from the tracks left by the constant passing of horses and wheels.

That was how the couple ended up unwittingly involved in the conflict over the lands. It went down as a war of nerves without any direct confrontations. There was the occasional army platoon with heat-stricken conscripts patrolling the encampments of retaken lands, but they never stopped and nobody said anything to anyone. The patrols kept going on their rounds and, sitting under some mango tree, the women of the *Defensa de Tierras* just watched them go by and vanish through the flickering steam into the distance.

Selene and Felipe went ahead with their own projects. "What do you think we should put up on the sign by the entrance?" he asked her one day.

"Animal Sanctuary," she suggested.

"Sanctuary? What does that mean?"

"Well, a sanctuary is a place where God's creatures can live free of harm, a place where one feels protected," Selene explained.

"I like that word, *sanctuary*, I like it," Felipe said, before falling back into one of his habitual thoughtful moods.

But then the additional river that separated them

from the hamlet now, the newly born Ramona had the last word regarding their plans, as it made it downright problematic for them to go back and forth. The changed landscape made it close to impossible for regular tourists to come visit the sanctuary – a source of income they had expected when their project first started – and the trek from home to school became an ordeal for Selene and Ariel. Those were the reasons why they ended up having to move back to the hamlet.

Independence Day

They rented a house in the heart of the hamlet. Selene painted the living room yellow and chose indigo blue for the kitchen; she added wooden doors to the rooms, hung shelves in the kitchen and – now that they had electric power – bought a fridge. So, for a change this time around, the living was easy. Well, actually, until something happened that ... oh God!

It must have been midnight on that September the fifteenth, Independence Day, when Selene was awakened by Felipe's code whistling, and then she heard his voice, garbled and rushed: "Open up, Selene, open up..."

She got up and stumbled through a drunken haze of sleep before pulling on the barrel bolt to open the door.

"That son of a bitch, he gonna get his due alright, I'll make 'im pay right now," Felipe growled and went straight to the dresser, rummaged through his underwear drawer, pulled out the olive-green nine-millimeter he'd picked up – stolen – from the barracks when he was discharged from military service, shoved the pistol under his belt, covered it with his shirt tail and rushed out the door muttering, "Mudafucka!"

"What's going on, Felipe? Why the gun? What's gotten into you? Please darling, wait!" But no, no matter what Selene meant to say, to plead for, her voice wouldn't

131

carry any of her words; and now, standing mute in the middle of the living room, she could do nothing but watch the door closing behind him.

It was often the case in Redención that, when a man got caught stealing stuff or molesting a child, the neighbors took the law in their own hands and, after beating the living daylights out of the culprit, they'd throw him in the tiny cell that stood for a prison in the hamlet.

"Well, that just might be what he's up to, my Felipe," Selene told herself. There was nothing but blind faith in her when it came to judging her man's good sense. The only notion she'd allow to enter her head then was that, just perhaps, he and other fellows were chasing after the creep who stalked children with his body all greased up to escape any hands that might try to capture him. One nigh not long before, Selene had witnessed how some guys beat that man to a pulp on the beach, and she thought him a dead one, as he waded into a wild sea to escape the posse that were going at him with their paddles; but the fiend survived.

No, the way she saw it, Felipe could do nothing wrong. That conviction was what stopped her from crawling on the floor to grab his legs, from putting her body between him and the door, spouting something like: "What are you getting yourself into? ... Man, think of your kids!"

Soon enough she heard the shots: two whip-like dry cracks that rooted her further down on the spot where she'd been standing for a while already. She held her breath, expecting to hear more of whatever, but all was silence for a while – until Felipe's soft whistle brushed the suspense away and she hurried to open the door for him.

Coming in from the shadow, "It's done aright, he dead," said Felipe. "Ángel's dead, he dead 'n done. That piece of shit, he had no business doing me wrong the way he done; and now what's worse, I'm fucked for real, I'm gonna have to make me-self scarce, disappear." Selene just covered her face with both hands. "Oh no, *ay no...*" that's all she could say and kept repeating non-stop.

That same day Ángel had finished work on the well in the yard – so that, from then on they wouldn't have to go all the way to the communal well to fetch water. With that taken care of, him and Felipe had gone out for a walk to join in the Independencia celebration. A *mestizo* from a village inland, that man Ángel would show up in town from time to time with neither a suitcase nor a backpack – not even a toothbrush – and after staying a full season doing whatever construction work he could find, he'd vanish just as suddenly as he'd arrived. He had a rich mouthful of big white teeth, and cheerful eyes. With Selene he had in common the olive skin, the same sense of humour and their shared devotion to Felipe.

"Stop it already with your *ay no's*, just get off it, woman," Felipe balked. "It is what it is, I tell you: Ángel, he's out there lying cold right outside the Centro Comunal."

"*Ay, no,*" she said it once again, even as she was going straight into warrior mode: "I've got to see him, I'm going out there. Anyone I run into, I'll just tell them I'm looking for you."

Selene couldn't tell how or when she took off

her night gown, put on a pair of pants, a tee shirt and, barefoot, perched herself on the bicycle. In no time at all she found herself on the main street – La Principal – which was deserted at that late hour, apart from a lone couple chatting underneath a mango tree. Then she saw a guy coming her way on a bike and flagged him: "Have you seen Felipe?"

The guy said no. Then she pedalled hard, making a beeline toward the Centro Comunal, figuring she was bound to find the lifeless body amidst the shadows of the bushes that lined the façade of the center. But there was nothing there at all. Felipe's car was parked under a coconut palm. All she heard was the sleeping sea, and silence. Not a single trace of wind wafted through the sticky night. Soaked in her own sweat, Selene went back home.

"Nothing, there's nothing out there," she told Felipe.

"Huh, if you say so, then mon's gotta be still alive," Felipe thought aloud. "Musta dragged he-self 'n got inside the car – I left the thing unlocked, stupid me. And now, shit, oh she-it," he cried out, pacing aimlessly around the living room like a madman. "If Ángel's gone 'n died right there in my car, that just means it's time for me to get the hell outta town. I'm fucked, no way in hell outta this one." He opened the door, pulled his shirt off to make himself no different than the night, paused for a quick second to wrap his arms around Selene. They kissed. "You take good care, please, and get in touch as soon as you can," she told him clinging to his hand, feeling numb, unable to wrap her mind around this thing happening to them right there and then. "Did anyone see you, what you did?"

"I don't think so," he answered, "there was no one around."

"Well, if there were no witnesses, then there's no problem, really. You get back in the house Felipe, wait right here, don't go yet," Selene commanded now, as she was getting back on her bike. "I'm gonna go back and see if Ángel is in the car, just to make sure."

On this second time round she went easy on the pedals, not wanting to reach the dreaded goal, delaying the moment when she'd be staring at their friend's corpse inside the car. She got off the bicycle, brought the kickstand down with her foot, craned her neck, trying to see through the windows of the Toyota; but there was nothing to see: they were tinted windows and it was pitch-dark where she stood. "I'm just gonna have to open this thing, oh God," she thought and felt her heart beating through her teeth. One, two, three ... she held her breath, pressed the handle on the door and pulled on it.

The car was empty.

"The gun," Felipe said, "we gotta get rid a the gun."

"Where then?" she answered.

Sitting on the hammock, Felipe studied the ceiling of the house attentively; he stared at the roof tiles for a good while. "No, that'd be too obvious," he finally concluded. "Better the well; the mortar must still be loose between the blocks." ... Selene followed him into the yard. And yes, the mortar was still moist and soft from the time Ángel had filled up and buttressed the sides of the well earlier that day. Felipe found a gap wide enough between the cinder blocks and planted the pistol as deep as he could in it, right there in the well that the deceased himself had built.

The couple spent a sleepless night, her seated on the hammock and him laying on the bed, on the alert for voices, or the sound of an engine coming to a stop by their house. But just as it would be in any other night, all they heard was the chirping of the crickets and the croaking of the frogs.

The neighbors had come out of their homes as soon as they heard gunfire; they rushed to the place where the shots had rang, found poor Ángel bleeding big time, picked him up and drove him to Emergencias in the hospital in Puerto. That was where – not deceased, thank the Lord – Selene finally found him the next day. She was taken aback as, sitting upright in bed he welcomed her entrance with his ever-generous grin and his beaming eyes.

"Bah, easy does it, no big deal: it was just a little scratch on my lung, they're draining it now, see here?" He put her at ease. … "A miracle," Selene thought as she saw the thin hose connecting Ángel's torso to a gallon-sized plastic container. A miracle it was indeed, because that midnight moment when, pistol in hand, Felipe walked into the Centro Comunal and found him there – of all things, tying up his trekking shoes, looking ready to leave town – and right away started bitching about stuff that made no sense, pointless accusations, Ángel, way out of character then, had gotten really pissed off:

"Show some civility, my brother, you're stepping out of line right there; what I feel for your woman is nothing but respect, you hear? Come on now, that's just you letting your liquor mess with your head. You better go back to your lady, Flinn, get yourself some sleep where you belong." That's what Ángel said, calling Felipe by his surname, as was his habit, while leaving the Centro Comunal, where he worked nights as a watchman. But Felipe kept going after him.

"Mon, you got some nerve playing smart aleck with me now, when you the one that's been way out of order 'round here all along. You stop right there 'n listen good: you the one gonna get some deep sleep like you deserve it, bro, not me – you going where you belong," he groaned and fired a first shot, which went through Ángel's groin, knocking him down. "Mother fuckin' somabitch," some voice cried out inside Felipe's head, "no way out 'a this one, you gonna have to finish 'im off, get it over with." And once again he pulled the trigger, let go the second bullet. That one went between his friend's ribs and out his back, grazing a lung and apparently missing the liver and whatever artery was in its way.

"Ángel, please tell me, what happened?" Selene asked, pretty much under her breath.

"Ah, nothing ..." the wounded man responded with a firm, loud voice, as if wanting to be heard by the doctors, nurses and orderlies, along with all the other patients in the crowded clinic – most of them with bullet or knife wounds themselves.

In one corner of the room two girls stood by a bed clinging to each other, crying softly. All of a sudden one of them let out a howl; then their weeping grew louder and, not long after, the two of them passed by

Ángel's bed, following a sheet-covered dead person on a stretcher. When they'd gone beyond the door and their yowls sounded distant, Ángel kept going: "What happened is, there we were, Felipe and me just walking about late last night shooting the breeze when we heard this gunshot coming outta the dark. Right away, oh man, I just blacked out 'n didn't come to my senses till some car brought me from the village to this hospital here. And then of course newspaper people – vultures all of them who's always hanging out at the doors to *Emergencias* – they ask me what's gone down and I just tell them what I know: that I saw nothing."

Somehow unable to fully understand the gravity of the moment, and yet refusing to acknowledge the actual fact that she was in dire straits, as she could be charged with being an accessory to a crime, Selene refrained from asking questions, and didn't confront Felipe to make him face the music, come clean regarding the reason for his actions. Instead, throughout the following days she acted as though possessed by some superhuman force; it was as if her existence had been taken over by a will not her own, whose only goal and mission on earth was to protect Felipe at any cost.

"As long as the injured party remains alive and doesn't go back on what he stated in his deposition on the event, we're in good shape," said the lawyer.

And Ángel would never change his tune; he actually went to the Police to record a plea for the case to be closed. The man stayed true to his word even when things took a nasty turn, when he almost died just as he was to be discharged from hospital. Feeling really well on the eve of his departure, he'd gone out for a walk and to eat some pork-rind tacos in the Parque Central. That night he felt his stomach turning; and next morning the doctor that went to sign his release form found him shivering, looking yellow and just about to go unconscious. That was his condition still when Selene went in to pick him up.

"I'm gonna bring him back home," she had told Felipe. "He'll be well cared for with us over here," and nobody around would dare challenge her decision, not even those who might be wary that Ángel could be cooking up some kind of retribution. Felipe himself, who for once in his life looked frightened and downright ashamed, paid heed to his woman's every word, with his tail between his legs. "It's all good, how you want this done Selene," he said. "If that's the way it's gotta be, the two of us we'll take care 'a him…but once he's here, there's no way in hell I'll be taking walks alone with Ángel – just 'im 'n me together out there, no way mon: I ain't that crazy."

Felipe was bringing up a conversation he'd had with Ángel on Selene's cell phone, when she stayed in the clinic to stand watch over their friend after things went south and ended up calling for a mighty serious surgical intervention: "You just wait till I get outta here, my brother: I'll get back to the village and we'll roam around together like we always do," the wounded man had told him, and declared, "Everyone in Redención will get a chance then to see what real friendships are made of, right Flinn?"

Selene would never question the purity of Ángel's intentions, the risk-defying extent of his fealty; and that was proven beyond any doubt the day she went to take him back home and found everyone on tenterhooks in the clinic. Along with a male nurse, she had to push him on a wheelchair to a special unit some distance away, where he was to be given a tomography. They went across the marketplace with Ángel falling sideways on the chair and growing paler by the second behind his sunglasses.

The technician's judgement was succinct: "This man is dying. I'm actually surprised that he's still alive. A blood clot has come loose from his liver. There is internal bleeding, serious."

Pushing the same wheelchair, they went back through the endless racket of the same marketplace, dodging traffic in streets infested with potholes, famished dogs and God-awful loudspeakers.

An emergency operation had to be done. Scooters kept coming in throughout the day to bring the necessary blood bags. "Here comes another one!" the guys on scooters would cry out triumphantly every time they rushed in with a new bag. By eleven that night, the eight pints needed to start the operation had been delivered.

"That wound, it was located in a mighty difficult place," the surgeon explained to Selene, and he went on: "I had to give it all I had to keep the wall of the thorax open just to be able to reach the spot." Then, pointing at a dark red jelly-like mass lying inside an aluminium tray, he finally said, "Look, this is the blood clot we pulled out." That thing was almost the size of a newborn.

After the ordeal – when nobody thought the man would come through alive – that's when Selene stayed in the hospital right next to Ángel. Then, the day the patient was at last given a clean bill of health, it was decided that he would be better off staying in a cousin's house nearby, because the road to Redención was an endless mosaic of potholes and that trek would be unbearable for him. A couple of months after, feeling well enough, the man Ángel went to visit the hamlet, just as he had promised. He showed up limping about and, as usual, flashing the same old, wide-open smile.

From then on, no one could ever make him say he'd seen the person that shot him twice. "My brother, Flinn – he done nothing wrong," he told Selene one day, dead serious. "There's no one can blame 'im for nothin'."

But Felipe still felt a cursed weight on his shoulders, he couldn't lower his guard: whenever Ángel showed up in town, he expected to be hit by a bullet every time there was darkness around him. That was why they went back to The Bush, because Ángel decided to move to the village for good.

About that, Horacio the healer would only say: "Y'all, the fifth sacrifice is still missing. Remember, can't be any less than five."

Laruni Hati

Selene was dragged into limbo by the seesaw of the hammock, that is until – whining quietly and wagging her tail – Sombra, her canine bodyguard and sidekick, broke through the maze of remembrances where she had gone astray. Not to be dismissed, the sweet yet tough-as-nails doggie was cocking her head sideways with her benign gaze fixed on the mistress as if pleading, "Come on, how long before we two go out again?"

"You're right, Sombra," Selene responded with an affectionate smile. "It's a good time for us to do our rounds."

She went into the bedroom and searched in her lingerie drawer for one of the kerchiefs that she barely used. Leaving the house with head uncovered to roam around the flooded plot by herself didn't frighten her as much as it instilled a bit of respect, and something instinctual made her want to cover her head just as the hamlet's women do whenever there is a storm. As her hand reached the bottom, it came upon a strange object. She looked, and looked again now focusing her eyes, unable to grasp what she actually saw there: her vibrator – its silver tip deflowered by something like the blow of a blunt instrument – looked like the corolla of a defaced flower with petals sharp as razors, the sort of object one could find in some Feminicide Museum, or else a child's tin pinwheel.

Selene felt the now familiar stuttering beat of her heart, as in her mind she saw how Felipe had rummaged through her underwear drawer – a most intimate space – had found the vibrator there, taken it from its soft cocoon and placed it on the concrete floor; he'd gone then to fetch his hammer and, in a calm and calculated manner, let go his ire with one single iron blow against the gleaming point. The proof was there on the floor right in front of her chest of drawers: a fissure the size of a fingernail.

Then what was most dreadful, Selene figured: how gently the man had returned it to its nest of lace and silk for her future discovery. He'd left it there like an anonymous message, a threat. Many years later she'd regret not having kept that thing: a work of art and a testament to survival. As though wanting to keep the fingerprints untouched, she took the wounded vibrator gingerly between her index and her thumb, dropped it inside a small sack she found in a corner of the room, and then went to dig into Ariel's treasure chest, his collection of river stones; three of those, the biggest ones, went into the sack that got shut close with a knot. With that out of the way, she stepped into the kitchen for a gulp of water. The door was open and in the swamped yard beaming goblins still stood beckoning her with redoubled insistence. Out into the flood she went and threw the bundle inside the canoe before unmooring it as she called out: "*Uoi*, Sombra, let's go for a ride!" The doggie, that had been wagging her tail like some wind-up toy for a while with her full body at the ready for the command, jumped off the pile of household stuff where she'd been on the lookout for the start of the promised jaunt.

With her ears pricked, her chest puffed, and proud as a figurehead on the bow, Sombra stood tall in front while, taking the stern seat, Selene paddled away. When they got to where she figured was the centre of the tilapia pool, she dumped the sack with the vibrator and the stones and held still watching the little bubbles left behind by the bundle as it bid farewell to her while sinking to the bottom.

"Down there it lies, for future archaeologists: a mystery to unravel." It was with that sentence in mind that Selene brought the ceremony to completion. Once done, she folded that event till it was as tiny as it could be and put it away inside the vaults of her heart along with all the other grievances.

They went over and across the wide esplanade in front of the house and headed straight for the islets. A burst of white herons taking flight startled them as they entered the mouth of one of the newly formed canals in the flooded terrain. Soon enough they came upon another lake – this one over a field that Felipe had chosen to grow yucca and sugar cane. They were just about halfway into the lake when Selene spotted silver gleams amongst the plants: little fishes the size of her hand. She was wondering at such prodigy – fish swimming in a yucca field: only in fantasy tales had she ever seen dry land mixing up so intimately with the sea – when her heart skipped a beat as she heard feet splashing through the water on the adjacent plot. The dog stretched her neck and her ears got even stiffer. Selene was left frozen on her wooden perch. Everything stood still, all but Sombra's ears, which fidgeted like antennae as she followed the sounds of steps in the neighboring plot, where the tips of fence posts could be seen now. All at once the splashes in the water stopped being steps and were now tapping sounds. The yucca field on the other side belonged to Hati, the wise neighbour. Gathering as much courage as she could, Selene called out:

"Hati, is that you? Who's there?"

"Yes, it's me out here, *numa* – my friend – here I am as I should be, salvaging my yucca from the flood before it rots …"

Hearing Hati's voice, Sombra started wagging her tail the way no other dog could: her body rocking from her waistline back, like a rumba dancer shaking her bum. Selene herself, no longer spooked, was just about to start wagging her tail. She rowed on as fast as she could – just to make sure it wasn't one of them visions that are known for leading one astray in The Bush – till she saw the moon-shaped face of her neighbor, a woman so tiny that the water reached up to her bosom in a spot where it would only reach Selene's waist.

"We've got our work cut out for us, numa, time to make *ereba* – cassava bread, you know."

She would pull on the whole plant after loosening the roots with the hoe. The task as a whole was done blindly, since everything happened underwater, but Hati kept pulling out handsome yucca roots, none broken up, and threw them into her dugout canoe, her *cayuco*, which she kept anchored to a tree trunk. The woman was well into her seventies, but you'd never see her taking a break; every time Selene passed by her house, there was Hati working.

"*Ayoo, ayoo, Laruni Hati, ayoo!*" Selene would

salute her and – waving a hand plastered with ground coconut, or cassava, or flour – Hati would respond to her call: "*Ayoo, Selenita.*" Then, if she had no time for a visit, Selene would go on her way warbling: *ayoo, ayoo, Laruni Hati, ayoo ayoo…* In the Garifuna language, Hati means "moon," and she called her friend *Laruni Hati*, Moonlight, because of how luminous she was. Hati, she would say, was to the earth what the full moon is to the sky.

Hati was boss in her home; she did everything herself, that is, apart from chopping wood, a task that fell to her husband, a very tall and burly man that everybody called Madu and who made his living as a fisherman. But he wasn't the only one to catch fish in that household: one day Selene saw Hati in the middle of the river, fishing; alone in her cayuco, she was letting go and retrieving the line as serenely collected as any other woman would have been while knitting on a chair in her living room. That woman Hati always made her foreign friend feel this urge to somehow live inside her skin, walk in her shoes; she always looked so in control of herself, so tranquil, in such harmony with life.

What Selene found most awesome was how, by her lonesome self, Hati made all of her *ereba* – or *casabë*, as the *mestizos* call it – always with those slight and measured moves of hers, as though none of it meant any effort to the old woman. All by herself she carried out a job that takes a team of women several days to complete: ten of them to peel the hard yucca roots and, once it comes back from the grinder, up to four to strain the white core so as to get rid of its bitter sap, until it finally turns into the finest flour. Then the whole thing goes into the hands of the expert *ereba* maker, who cooks enormous white and crispy crackers on a baking plate – the *comal* – all of them made of nothing but yucca: neither salt, oil or water added to the mix – a preparation as pure as the spirit itself. That whole process was brought to completion by no one else but Hati. All of it took place in her kitchen, made of cane reeds and palm leaves. Once the baking was finished, the cassava crackers got piled up inside flower-printed cotton tablecloths in impressive columns that would quickly grow small when word was passed around that in her house there was fresh-as-dawn cassava bread, *águyulugu*. Hati didn't even have to go to the marketplace to sell her stuff: customers came to her own doorstep, most of them town folk, but also hoteliers from Puerto – which was how far the fame and demand for Hati's *ereba* reached.

As she came back home from school every day, Selene was wont to make a stop on her bicycle ride so she could sit with Hati in her always cool kitchen, drink some coconut water and moon over the collection of instruments for *ereba* preparation that hung on the walls like museum pieces. There they were – in various sizes and woven with reed fiber right out of the mangroves – the strainers and the snake-like pipes to squeeze the bitter sap off the ground yucca. As she squatted down sipping coconut water or sucking on an orange, Selene would let her eyes fawn on the aged mahogany troughs and bowls – surely bequeathed from Hati's grandmothers – where yucca turned to flour awaits its transformation. The living museum that was Hati's kitchen was an endless source of wonder for Selene.

"Do you need a helping hand, Hati? You've been chest-deep in water for a long while, you could get sick, you know," she told her.

"No, Mama, I'm good 'n done for the day," Hati answered back letting go a cackle that put her toothless gums in full display.

"Well then, climb on the boat *mujer*, I'll give you a ride."

They hitched Hati's yucca-loaded *cayuco* to Selene's boat; then the Harutu woman held Hati by her arms with both her hands to help the elder one climb aboard. Right away Selene was surprised by how weighty her friend was – something that belied her slight frame – and more so when the old woman let go an involuntary groan of pain as she got on board.

"*Ay, muchacha!*" Hati exhaled as she sat down and then explained: "All of its exertions have caught up wid this body a mine." This while she rubbed the cluster of knots that stood for her hands, her elbows, her arms. "It's most of all when it rains that my bones hurt like there's no end to it," she concluded and went on to rub her knees and legs, as well, over her soaked clothing.

Seeing her friend's usually luminous face now shadowed by pain, Selene felt her heart shrinking. How could this woman who always stood straight as an arrow, who was so strong and worked ceaselessly, how could she be a casualty of arthritis? It was something she could have never imagined. Old Hati wouldn't ever show the slightest hint of her suffering. "Ay, Hati, I had no idea. You shouldn't have come out to work amidst this flood, *mujer*."

"Don't you worry yourself, *Selenita*. Neither this body, nor my yucca field, or the bed where I sleep, none of those belong to me … and these pains aren't mine either. All there is down here my Lord has sent to me, so that Hati may take care of all that's His. And just as God lent me everything I have, He might as well take it away; so then there's no point in me worrying, is there now?" She closed off her argument with another sparkling cackle, and moved on to scold Selene for walking about with her head uncovered. "Ay, *Selenita*, you without a kerchief in this here Bush and with this weather, God forbid!" It wasn't until that moment that Selene recalled the ever-important kerchief of the Garifuna women.

The work of uprooting yucca is hard, Selene knew that well: there was the occasion when, after a prolonged absence of her son, Felipe's mother got to their house and found her sprawled in bed like an empty sack; the elder's remedy had been to take her out to the yucca field to harvest the roots. There's good reason why any backbreaking task is called a yucca in Redención. That day Selene learned in her own flesh the meaning of yucca, when, warning her no to break them, Mother-in-law put her to work pulling the tubers from a dry and hardened soil. That was then the only consolation she got from Doña Chola, who, for all other matters, was always kind to her. Selene learned everything there was to know about yucca; she became familiar with the sweetness of its pulp and the bitterness of its sap. But it would be a long while before she learned that for the Garifuna, displays of suffering are loaded with evil omens, and that is the reason why you never offer your shoulder for someone to cry on. There was the time when her tears landed on the jet-black fuzz that sheltered Felipe's chest, and right away he pushed her off grunting: "Back off, you're gonna jinx me!"

"Hati, this is one huge bunch of yucca you got here! That's gotta be a whole lot of work ..."

"Oh *numa*, just about enough, I tell you! And to top it off, I need to keep everything together at home, so that when I'm done baking there won't be any need for me to go out and get drenched no mo'. It's just that my guy Madu, once he starts drinking – and even more when the weather don't let down – there's no end to his shenanigans. So then, gotta find someone to get me the coal now, 'cause when I went by El Búho's gazebo, Madu he was already passed out on a bench." Hati let out another one of her contagious cackles. "And how's things with that Felipe of yours, *numa*?"

"He went to town, on account of checking the flood, he said." A comment that brought on another burst of laughter, this time shared by Selene. As they went across the lake, their cracking laughs had fish fleeing back and forth between submerged plants. But when they got to the new, narrow canal, Hati started talking under her breath, whispering as if they weren't alone, the two of them.

"Ah, Felipe, lemme tell you: he's the reincarnation of his grandfather, Cirilo Flinn, that was his name. ... Cirilo owned all of these plots, earned them with his machete, farming them and later raising cattle. The man got to be so rich that on country fair days he'd show up in town with his satchels full of gold coins, riding this big stallion, Colorín – his favourite, 'cause that horse was just like him, black as night. Cirilo wasn't from around the village, originally that is; he was born over on the other side a the mountain, in a tiny hamlet way out there by the Natural Reserve; and Amada, his wife, she was born there too. He was twice her age, so she must have been fifteen at best when Cirilo eloped with her. Amada was a hard worker, even though she was slight of frame. She was crazy about him, that girl, and stuck around with her man in all of his adventures. Go figure.

"Cirilo had a flat face, rough on the edges, not like your Felipe's; that pretty nose and those high cheekbones of his, he got them from his grandma... So, Cirilo and Amada arrived here machete in hand, 'cause there was land to be worked, that's why. They broke through and found their way as newcomers, and soon the whole town started looking up to them – this place that's known for being jealous of outsiders. They started a yucca and cassava business and gave work to a bunch a people in town. Then they got to planting new species of trees; there's even a mango he planted hisself – famous too 'cause it gives the sweetest fruit – that we all call the Flinn mango to this day. Uh, 'n there's more: Mada – that's how we called her – she knew all 'bout healing, that woman, she sure did. If a dog bit you, or even a snake, she'd cure the wound with a burning piece a coal right on the bite. No one 'round here ever knew nothing better than Amada's ointments for the sores left by mosquito stings. Then she'd tie the string on newborns' navels like no one else could: they always ended up with pretty belly buttons. Just see how it is that all her children and grandchildren, all a them have these round and flat bellybuttons, real nice..." Turning to herself, Selene saw Felipe's belly button: it was as big as a *diez-centavos* coin, a silk-covered drum where she played at make-believe calls to the ancestors. But Hati was still going: "Not like the rest of them folk around here, all a them with their belly buttons showing up like a third leg." This time the ensuing cackle sounded crafty. "And it's just because a their navels that Cirilo's children can be told apart from others here, 'cause Amada made sure that no child of his would be stillborn or die at birth, and she never refused to care for any of his other women either…it was plain hard to tell how Mada could handle the rides between life and death as good as she did, the power she had. Just imagine, if you can, those hands of hers, so skinny, those fingers like tender reeds, all covered with blood, or marked all over with calluses from working the land. Oh but then, on Sundays, before arranging it in perfect braids, she'd rub oil on that hair a hers that was so hard to comb, being rebellious and still so smooth, just like Felipe's; then she'd pull a fresh dress out of her trunk, put on a nice hat and go visit the homes of women in labor, men wounded in the banana plantations, old arthritic folk. She'd always walk in with little presents: a few coconuts here or some lemons there, whatever; thing is, she'd never show up empty handed. And in Amada's house there was always a bite to eat or a pillow for whomever dropped by, and that's why people loved her so."

All the while that Hati spoke about Cirilo's wife, with her mind's eye Selene kept seeing the image of Doña Chola, Amada's daughter and Felipe's mother. Hati went on to finish off her yarn: "Then, to all of us that had done work for him, one at a time Cirilo started giving small plots for us to call our own. I was the *ereba* maker for Cirilo Flinn; his favorite, mind you; but he didn't take advantage of me like he did to so many others, and that's 'cause I was the best of all his workers."

Selene felt a sharp, stabbing pang in her knee, which she had kept bent for far too long: the right knee it was, the one she'd fractured. She closed her eyes and took a deep breath. At that very moment, one of those memories arose that used to haunt her, lurking in the hidden corners of her brain to take her by storm at the least expected times – remembrances carried perhaps by the smell of coal, a stroke of light at sunset, the color of clay, the pain in her knee, the leaping of a fish; just about anything could unleash them.

Coral

Having put Ángel's mess behind them, they went along with Horacio's advice and moved back to The Bush. "That'll be just so you two can live free of the prying gazes of busybodies and shut out the gossip in town," that's what the healer told them. So Selene stopped working at the school and it was decided that, until they'd settled properly back in the farmstead, it was better for Ariel to spend some time with his grandparents.

That was the time when Felipe downright fell to his knees before her: "You are a goddess," he told Selene. "You saved that man's life and then went and kept me outta jail, you did." He totally gave in to his love for her like he had never done before. "I don't need no other woman," he'd tell his lover, not knowing where to start kissing her, caressing her. They became complicit in everything that went down. The four walls of their bedroom weren't enough to contain their lust: off kilter, on fire, they'd mount their bicycles and, surfing the breeze under star-cloaked skies, go to make love on the beach or by the rocks at the other end of the bay, or else to just meander around the hamlet's pathways. There was a couple of times when, out of the blue, they climbed on the Toyota and went all the way to Puerto, this while a line from one of Selene's favourite poems haunted her: "...*quavering, ravenous, on the hunt for ghosts.*"

Then one night, when they walked by Redención's

pool hall, they ran into Coral.

The street was dingy. They were well over a block away from the hall when towards them came an ebb and flow of buoyant conversations punctuated by the collisions of billiard balls. Bob Marley's peaceful voice held sway over the gathering; then, blending with the steam of the sticky night, it slipped away amidst the dark alleyways that flowed into La Principal, the main street: *Turn your lights down low…* In the shadows, one could glimpse silhouettes busily engaged in a nocturnal marketplace for goods unseen. The night was still young and there were people strolling down the sand-covered street, so Felipe and Selene got off their bikes. They were just beginning to push on the handlebars when Selene recognized Spooky's famed figure, camouflaged by the shadow of a mango tree on the corner across from the pool hall. That was a mountain of a man, a giant: he was twice as tall and four times as bulky as a guy that had just approached him. Leaning on the tree trunk, Spooky looked the other way, oblivious to the skinny man next to him, to his gesticulations as he cajoled excitedly offering him some object. Seated on a small bench a few steps away and protected by the same tree's shade, there were three young fellows smoking. A familiar scent stung Selene's nose as a disturbing heavy smoke that smelled like burning plastic wafted her way – the same smell that crossed your path wherever you went – the smoke that was wasting away the young minds of the village. The cigarette that kept going from hand to hand looked like a Bengal light that released a loud spark every now and then. The teachers in school had been well instructed on how to recognize crack:

"They call it crack because of the banging sounds the substance makes as it burns," that was the description given by an expert on addictions who came to town one day from the capital. The schoolteachers were having a campaign against the problem, which had become a full epidemic, and Selene herself had been part of the prevention committee – that is, before she was forced to give up her teaching job because of the charged situation caused by Felipe shooting Ángel. It was indeed a serious problem: the cocaine that travelled through the hamlet wasn't enough for the young people, no way – mixed with baking soda, they "cooked" the white powder to bring out the alkaloids and turn it into crack, a more threatening substance, since its intense and brief high brought about a new generation of almost incurable addicts and, along with it, a new wave of crime. Crack was the lowest of the low in the process, and even the capos stayed away from it, on account of the stuff making people downright insane.

When they passed by the mango tree, the skinny fellow turned towards them, offering a cell phone: "Look here, brother," he told Felipe. "It's outta-da-box brand new, picks up *why fy*. You take it, mon, give me five hundred now, tomorrow you get 'em back ... well, three hundred, bro..." The young man's desperation horrified Selene: he looked like a castaway, someone hanging on to life by the skin of his teeth. Felipe, who was in one of his joker moods, thought it cool to have fun at the expense of the poor wretch – something about which Selene was none too pleased: there was no point in being cruel, and then again, she just wanted to keep walking, get out of that place.

"Alcaloide, mon, you tell me now, what makes you think a cell phone is what I need, me bruda?"

"Ah, so you can call your people, mind your crew, check up the scene," answered that pathetic bag of bones everyone knew as Alcaloide. Selene would never feel fully comfortable with the cruel sense of humor that people showed when making up nicknames in Redención – always mocking a person's whatever misfortune. There was, for one, a kid in school the others called Dancin' just because he had a condition that made his legs twitch as he walked; then there was another boy who had learning difficulties and that one they called "just thinking," because every time someone asked him, "whatcha doing?" the little one responded, "oh, just thinking."

Alcaloide wouldn't give up, though: "It's the thing to have, so you keep up with modern times a'right. This is the twenty-first century, boss." The guy couldn't stay still for even a second, kept taking jumpy steps from side to side as he spoke. He looked like a praying mantis, with his long legs way out of proportion with the rest of him, his body all bones and his bulging eyes.

Felipe put an end to the chat with one of his mad wisecracks: "Oh but what you don't know, me brother, it's I'm just a little black chap born in the year zero."

Even though the whole thing was annoying to Selene, she did find Felipe's quip amusing – perhaps because there was something of the truth in it – but she remained stone faced. Bob Marley's voice changed tempo now: *Sun is shining, the weather is sweet, make you wanna move your dancing feet…*

They walked for half a block before reaching

158

the pool hall. That's where they saw her, both of them at once. There she was, with that pretty face of hers, seated on a bench right outside the hall drinking a beer. Seeing them come by, she lit up in a smile that gave a quick glimpse of her gold tooth. Felipe knew her from way back; Selene had just crossed paths with the woman, nothing more. After the initial greetings, Coral slipped her hand into her cleavage and, pulling out a joint, signalled for them to follow her. Felipe went to the bar, came back with three beers and put them in the basket of Selene's bike. Then they headed for the beach pushing their wheels. Once there, they sat under a straw hut to smoke the reefer while doing sign language with Coral, who was deaf-mute. She was upset – had gotten into a kerfuffle with her lover's mother not long before: the old lady didn't appreciate Coral coming to her house. Fact is, most folk in town treated the young woman like a pest; they bad-mouthed her because, in spite of her disability, she refused to lead her life like a victim; because she was beautiful and often unruly; and to top it off, because she loved beer and partying. "*Puta* – whore," the woman had called her, and Coral was so pissed off that she even succeeded in articulating the word as best she could. But there was more: instead of defending her, the man had kowtowed to his mother.

"That's shitty, people can be real shit," Felipe kept saying and shaking his head. Selene did nothing but listen: being an outsider, she wouldn't dare speak evil about anyone there, just in case she crossed the wrong person. Nonetheless, in her heart she felt nothing but true sympathy for Coral.

When they were done with the joint, the

conversation petered out until, sitting on the reed bench, the three of them went quiet, just looking out into fluorescent waves. Felipe's gaze rolled now across the small nose, the lathed cheekbones, those untamed little braids, that smile given an aura of danger by the gold tooth. "Mesmerizing," Selene thought, while Coral kept staring at the darkness, getting a kick out of being watched.

"Man, she's pretty," said Felipe, and Selene couldn't but agree with him. Verging on euphoria, a swell of blood ran over her body. It was a sensation she had never felt before: the attraction between Felipe and that woman was turning her on. Right then Coral cast an oblique look at her, as if asking for forgiveness, or a go-ahead. Selene gathered herself enough to pose the question:

"Do you like him?"

"Yes," was the answer, as Coral lowered her eyes, embarrassed.

Felipe looked at Selene, Selene looked at Felipe, Coral and Selene looked at each other, the three of them exchanged looks and then he pointed away with his head: "Let's go home."

They walked back the way they'd come, Selene, Coral and Felipe. Together they made their way across the hamlet pushing the bicycles till they reached the sandbar and went around it on the beach side; once on the path to The Bush, they climbed on the bikes. Coral rode with Felipe and Selene went behind them, thrilled to be heading toward mysteries; the perfume of the night blended into her mane. The trio had barely entered the house when their kissing began; tongues and fingers got busy pulling on belts and girdles, unbuttoning garments and, leaving on their wake a trail of rags, all three finally stumbled into the bedroom. They flopped on the bed, beaming. Selene unhooked Coral's bra and started kissing her breasts, which her hands couldn't grasp whole. Fully at ease, Coral leaned back on the pillows looking at Selene with half-closed eyes; her breathing was deep and measured. Felipe was in turn occupied with rumps, thighs and groins. The women covered him with kisses amidst shared smiles. Selene went to search for condoms in her man's drawer – being always on guard, she certainly knew where he kept them and how many there were. She ripped open a cover, pulled out the thing, and Coral put the latex nipple between her lips. Felipe, lying on his back in awe, enchanted and eager, watched how the two women were about to lay the preservative on him. But he could no longer hold back and burst like a new-born spring. Struggling to get back in charge, he rubbed his cock, kissed Selene, kissed Coral, caressed both pussies – reckoning they were quite alike, as he would later tell Selene – but in the end the deep vertical crease on his brow proved his defeat. Exhausted by the lovemaking he and Selene had done before leaving home, by the relentless pedalling, the day's labors, the spliff-and-beer mix, he fell asleep, vanquished. Selene and Coral spent the rest of the night fondling each other till satisfied when dawn was near.

From that day on Coral just bloomed, everything about her said "happy." She went by the farmstead almost daily and helped Selene cleaning fish as well as with house chores and farm work, of which there were more than enough. Selene herself wholeheartedly took to her newly found freedom. "Really, how fortunate I am," she thought, "having a mate with whom I can explore the entire universe." She felt fulfilled in a new life with neither limits nor fears. During the nights that she and Felipe spent alone together, which were becoming scarce by the day, Selene danced for him as she had seen table-dancing women do in a Puerto strip club where Felipe had taken her once. Whenever there was a full moon, they walked out into the yard with the boom box and she danced to some *bachata* beat: *Quítate la ropa, desnúdate toda y no temas a mi amor* – Get rid of your clothes, go naked and don't fear my love.

But then Felipe started having outbursts, tantrums: "Wayward is what you are, yo mamma didn't know how to control you; obedience, that's something you know nothing 'bout," he'd bark at Selene when he saw her smoking, or for whatever misstep, no matter how trivial.

Coral jumped to her defence whenever she saw Selene's eyes drown in tears. "Let's get out of here," she sign-talked to her when Felipe was in a foul mood, but Selene wouldn't go along with her friend. The way she saw things, those were issues for her and her husband to deal with on their own – because Felipe was her man and she his woman, even if that wasn't written on any document out there, nor had it been declared before any saint figure anywhere. And then again, when Felipe got over his temper blows, he would rekindle his love for her, taking Selene to heaven itself.

Around that time he decided his next great project would be learning how to do car body work. He hauled scrap metal to the farm, and his friend Hilario showed him the ropes in a lean-to they put together a few steps from the kitchen. Good Hilario: a man as charming as he was pint-sized; in a town of smiley people, he was the one with the brightest, most permanent smile. And just as any other sentient being did, he had surrendered to Felipe's charm, had become his staunch, unquestioning follower – yes, like the dogs that left their homes to follow him, like he horses that yielded to his commands, like the women who offered themselves to him, like all the men that wanted to be friends of his; and like Selene as well, who had unthinkingly given up on her own life, as though hypnotized, in order to take care of him, and fervidly wished she'd have no other choice but her Felipe.

"If you asked Hilario, he'd drop his pants in a jiffy, of that I'm sure," Selene said one day in a fit of jealousy over the man, since it wasn't enough for those two to spend the day making an unbearable metal-banging racket next to her kitchen, but come sunset they'd go off together to wherever it was they went in town.

Selene felt then that with each hammer blow on metal sheets Felipe was discharging his animosity towards her. In retrospect, when the whole thing became ancient history, Selene came to the conclusion that getting into car-body work was the worst thing Felipe could have done to her: it was a desecration of her home, something that she felt was the most sacred thing to her. Around that time she started smoking pot in earnest, because getting high made it easier for her to endure the ordeal without making a fuss – a turn of events that, as was to be expected, brought about many a spat.

"Go ahead, get your joint-rolling doctorate!" he'd cry out loud every time she rolled the first joint of the day right after breakfast. And that only made her smoke another spliff – just to feel free, to find shelter in rebellion. With so much quarrelling going on, Selene would at times run off to Puerto, to Viola's hotel where she asked to be given the room on the fourth floor, up there with the trees, just to be able to smoke her reefer in peace. Soon enough Felipe would show up looking for her, and they reconciled getting high and making love for a couple of days.

It was as though they had discovered each other's well bottoms; they baited, spurred one another, pushing themselves to plunge into that well, reach bottom and then go beyond that bottom. They would take turns in attempting to deliver themselves – him, her – but then the other would be pulling both back down into the pit.

One of those nights in some hotel, when way too late she said they should go out again just to buy more marihuana, Felipe tried to stop her: "Selene, we've done all and everything, we've had enough to smoke already, let's get some sleep." Her answer, with a hand gripping the doorknob, was: "You know, I am a bottomless well, Felipe." She said that and bolted out closing the door behind her.

It was a game that gradually got darker, more pathetic, until their energy and their will finally died down; but that came to happen after a long time had gone by.

If someone made her feel at peace during those times, it was actually Coral: she'd just shrug her shoulders meaning, "who cares, none of that matters."

Fed up with the constant hammering of the metal workers, Selene shot back one day, "Who are you to tell me not to care, you can't hear a thing," and at that Coral just laid a hand on her solar plexus and nodded, signifying that she did hear, in her own way. She turned around and grabbed a tray with the fish that had to be cleaned, then threw on top of those a knife and some lemons before signalling for Selene to follow her. The two women ended up settling down under one of the straw huts Felipe had built on the outer side of the plot.

"Felipe, Coral needs money to buy a mattress for her and the kids," Selene told him one day. Coral had four little children, the youngest just months old. All of them were cared for by their grandmother because of what the family saw as Coral's "unfitness." That was too the reason why she wandered about like a mare without a rider.

And well, that time, even as he was known for his generosity, Felipe refused to buy a bed for Coral. "So now you wanna buy a bed for your woman, is that it?" He was about to have a conniption, and Selene did not risk taking things further, there was no point in reinforcing his jealousy. But no matter what, that day she felt lousy for not giving a hand to her friend in need – that sweet girl who jumped with joy the moment she saw her; the one who had once rented a taxi to bring Selene out of The Bush on account of another fracas with Felipe; the one that one day let her friend wear her own sandals (which, truth be told, Selene never returned). ... Ah, Coral coming by once on her pink bicycle to bring her a breakfast of fried plantains, beans and a half pint of rum. Yes, that was one occasion when Felipe wasn't around and then her friend Coral meant to share a kiss, but Selene turned her away. Why? Because that was something they did along with him, with Felipe, it was something of his. And yet Selene made it clear, had to: the friendship between them as two women, that was beyond question.

And so that day Selene told Coral: "Your wanting me, it is my honor, but I can't, not without Felipe. Believe me please: I am your friend, always will be...

Dru, Dro, Dri, Dre...Drama

Selene and Coral became just about inseparable, that is, until the day Selene had to spend two days in the capital, and found the tell-tale signs when she got back home: Felipe's watch left behind under the bed; stained sheets; her man's evasive looks. Right away her guts tightened up – a visceral spasm that felt like a conflagration in her innards.

"Did Coral come here while I was gone?" Selene asked, and he said no. She said nothing, got on the bicycle and rushed over to the village. When she found Coral, doing her laundry by the well behind her house, she got off the bike and signalled – first, pointing with one finger: "You." Then, rubbing left and right index fingers and right away miming the gorilla-like gesture Coral had made up to signify Felipe's person: "Did you sleep with Felipe?"

Calm and collected, Coral nodded, articulating "Wednesday."

Feeling downright cursed, Selene got back on her bicycle and hit the pedals with a vengeance on her way back to the farm. She burst into the house and started hurling dishes against walls; the chicken-shaped clay pot, the radio, the fan, she smashed those on the floor. Then she picked up a hammer from the dining table, went straight to the brand-new oven they'd just bought and hit its door with a light yet deliberate blow, which unleashed a cascade of glass that somehow assuaged the fury in her heart. But the woman wasn't done yet: with one single kick she sent the tiny blue wooden stool flying – that shaky, jerry-built stool that kept getting knocked over but followed them to whichever new place they moved into, and always got re-painted to fit the new décor.

That's how she fractured her knee, something she wouldn't come to realize till much later.

Hilario, who had been chatting with Felipe under the mango tree, took off like a bat out of hell, and Felipe just hollered from the hammock where he sat in the yard: "You break one more thing in there, woman, I swear I'll set all a this shit on fire."

Once again Selene had to put distance between herself and the farm. When she reached the sandbar, though, pedalling on loose sand felt like being in one of those dreams when you get nowhere, make no progress no matter how much or how fast you run. So she ended up having to ride the bike in first gear all the way to the hamlet, crossed it from end to end, and this time around found Coral swimming in the surf. She stayed on her wheels waiting for her friend to get back to the beach …

"Climb on!" And Coral, still soaked, did as she was told.

This was the fourth ride she took to and fro, now with Coral perched on the crossbar. She pedalled back home as though hounded by demons. Her passenger, as usual, kept an aura of calm repose – because Coral's deaf-mute condition granted her the privilege of being able to pretend to be oblivious whenever it suited her, a privilege she readily wielded as her weapon.

The women went past la Principal, which was

now lined with curious, dilated, morbid eyes. As they left town, people on both sides of the highway craned their necks like vultures smelling carrion. Soon enough and, following a habitual pattern, tongues got unleashed and what folk didn't know, they invented.

Throughout all the comings and goings, Selene didn't even feel the pain from her fractured kneecap.

When they got to the farmstead, Felipe stared at them from the swaying hammock where he lay under the mango tree. Selene parked the bicycle in front of him and right away noticed how the vertical groove on his brow looked deeper than any other time.

Still on the bike, she barked: "Okay now, Felipe, go ahead and tell me once again that Coral didn't spend a night here with you when I was gone." Coral was still seated on the bicycle's crossbar, eyes wide open and mouth agape, wondering what the problem could possibly be. Felipe just got up off the hammock, grabbed the machete he'd left planted on the ground and disappeared in the thicket.

Selene took Coral into the house, where Ariel – who happened to be visiting them that hell of a day – was busy sweeping the debris: the gutted fan, the crockery smashed, the glass from the oven door sprayed all over the floor. In the child's brow Selene noticed the same crack she'd just seen on Felipe's frown. But really, there and then all she could see was her own anger; even Ariel's presence wouldn't bring her to her senses. The kid fled into his room and slammed the door behind him.

Aghast on seeing so much damage, Coral kept asking with her gestures: "But why all of this, why?"

Selene had her friend sit on a chair: "When I'm not here" – index finger on her chest followed by waving hand – "you" – index like a dagger pointing at Coral – "don't" – index going side to side forcefully – "come here" – index sweeping the space that Selene was attempting to reclaim as her own, a bit too late already.

Having turned her eyes away, Coral got absolutely nothing of that message; she took herself out of the house and crossed the bridge in a sprint. Selene shut herself up in her room. Looking out the window of his own room, Ariel saw Coral leaving the farmstead.

A few days later, when Selene was tutoring the child as he worked on decoding his syllables, clearly and without hesitation the little one wrote down his first word ever: dru, dro, dri, dre... drama.

Madness

When the cooing of the pigeons that nestled nearby woke her up, Selene kept her eyes shut. Echoing the bed sheets, her eyelids had fallen prey to gravity. "Here I am, on the other side of everything, in this sand-covered bed," she scribbled with her mind's pencil. "There's no point in attempting to move: I know there's no strength left in my arms to even try." Drawing her hands over her pubis now: "I am an empty room ... just as empty as this room I call my own."

She took a stab at moving her right leg, but something kept her from doing it: a limp and whitish swelling, bloodless; a talon throttling the juncture between thigh and lower leg – a numb, dull cramp that kept her motionless. She'd been lying flat for a good while when Felipe walked in, measuring his steps. Only then did Selene open her eyes, as he crossed the room and sat on the bed.

"Felipe, don't lie to me, come clean, tell the truth. It'll be best if we talk it over, you and me. It's only when we lie that we betray each other," she told him with a feeble yet deliberate voice that made him drop his guard at last.

"Yeah right, truth is ... well, yes Selene, Coral slept here when you were gone. But really now, it was just that one night, and she left at dawn next morning, I swear."

Even though she was well aware of the whole thing, hearing it coming from Felipe's lips made her feel as if lightening had struck her body; her heart got ejected from her bosom and her mouth went dry.

Felipe lay down on the bed, lifted both arms, clenched his hands together and made a grand show of thrusting a dagger into his chest:

"So there, that's what you wanted, right? ... What you were so damn afraid of finding out, the thing you feared the most, you got it now: the admission, the certainty... There you have it, the knife."

The side of Selene that, while detached from her, kept watch over the goings-on, couldn't but admire the histrionic ability of the man who was staging a hara-kiri move as he lay on her bed.

From then on she chose to shut her mouth and kept everyday exchanges with Felipe at the bare minimum. Isolated from the world, she went adrift on the aching tides of her swollen knee, which had become her universe. Her days subsided into a sluggish and dull pendulum swing. She would see her man only at night when, shadow-like, he fell exhausted next to her.

Then amidst the dense billow that life in The Bush had become, there was an early evening when – for once not feeling the urge to hit the trail after bathing, even as he'd pulled out fresh clothes to go celebrate Easter eve in town – Felipe flopped down on the bed next to Selene and drifted off to sleep. The spiralling voices of golden orioles swaddled the dusk as it fell surrounded by scarlet strokes, and solid shapes became silhouettes.

Suddenly, somewhere in the distance: RAT-A-

TAT-TAT, a shooting burst ripped through the silence.

"Someone's gettin' dead," Felipe groaned.

Shots rang out once again: RAT-TAT-A-TAT. Those were from a semi-automatic, the kind of bullet that not only breaks the skin but bursts inside. A sound of death, unmistakably cutting, categorical.

"I'd say it's gotta be over in El Puerto, the way it sounded," he sentenced. "Mark my words, the newspapers will prove me right tomorrow."

As the day gave in to utter darkness, a chorus of frogs overtook the birdsong all around. It took Selene the longest time to fall asleep; no matter how much she tried, it was impossible to erase from her mind an image of bodies falling like sacks.

"Coral got killed last night…"

It was Horacio the healer who broke the news to them, as he came in for the healing session so early that the couple were still in bed. "The deed went down over in the Barrio Matamoros. There's no one can tell now what that woman was doing over there if not looking for her death," he told them through the window while still standing out in the yard.

An abrupt river of tears started pouring down Selene's eyes, overwhelming her inside and out. She feared she'd drown in that deluge, squirmed out of bed, went to Ariel's room and threw herself on his empty, neatly made bed. A backpack hung from a nail on the wall. In apple-pie order on a small wooden table: a tiny plastic airplane, a rubber ball, a couple of books, some pencils. A fine layer of dust coated everything in the room, marking the time since Ariel had lived in the house. The child's bedroom, painted blue and attentively arranged, was now downright abandoned.

Felipe and Horacio ended up in the kitchen and, while brewing a herbal tea for Selene, the healer proceeded to tell the story, as he knew it:

"Coral, as we all know, is a bit too restless…" Horacio picked his words carefully, since he was aware of how close the couple had been with the deceased; he made sure as well not to speak about Coral the same way that people in town spoke of her: the crazy one, the hussy, Jezebel, degenerate, pervert. "Who knows how it was that she ended up in that neighborhood full of Mara gangsters," he picked up the thread after a long pause. "Her mother says that afternoon Coral signalled her brother to go out with her and the two of them left the house, saying nothing but 'we'll be back.' … There's people, too, who say she was a small-time pusher, that she'd gone to Matamoros looking for dope to sell; but I know nothing 'bout such crap, me brother."

"No mon, I wouldn't bet on that, not me," Felipe broke in. "What Coral is all about, you see…" He had to pause – the cascade of images and memories threatening to overpower him. "Coral likes partying, is all, and there ain't nothing wrong with that, is there?"

He spoke in the present tense, just like that, without thinking; it was the natural thing to do, couldn't be any other way.

Never again was Coral's name mentioned in the house. Selene felt disjointed, broken down. She did not speak or move more than was essential, and saw everything as though looking from afar. Horacio went to The Bush every other day to treat her knee with mud poultices, and she wouldn't say a single word during his visits. Good thing was, the swelling subsided bit by bit under the healer's care. Meanwhile, Felipe spent his days in the yucca fields, avoiding her as much as he could. She felt rejected to the bone.

Then there was the night when they had a go at making love, and out of the blue he told her, "I want to do it under the stars, out there by the cliff." Right there and then she got this dreadful notion that Felipe meant to kill her... "The woman, she went crazy, Lord," he would say afterwards. "She took off running and jumped into the waves down there. Nothing I coulda done, it was so dark, she went so fast, so sudden." There couldn't be any other reason why he'd want them to make love by the cliff at night, and with her being in such wretched condition: emaciated, her knee all swollen, a complete wreck. She pushed him away, rolled over on the sand-covered, sweat-soaked sheets, wrapped her arms around her ribs and, making herself as tiny as possible, did the best she could to fall sleep.

"It was on a bed of lilies where I drifted all night long in the moonless garden with goblins riding horses whispers and laments spreading amidst boughs you try to hold me in your arms your hair shedding delirium petals on the headrest but I take a bite out of you in my teeth the sensation of a smooth skin so hard I am the madwoman of the dawn..." Selene wrote on the notebook she held tight to her chest like a shield, the one she kept under her pillow when she went to sleep.

And, the day came when Felipe, who was dying to know what Selene kept with so much zeal in that notebook, seized on a passing inattentiveness of hers

– a split-second opportunity – and dove into it greedily. His eyes went over the letters one by one, hurriedly squeezing the words, anxious to make them reveal their secrets to him. "... Last night she came to lie next to me on my white bed with its new pillows between my clean sheets her open wound pouring and me going out of my way to bring order into the chaos that was breaking in swept everything in her wake while all of her leaves kept falling off. Then I came to a park pitched camp there placing my little fish in the centre figured out the way to flood the field to make a lake is it possible? I wondered got down to work a cup-full at a time."

"Poor thing," Felipe told himself. "She done gone outa her mind."

Selene spent her days all by herself in the house, with her only company being the little dog Sombra – Shadow – whose name fit her to a tee. The horses came sticking their muzzles past the kitchen door, following the aroma of ripe bananas and mangos – the woman's only sustenance during those days – and the cooking space was steeped in animal smells. Out in the yard the chickens were an almost human presence as they busily scratched around piles of dry leaves that no one would rake away. Selene's character, her nature, got to be so ghostly that there were times when even the bare-tailed opossum climbed down from the rafters in her very face, and it was only Sombra's growls and barks that managed to chase him away; the intruder would then disappear leaving behind a sharp, Creolin-like smell, or else he would lie on his back playing dead till free to run away when no one was looking. Selene feared him like the plague; and actually, they would spook each other, woman and critter, whenever they came face to face by accident.

There were moments when, with her soul taking flight from her body, Selene saw herself as another one of the women who inhabited a gallery of their own in her memory: castaways, women gone insane. The first one, a girl just about nine years old, who lived in the Madre Keller orphanage where she and her mother used to go bringing presents for the forsaken kids: dollies that Selene would put aside, were sent to the "hospital" where hairless dolls sat on shelves waiting for new manes – blondes, brunettes – or else a missing eye, the absent arm, the chopped-off leg. Mother and daughter would show up at the orphanage afterwards with the rejuvenated dolls and bags full of other toys, clothes as well. It was there, in Madre Keller's patio, where that nine-year-old girl spent her days – the one with roughly sheared hair who'd grown up tied to a donkey and brayed instead of talking. Then in Selene's memory, the image of the donkey child merged with that of Tomasina, a teen-aged girl she'd seen many years later in the Madre Teresa asylum in Guatemala, where she'd worked as a volunteer in one of many education brigades. On full moon evenings, with her tresses all hacked and her gaze lost in the void, Tomasina would peel off her clothes and go out dancing in the street. In Selene's museum of demented women there lived, too, a wheelchair ridden old lady that would often rip off her knitted cap to show a head where sparse hairs allowed glimpses of her scalp, while she cried out: "Look at all them snakes how they bite me, look it how they go on climbing from my feet and up my legs, oh how they bite me, these snakes."

And then the white-haired woman with ragged skin and lust in her eyes, who wandered about rubbing her crotch and her breasts nonstop. All of them were women who, as Selene saw it, had gone beyond "the line," the subtle, even invisible boundary that since her childhood she imagined as something setting reason apart from madness in people's insides.

On occasions when her grandfather took her to the theatre or a ballet performance, "What is it that stops me," she would question herself, "if right this very moment I choose to get up from my seat and climb on that stage to dance and howl?" And her response: "Nothing, just my mind," as she imagined the borderline between sanity and lunacy being nothing but a very flimsy gossamer, like the ones they use in theatre stages and look now solid now translucent as different lights hit them. Since she was a child, that's how Selene had seen reality, good and evil, her feelings and her moods. Everything was relative to her, and that was why it always took so much effort for the woman to choose sides. But those days the one thing clearest to her was that she had gone through the gossamer into the other side; and that because, truth be told, the horse-riding goblins and the woman with all her leaves falling off, and the little fish in the middle of the park, and her making a lake with cups-full of water – those weren't dreams; those were factual realities.

And, when Felipe read Selene's journal, the man actually saw a reflection of himself in it: he too had seen the gallivanting goblins in moonless nights, but then he'd found it so much easier to determine that through all of this his woman had lost her mind.

He felt his sentence confirmed the day Selene started taking her clothes out into the yard. It was a selection from the outfits she'd worn in her nights out with Felipe: dresses, jeans, blouses, her finest lingerie – out of which she kept just a couple of cherished pieces. She bundled everything up, doused the pile with fuel and tossed a lit match at it. It took a while for the purple dress to catch fire; as it was made of polyester, that garment downright refused to give in to the flames that seemed to be reaching for the sky; it just floundered and writhed ever so slowly, like caramel swirl, until the thing finally disappeared. When all the clothes were burnt and there was nothing left but smoking ashes, she went into the kitchen, brought down a bunch of sage she'd left to dry hanging from the rafters, came back outside and threw the cleansing sage into the remaining embers.

Being done with that, she picked up her notebook:

"Coral has gone and died, with her pretty little face
With her honey skin, woman-child.
Her death, instant death
I did hear it from my house
Early evening on the eve of Easter day
Shots, semi-automatic shots.
Who would have thought it was you
Ay muchacha, with your pretty little face!
And Coral, I've got to ask you,
Ay, Coral, I tremble at the thought:
Was it all of us that killed you?"

When she was done writing, Selene put the notebook away inside her suitcase. She then went and took a bath next to the well, for the first time in what felt like an eternity. It was while doing her final rinse that she saw her mare La Blanca, wounded, looking as if she'd been in some kind of skirmish as she crossed the bridge with heavy steps. When she came closer, Selene noticed the lacerations on her back. First things first, she had to be washed and brushed head to toe, staying away from the wounds yet making sure those were left thoroughly cleansed. After that, Selene diluted some calendula tincture and washed the sore spots; as well, she gave the mare some sugary pellets steeped in the same wonder flower. The two of them, now well bathed and prim, went and took a deserved rest under the mango tree.

Inasmuch as Selene recovered her strength, remorse increased. Lucidity was torture: "If Coral had only stayed here with us, she wouldn't have gone out there… and then what have I done, what horrid way to pay my debt with that woman – my poor dear Coral, thinking she had found a sanctuary here… A scab, that's what I was, behaved just like the worst macho … Ah, nothing but vanity! But how could I even pretend to be an equal to Coral, with that goddess body of hers, with her oh so natural sensuality? … Stupid me, how in hell could I act so blindly, so selfishly," she moaned hitting the walls. "I wasn't being generous, God damn, only controlling. In aiming to contain Felipe's sexuality I did nothing but stoke it, made myself an instrument for the desire between him and Coral, that's all. And oh God, I was just using her. It's all my fault, it is," she wouldn't stop racking herself. Then if by chance she sensed her reflection on the dresser mirror, Selene couldn't recognize herself in the image of that scrawny and disheveled being that stared back at her: it looked like someone watching her from way afar and in a time long gone by.

Felipe, knowing himself incapable of doing it, brought Ariel back to the farmstead to be by Selene's side. During his father's absences, which had become more and more frequent, she and the boy got in the habit of taking strolls at sunset. Ariel, whose head reached only up to Selene's chest, would wrap one arm around her waist, and she would throw hers over the little one's shoulder.

"Ariel, will you go on loving me when I turn into a little old lady?" she asked him in one of their outings.

"Yes, Selene," he answered back.

"And, will you also take care of me?" she kept at it.

"Uh, well, isn't it the same, Selene? Love, care – it is the same," he retorted, on the verge of irritation, wondering why Selene couldn't get it that loving a person and taking care of that person are one and the same thing.

Replica

They had gone to bonesetters and healers, doctors too; the X-rays they put her through in hospital showed nothing at all – must have been because their machine was an old wreck. The swelling kept coming and going, and Selene felt relief only when laying still. That's the reason why they had to go back to the house downtown, where life would be less burdensome.

On moving day, Felipe, Ariel and Selene left in the car – Felipe at the wheel. Patatiesa, who was there to help them, took the reins of the cart pulled by el Rey, with la Huraga and La Blanca following right behind. Sombra rode atop the bundles with her chest sticking out, as was her custom: a miniature sphinx. The coati named "Coati" – which Felipe had bought from an Indian not too long ago – did all kinds of balancing feats on top of the bicycles lying on their sides; his black domino mask made him look like a bandido as he kept his gaze fixed on the road while wagging his splendid tail.

That was that, early on a January morning the procession entered the village like a circus caravan.

The house downtown was nestled in the middle of a square garden planted with fruit-bearing trees: mangos, avocados and oranges. All kinds of snakes lived in the garden because a creek flowed nearby; they were half a meter long, as thick as two fingers, and had bright electric colors in shades of green and blue. Even though snakes scared the living lights out of Selene, there was a day when – as she sat on a tree stump – one of them slithered across her foot, and she just stared at it, dazzled by the critter as if bewitched.

Some guy named Aguilar had built that house for his mother, a woman who had been, as people had it, the last true sorceress in Redención. The gossip in town was that she could turn into an animal – a bird, or even a hog.

It was a square building, the house, with four doors looking to the four horizons. Thing is, that Aguilar fellow – the woman's youngest child, who was an accomplished outlaw – had designed the place that way so he could fly the coop at a moment's notice, as he had in fact done the night he went and killed a man.

Horacio – who was still looking after Selene's knee – found her swinging on the hammock as he came in one day bringing clay and herbs for the poultices; Felipe was making lunch and Ariel was away at school: everything there gave the feeling of a contented family. The three doors in the living room were wide open and sweet breeze streams bathed the house through and through.

"Brother listen, when you're done with that, there's something I've got to show you," the healer told Felipe, who right away added water to the rice, covered the pot and went to sit on one of the dining room chairs, inviting the healer to sit next to him. Horacio pulled a long rolled paper out of his backpack and spread it over the table. Selene, still on the hammock, craned her neck to check the outlines of something that looked like a blueprint.

"Felipe, look it here, I've been working on these things, you see, 'cause I have a real clear memory of something done gone down a few years ago; check it out my brother," said Horacio, serious, and the man went on to tell the story while his index finger followed the lines on the scroll: "You do know, of course, that your landlord's brother, that guy is nothing but trouble – he even made a move to steal this property from his own family – and the man's still in prison, paying for things that happened when he was living in this here house, right?"

Felipe and Selene nodded in agreement: they knew all about that.

"Well then, the way things came to pass, let me tell you," Horacio kept going: "Aguilar got 'imself mixed up in some kind of quarrel, a dispute with some guy in the shop that's located right here, look" as he pointed at a spot marked with a red cross right beside the Centro Comunal. "You see now, that's just a few steps from the place where you had your altercation with Ángel...Then your landlord's brother came to this house": Horacio's finger traveled from the red cross all the way to another cross which marked the location of their home. "He picked up his weapon, went back to the shop and let that fellow have it ..."

Felipe shared knowing looks with Horacio, and right away Selene got the message too, it was as clear as daylight: the cursed confrontation between Ángel and Felipe had been an exact replica. Nothing seemed to make any sense at first sight, but one could hardly overlook the similarity between the two events.

"Protect yourself, *hermano*, protect your family

now that y'all are back in town. Gotta hang a cross on each door – four crosses, I'll put them together for you. And don't you forget now, there's still a need for a fifth sacrifice. That one calls for blood to fall on this ground we all walk over.

It is Much Easier to Tie a Knot Than it is to Untie it

Hati's whispering voice brought Selene back to the here now:

"Cirilo Flinn was thick-skinned, tough as shoe leather. There was the time his horse kicked him right in the mouth so hard it left his lower lip hanging lose – real bad. Well then, man pulls his machete out 'n he done cut it off all the way – jus' like that, *numa*, jus' like that! There's no end to the tales you'll hear 'bout old Flinn, Felipe's grandfather, you know. People say *toughness* was what he left as his inheritance to his eldest daughter, Doña Chola, and that would be your husband's momma now. That man Flinn, he had the devil's temper – so mean, his woman died howling in pain after he done hit her back with the flat side of his machete, the planass, till her skin came loose, flayed all over. Then – Lawd bless 'er soul – as the woman was bed-ridden, on 'er way outa this world, to all concerned she done become a phantom, or even something less 'n that: nobody would pay her no mind. Her grandkids 'n their pals, they just went on their ways without a single word for her, coming in 'n outa her house like she wasn't there no mo'. I got to see it with me own eyes the one day I went to visit her – *numa*, I did. The poor woman had crawled all the way to the window, and there she was shouting at some boyfriend one of her granddaughters had those days: 'I ain't dead yet, no way!' she screamed. "When you come into my house you ask, 'may I come in', 'n then you greet me proper." But the bastard just went past her like there was nobody there talking to him – poor Mada! – Worst of all, by that time Cirilo, well, there was nobody could tell nothing 'bout his whereabouts."

"Jesus Christ!" Selene cried out. "How is it then Felipe tells me all the time that Cirilo idolized his wife Amada?"

"Ay *Numa*, you know what? let me tell you: There's a right-side-up and an upside-down to everything ... God forbid, *mujer*, but there will come a time when you'll get to see how it is that men behave 'round here: they beat their women just to make sure it's known 'you're mine,' and after the beating there's always the lovey-dovey make-up scene; so, we end up falling for their games, well, that is, till one day you've just gotta turn 'round and say 'no mo'... But lemme tell you, *Selenita*, it's much easier to tie a knot than it is to untie it."

Felipe talked a lot about his grandparents, always putting them in the best of lights. According to him, Amada had led the life of a queen, ever so happy and contented as she took care of all the children her husband sowed wherever he went, just because she never doubted how much Cirilo worshipped her... That story never failed to disturb Selene.

The two women were startled by the white burst of a heron that was busy fishing not too far away. They kept going down the channel that flowed into the central part of the plot: the house stood on the left, with its thatched roof and its two solar panels looking up into the sky. Selene had painted the whole front red and made the window frames stand back in olive green. She had solar energy installed on it, as well. "Weird, how there's always lights on and off in there, but not a pole or a cable to be seen anywhere?" the neighbors wondered, declaring it a matter of witchcraft. In the distance over to the right, you could see the abandoned batch of huts and huge palapas that had been once the *Casa del Casabe*, with their palm roofs all worn-out like old raven wings. Giant dry leaves hung from coconut palms while others bobbed on the water like forsaken canoes. Amidst it all, heavy with young sprouts and oblivious to the flood, along with mango and orange trees the punctual palms were busy realizing their springtime designs. "Will I get to eat those mangos, to drink the milk from those coconuts, to squeeze those oranges right into my mouth?" Selene wondered, as she was living by the day – her future being increasingly uncertain.

"Look, Selene, just you look at those roofs that everybody said were gonna fall apart; look how the mean wind didn't bring them down, as much as it tried; they still there even if the manaca palm already rotted away all over them," said Hati pointing at the ruins of the Casa del Casabe, and using her hand to protect her eyes, squinting now under the glare of sunbeams that were starting to break through the still hovering storm clouds. And she concluded: "He really something, your man Felipe: that was his job: a mighty good worker you got there."

Selene felt her chest tightening. "My man Felipe?" she had to ask herself.

The elders in town that had known Cirilo couldn't be but amazed at how Felipe the grandson was a total dead ringer for his grandpa. Felipe could chop down mahogany and San Juan trees all by himself. He didn't fall prey to the allure of the spirits of the forest, something that made victims of so many men that went in search of rattan. His works were things worthy of Titans – but once those passionate artist's hands of his had finished magnificent thatched palapas and the planning stage started, Felipe would come undone. As if the last breath of his power had been exhausted, he'd end up throwing himself on the hammock and sleeping for days on end – the back of his right hand over his forehead, left hand clasping his erection, as though nothing at all was happening around him. Or else he'd disappear for a couple of days of wild sprees in town. However that might be, every time he came back around it was always looking into some new challenge, a new design.

All in all, however, there was another being that lived within Felipe: a reckless and menacing person – the one that ruled that day when the man brought the tip of his machete to rest between his woman's panic-stricken eyes. That came to happen just because Ángel had gone to the house looking for him and he wasn't there that day; so right away Felipe got this crazy notion that his pal had come to their house just to meet his wife… One single drop of blood slid down Selene's face, drawing a North-South longitude line on it. The telling scar remained there forever: a dwarf star floating on her brow like a third eye. On that occasion it was perhaps his grandfather that got such mean things into his head, as was his wont when he showed up in his grandson's dreams – just as he had done the day when Felipe woke up demanding that Selene start formally learning the Garifuna language only because Cirilo had said so: "That woman of yours, she better learn to speak in our own mother tongue," he had told his grandson in a dream.

Come to think of it, Felipe's fragility showed through only when, in making love, the man would cling to Selene's breasts as if holding on to a piece of driftwood that would save him from the wreckage at sea.

Hati pulled Selene out from the maze of thoughts where she had lost herself once again, when – sitting on the boat behind Sombra, a figurehead on the bow – the two women were coming near the road: "May the Lawd bless you, *numa*, and girl, if you feel like you're up to it, do come over to my place tomorrow so you can help me peel the yuccas, there; and we'll keep the chitchat going as we work, you hear aright?"

"Yes Hati, I'll be there tomorrow, God willing, that is," Selene answered, spouting the formula she'd learned from Felipe: a phrase that was supposed to keep one's chances open just by leaving things in the good Lord's hands.

They crossed the bridge and reached the main gate. The path leading to the hamlet had turned into a muddy brook already. As she was grasping her knee, Hati had some trouble getting off the boat. She waved, unmoored her own canoe and took off pulling on it, with the water reaching up to her thighs.

It was getting hard to row without scraping the

ground under the boat, so Selene left Sombra on board, jumped into the water and, just as Hati had done, returned home pulling on the thing behind her. Somehow as if her eyes had taken flight, from the heights she saw two women dragging two small vessels through The Bush now flooded, deserted.

Contraband

Arriving home, Selene moored the boat, opened the lock and walked into the musty smelling living room. She flipped the light switch on, but the bulbs barely shone because, after several sunless days, the solar plant charge was all but depleted. Where there had been only a pool of water, under the heaps of furniture and the bundles that hung from the ceiling beams there was now a wall-to-wall carpet of mud. First thing in the morning next day, she'd start by scrubbing the floor clean. Once done with that, it would be off to the hamlet to get Ariel back home – she missed him so. On their way back, they'd stop to visit Hati and help her peel the yuccas, as promised. Having learned from necessity that it's always good to have a plan ready to go, she had one set in her mind. Even if it just meant facing one more day, taking the next step forward. What mattered most was not to lose one's footing – just as the tightrope walker won't take a pause midway over the void, or the cyclist won't stop pedalling as he rides his bicycle. Selene felt the ground move under her feet; it was as though the boat were still rocking, but this time in her insides. She plopped on the hammock and right away the ropes started moaning. Then, as she drew the swaying on the mud with one big toe – the pendulum bob of a grandfather clock that had survived a shipwreck – it dawned on Selene that her face was boiling hot, and she closed her eyes. Felipe's absence quivered behind the veil of her exhaustion like the dwindling flame of a candle; and surrounding that light, the shadows of Cirilo and Amada were acting out their drama, resembling the marionettes in a Balinese theatre stage (or was it not Felipe and Selene? Felipe's parents perhaps?). They swirled nonstop around the candle as though riding a carousel; rushing about, flapping their arms in the air; fleeing from and chasing each other; now hugging, now rejecting their embraces. An echo of Hati's whispers flurried inside Selene's brain, inebriated now from too much oxygen, the raging fever: "There's a right-side-up and an upside-down to everything …"

She left the hammock alone with the nagging of its ropes and headed for the bedroom, taking off her parka on the way. Once in, she climbed on the platform they'd jerry-built with buckets and planks, sat on the bed and cleaned her feet with a wet towel that had been left nearby. She pitied those feet that seemed not to belong to her and that didn't even look like they matched as the ends of the same pair of legs. The right one was a lump colored in a furious crimson red; oozing some sort of dense substance, which was turning into a yellowish scab, an old cut straddled the instep; it had purple-pink edges, like parted lips. The left was bony and covered with veins and tendons that resembled roots: a miniature mangrove. Selene didn't even bother to get the mud off her toenails – ten black crescent moons. "If the jungle swallows me, so be it," that was her thought as she heard the faint rustling of termites gnawing on a roof beam.

Before falling asleep slumped across the bed, she took a shot at counting all the times they'd gone from The Bush to the house downtown and back again.

The reason for their latest move to the farm was that, after Horacio's revelation, the house in the hamlet got to be too scary for them; and also because Ángel decided to return to Redención: he'd come to do construction work on a hotel that was being built on the road midway between the village and The Bush. And so it was that, the same way they'd arrived in town, the family migrated back to the farm with all their belongings. Coati was the only one missing, because he'd disappeared one night without rhyme or reason. A disconsolate Selene cried rivers, imagining what his final fate could have been: it wouldn't be too far fetched to imagine him being stolen and made into a stew. "Damn, I knew it from the start that once in the hamlet the little guy didn't stand a chance," she told herself and cursed them all, "Cannibals!" Coati was by nature rather restless, and yet – always the loyal companion – he would keep steady and still next to her with his long, pointy muzzle and his fluffy tail, not budging for a second whenever the fevers hit or the blues took over her soul. For all she knew, one suspect among many in the crime had to be her own husband, who'd just stare at her wide-eyed and tight-lipped every time she broke down crying. ... Drop by drop all the memories, vivid at first, started going dim under a cloud of fog; they came in slower and far between, until she finally fell sleep.

The crowing of a cock woke her and she remembered Wetback, her own little rooster, the one that always sung out just after midnight, as though he sensed the coming of the new day way before all the other roosters in the neighborhood. Selene heard the plaintive cry of the present cock protesting in the yard: *Ay Felipe, where's Felipe hanging if not at home where he belongs?* And at that, old sadness drove her grey hand into her chest. She kept herself still, rolled up in the sheet for a good while, thinking about Wetback, who spent his days looking after his young siblings: two little chicks that were left orphaned not long after hatching, when the opossum had their mother for lunch. "Faggot rooster, mon, playing fucking nanny is all he can do, no way," Felipe would bark when the devil ruled his day and everything rubbed him the wrong way.

When the luminous hands of the clock on the night table pointed to four in the morning, Selene got up and shuffled into the living room. She groped around looking for a match to light a candle, because by then the solar plant had called it quits altogether. After setting a pot of water over the fire on the stove, she went looking for her abandoned notebook; thing is, there was a sentence in her head that refused to stop nagging her, it needed fixing. She pulled the journal out of her suitcase and opened it only to come across a bunch of unfinished sentences, senseless paragraphs: "Last night she came to lie next to me over my whi it with its new pillows b tween my lean sh ts a pen wound I going way too bring order into the chaos whi her leave fall in ..."

"Well, I'll be damned," thought Selene, "feeding on the rafters in my house hasn't been enough for these motherfucking termites; now they've started gnawing on my words, as well."

Just as she was badmouthing the termites, from somewhere near the house there came the tingling sound of a chain. If not for Sombra raising her head and pricking her ears while resting rolled into a doughnut on a table, Selene would have thought she was imagining things; but, first from afar and coming closer by the second, she did hear the grinding of a cart. Sombra started barking as soon as it was clear that the thing was approaching their home. Selene stretched out her arm to cast some candle light beyond the kitchen door: standing in a corner there, a machete was on guard as usual, just in case. Felipe had left the house on foot, so, who could it be? She crossed over to the window by the kitchen sink and opened the blind. Phantom-like, the silhouette of a horse cart slid over the bridge. With the first flash of light, she barely caught sight of el Rey's broad white chest. Felipe rode the cart standing up, the reins tense between him and the stallion. He'd let his hair down – dreadlocks falling free over his shoulders under the wide-brimmed hat he wore when working. As he got close enough to the house, her man let out their coded whistle signal: a long one first, followed by a short and vivid second and, as a full stop, a sharp and brief last one. Selene opened the door making sure she wasn't seen and then, along with her own heart that wanted nothing more than to rush over and hug him, Sombra dashed off to welcome her master. Felipe jumped off the horse cart and pulled a sack from it with obvious effort; the bundle fell to the ground with a racket of metal clanging against metal. He then grabbed a black canvas satchel and brought it into the house.

Being unable to escape the moment when they'd come face to face, Selene was on tenterhooks. Once she could at last breathe fully, Felipe crossed the threshold of their home. His eyes – darker now than usual and entrenched under the brim of his hat – scanned her face like laser beams. Whatever it was that he saw there, the man stopped in his tracks, threw his weight against the doorframe and sucked on his teeth. Selene braced herself with one hand on the edge of the sink. Making contact with the cold tiles was enough to confirm that this wasn't a dream – another one of those twilight dreams – and she remembered to breathe again.

"Hear me out, look it here…" Those were the words Felipe used whenever he wanted to tell Selene something of consequence. She had in turn become somehow immune to life's blows while living with him – just because people end up growing used to all kinds of things: living without running water, living without peace, living in fear…"You already know that there are times when the bad weather gives us a break, opens a door: stuff ends up on the sandbar," he went ahead with his report. "Things like the iron pieces in that bag out there, or the couple kilos of *white lady* I got here in this satchel…Me, I just couldn't let this one go, no way…All we need to do is keep the stuff here for a little while." Then, as if trying to convince himself, he added: "That's all we gotta do…" and disappeared in the bedroom with the black satchel still in his hand.

Selene stayed where she was, still bracing herself against the sink, with her fingertips going over the tiles covered in replicated designs, Moorish figures in relief like the maze within the brain. Felipe went back out into the yard, squatted by the sack, threw it over his shoulder with a strained swing, got back on his feet and brought it into the house going right past Selene, who stared at him agape, knowing now that he had gone on another night foray into the beach searching for remnants of drug cargos left adrift along the shore, and this time around the cursed white lady had finally made its way into their own home.

When Felipe placed the big bundle on the floor there was again the sound of metal crashing. He proceeded to settle down on the blue wooden stool with that cumbersome bag before him. And then, like a kid unwrapping Christmas presents, new toys, he started going over the contents of that sack. It was nothing but a bunch of rusty metal.

"Uh look, we got us a bazooka here!" the man commented to himself, captivated by the sight as he pulled the thing out of the bag. With the care and attentiveness of a child, he pressed the shoulder stock against his right armpit and held the weapon in both his arms, which looked to be as long as the cannon itself. The ammunition rounds came next – two of them, like iron fists. Felipe went about checking and handling the fruits of his plunder with knowing ease. "I'll take care of these in a jiffy, all we need is some backing soda …" He had learned a bunch of things while doing his military service: the handling of automatic weapons, memorizing numeral-and-letter cryptographs, as they call them; even various ways to immobilize a person with the least effort.

"And check out these goat horns, oh wow!" Looking dazzled, he pulled out two submachine guns, one after the other – the kind with curved magazines. A pistol came out next, also covered in rust; Selene recognized its shape: a nine-millimeter like the one Felipe used to have – there was no way she could forget that gun. Felipe pulled on the clip a few times with delicate touches till he managed to make it come loose; then, after loading it in again, he gripped the gun firmly with both hands and checked the sight while stretching both arms out and aiming at the open door. That one weapon he didn't return to the sack as he had done with the other pieces; it went instead into the waistband of his pants.

Selene's forefinger kept going over the designs on the tiles as if drawing traces on paper. She was seeing everything sharp and clear; her mind was working fast: anticipating Felipe's every move, she knew beforehand when he'd unload and load the clip back in; the exact gesture he'd make when checking the gun sight; even when he put the gun under his belt as though it had always been his own. She knew what was to come before it happened, and drew a plan with equal sharpness in her mind: her excuse would be that she was going to pick Ariel up in the hamlet and go with him to el Puerto to stock up on provisions and supplies; that would explain her getting properly fixed up and holding a purse with her passport well encased in it. She'd be bringing clothes for Ariel, on the pretext that they were going to the big town. A surge of power flooded the woman, knowing now that she really could leave it all behind, not looking back and never again seeing Felipe. She'd be gone without further ado; yes, she'd walk away, following in the steps of so many in that land who are forced to live in exile. She'd buy her ticket in Puerto, along with anything that the trip called for. Ariel and her would climb on a bus, so she could take him back to his aunt's place, just as he had wanted to, and after that she'd go straight to the airport.

Just then Felipe's gaze met Selene's once again.

"What is it, woman, for fuck's sake you look like you've just seen a demon," he grumbled.

"Well, tell the truth, *I am* seeing one," Selene shot back.

"Don't give me that bullshit," he went on the defence with an aggrieved tone. "Stop playing goody-goody, you weren't born yesterday, come on."

Trying to foresee the next move of that animal he'd turned himself into, Selene fixed her eyes on the man's face as he stared at her from the shadows across the living room.

"Bah, fact is women like you, they come looking for adventures in the Caribbean and always end up spooked out of their minds," he barked now. "Don't tell me you didn't come out here just to get yourself some good old black cock. And don't you say you'd never heard about how things go down over here. I can always tell: I've come across many just like you – well born and bred little dames – and let me tell you: those are the worst, that's for sure. Let's face it: you used me to make your fantasies real, so don't come around playing Mother Teresa now ... So then, it's like I'd believe you if you said you never jumped in bed with that friend a yours, the one with the hotel? Come on!"

Selene stared at him flabbergasted, totally taken aback, unable to muster the will to defend herself in the face of such sudden barrage. And he went on, not done yet: "How could you not jump her bones after all, when that woman's got an ass to die for!"

For a moment there, Selene was about to burst laughing, but he kept throwing shrapnel at her: "Then to top it off, you're an expert through and through when it comes to getting a man's head full of ideas."

"Say, what?" Selene growled, transfixed. "Man, you've got some nerve telling me you feel used, how could you Felipe, for God's sake! ... Do you really think that this has been all about fucking and nothing else?"

She'd never said that word aloud, fucking, and it shook her to hear it come out of her own mouth, but she kept going: "Do you really think that it was for need of cock that I've spent five years breaking my back working here? No, I'm not that screwed-up, believe you me *papito*, and sorry if I hurt your feelings..." Even if she wasn't used to spewing out curse words, Selene started letting them fly like hand grenades, aiming to bruise, to smash, to bring the house down once and for all. "A woman doesn't need to work that hard if what she's after is simply a good fuck, because men are nothing but dogs looking around for a hole to use, and you all believe that us women are into the same crappy games you play." And she went on, riding a wave of rage: "Now tell me, what the hell are you talking about when you say I got your mind full of ideas?"

Then Felipe, who had never before seen Selene that furious, made his tone less aggressive: "Well, that day we were working on the road, didn't you tell me that without arming themselves the Defensa de Tierras people didn't stand a chance, or something like that, anyway? ... These weapons are for them, Selene, for the Grupo de Defensa. You get it now?"

Selene opened her mouth but not a single sound came out of it. Yes, she had spoken words of that sort – true, that – but only out of anger, despair, and only in

202

a figurative sense, on that occasion when they found the road blocked by rocks for one time too many; and yes, she had said that indeed, couldn't deny it. But, go figure, for Felipe words were seeds that remained ingrained in the pit of his brain and grew from there till the ultimate consequences became realities.

"But look it here, Selene, can it be that you still can't get it into your head how it is that anything you 'n me talk about ends up becoming a done deed? Me, I'm all about doing things, but you, you think too much; that's got nothin' to do with actual living, woman. OK now, wasn't it you who wanted to live in the countryside and raise animals? Everything you wanted, all of it, you've got it right here – ah but no, there's no way you'll appreciate the things I do, and why? Because you was born in a golden cradle, that it. What the fuck am I worth as a man if I can't give you anything? And only 'cause you always can do all, know it all. Hear me out now: there's no use to a woman that seems to never need a man. You think that there's nothing you can't fix, so let me tell you, what you're missing is humility."

His words smacked Selene right on the forehead like a lead pipe. "He's right," she thought, "I haven't been humble enough." Her wanting to do everything for that man, her need to impress him at all times, to give him anything and everything, all of that had made him feel small, and feeling so small, he was driven to constantly test and push boundaries. "Poor Felipe: I have never felt such need to do good, only to end up doing harm," she told herself. And it was all because of the shit-head arrogance that made her believe she could have her way in that realm where only the strong have the last word. Just think of how not even the seeds she planted got to sprout in a land that wasn't truly hers. She took a pause, though, realizing where that train of thought was leading her. Once again it had to be "poor Felipe." Once again she'd fallen under the temptation of making up excuses for him, understanding him, explaining his motives – and blaming herself. Always standing up for her Felipe, she'd been the one to get the man out of whatever troubles he got into; she'd hidden him, justified and defended him against all and everyone – at times even sparing him the ire of Doña Chola, his mother. She declared herself the sworn enemy of those who attacked him, even after he had come to terms with them.

Sticking up for her husband was something she never recoiled from. Like that time they were bathing in the river and a group of soldiers came looking for him because of some shady business he'd gotten himself into. Selene was swimming in the middle of the river and saw the uniformed men approaching them. Sitting distracted on the riverbank, Felipe had not seen the troop coming, so she started flapping her arms and yelling: "Out here, help, drowning, help, I'm drowning!" And him, knowing his woman was a good swimmer, figured out something no good was about to happen; he looked around and saw the soldiers coming fast toward him and right away cried out: "You'll have to excuse me, gentlemen, but I gotta go look after me lady before she goes 'n dies on me." With that he plunged into the current and swam away from his would-be captors. The couple went across to the other bank and hung out there for awhile laughing their heads off as the camouflage-clad soldiers went off shuffling those steel-toed boots of theirs on the dust, with rifles weighing them down under the midday sun.

But the haggard man with a hardened face that stood before her right now – even his lips, the color of muscatel grapes, looked thin and cruel – that man looked like a stranger to her.

"Have you ever killed a human being?" that was a question Selene would have wanted to ask of him, but she dreaded what his answer might be, and so she said instead: "I thought the life we had dreamed of together, this life you're wiping out right now … Felipe, I thought we were in this together, a real team, but that's evidently impossible in this place where men downright believe women are objects they own. You've never felt like listening to me, not ever: all the times I've tried to tell you how I feel, what I need." As she spoke, Selene kept beating her chest with one hand. "I've gotten used, adapted to this kind of living, or at least I've tried; but it's clear that you can't ever see what it is that I truly need: just like anybody else, I need to have peace, to feel safe in my own home. Even animals, no matter how strong, they all need that: a sanctuary. Do you remember that, a sanctuary? … But here every man – the gardener, the milkman, any man – as long as it's a man, that person stands above me, rules over me: my voice means nothing in this house …"

That's when Felipe plunged the dagger to the hilt: "You, you stand right here, underneath our balls, that's where you stand …"

Selene felt as if a scrotum, a giant bull sack had just grazed her face with its flabby skin covered in coarse hairs; but, holding back a retching wave, she kept going: "You never asked me if what I really wanted, what I felt was right *for me* was to go and risk my life, put my skin on the line or end up in jail with you. I'll tell you what: it's not up to you to decide how I live my life, Felipe, don't fuck with me!"

There was no stopping the bonfire in her gut: her mouth was brimming with a rush of words that came out exploding like bursts of fire. "And I've had more than enough of your blaming me for where and how I was born; that's something I didn't choose. I broke away from my social class, turned my back on my people. I've always been on the side of the poor; I've lived here with you, all of me – body and soul – without ever questioning why, pulling water buckets from the well like all the rest; and mind you now, no hardness, no harsh turn has ever brought me down. But there's nothing I can do if you and everyone in this damn town go on believing that I come from privilege, that because of that I never need anything, that around here my only job is to serve you all, that Selene's here just to give, give, give …" Her voice started coming out as though splintered, in pieces, bleeding, in torn-up syllables interlaced with tears: "I'm all dried up inside. You guys think that suffering is something only you have had to live with. But please listen to me just for once: we all have loads to carry, sorrows and pain to deal with. It's true I've never gone really hungry, and neither did I have to sell oranges on trains just to pay for my schoolbooks, but …"

Felipe broke in with a roar: "*Aghhh!* There you go: that's the reason why a man shouldn't go 'round telling others 'bout his private stuff, 'cause there always comes a time when they turn 'n throw it in yo face…"

Even as Selene was put off by the way Felipe used the third person plural there, implying he'd had many women, she retorted right away, mortified: "There's no shame in that whatsoever. I apologize, Felipe, didn't mean to offend, it's no offense, really: I deeply value …"

But Felipe didn't let her finish: "You treat me like a little kid, Selene, like I'm useless! It's like just because you got an education you think you can look down on us, put people like me down," he poured out a straggling resentment of his. "All the time you say everyone's free to choose their own fate; but let me tell you now, that kind of freedom is only for people like you; in this world some are free, others not so much."

"No, you listen to me!" Selene hollered, instantly feeling shocked at how exasperated her voice sounded. "The house where I was born, it was chock-full of secrets that impregnated everything like some toxic gas. I had to sacrifice my own blood there just to keep up with appearances, to follow form with due respect. That's another kind of wound, and it leaves scars that remain open forever. I'm fed up with having to apologize, asking for forgiveness, I'm not about to live the rest of my life on my knees."

When she paused at last, just to take a proper breath of air, in that moment of silence a steep cliff got opened that echoed back all the words she'd said and, appalled, she fell silent. She had never dared to speak to Felipe like that, but what was said was said and there was no way to swallow it back in. Tears started pouring from her eyes like waterfalls.

Felipe, who'd been staring at her during the whole outburst with a sceptical air, lowered his head; but then, he got up and rushed stumbling toward her with his eyes shooting flashes. "Selene, Selenita, look, I mean, is there anyone can understand you?" he pleaded now, stretching out his hands in an attempt to touch her; but she stepped back, recoiling from his approach.

"Felipe, do you really *not* know what the difference is between a thought and an action?" she yelped, at her wit's end. "If I tell you that it wouldn't hurt to kill those bastard coup plotters that forced their way into the presidential house, that's no reason for you to go next day straight to the Capital and hang them from a lamp post. ... Damn, Felipe, you're really a nutcase!" At that, he almost broke into laughter, and Selene would have laughed, as well, if she hadn't been feeling so distraught right there and then.

"Look, Selene, just listen to me a minute here: you know the way the river flows," he picked up his own thread, now on his knees, would you believe? "There's a lot of contraband passes through here, that's fact: so there's times when them dealers gotta get rid of their loads on account of their gangs fleeing from the man chasing them, or when bad weather brings their boats down too; so what happens is, the loot ends up in the sandbar – just like that, an easy pick. Now tell me, do you think those four by fours that go by kicking up dust storms, do you think those are just cool tourist cars moving tourists around? So then, why shouldn't we take advantage, ain't harm in grabbing a little profit here 'n there for the children of our hamlet, uh? We be the smallest fish in that big sea out there, I'm telling you ..."

Selene had felt rather apprehensive for a while already that Felipe's restless rambles from The Bush down to the beach, and back again to The Bush – that those weren't just games, entertainment. She took exception: "Yeah, I know, but then the ones that end up crucified, those are the hamlet's children too, the ones that do the dirty work for all the big kahunas so they can swing by untouched to pick up the goods in their huge pickups, with their gold teeth and their chests full of bling, with their diamond encrusted rings and watches. Yes, I know."

"Selenita, let's not fool ourselves: them dudes with gold teeth, they're also small-fish crowd, even if they be just a bit bigger than us. They the ones on the frontlines, in the line of fire. The true capos, those are eating lobster in their castles – the lobsters we fish out, and the conchs that's the cause of divers' bodies ending up a useless waste from decompression sickness … stuff like that, Selene, it makes one angry, pissed to the bone, God dammit!" With those last words his voice broke and he looked away, to hide the saltwater that was churning in his eyes.

Well, there it was again: Felipe once again knotting up her mind, getting the upper hand on her, distorting her coordinates of good and evil, threatening her grip on reality. It felt as though she'd fallen into a parallel universe. "Could this be what going crazy is all about?" she thought, "when everything the mind imagines turns into action, when the meagre line that separates us from madness fades away and there's no limit to what one can do?" By that time Selene was all but certain that she and Felipe were going insane. During the five years of their life together, a man had almost died, a dear woman had a violent death, and now this: they had gotten to the far out point of keeping coke under the bed and a sack full of automatic weapons, even a bazooka, in the living room. Nothing could be further from their bright, life-nurturing projects.

"I've got to get out, I need to think, need some fresh air. Besides, there's nothing left to eat here. I'm gonna go look for Ariel over in your folks' place; then we can go shopping for supplies and groceries, him and me. I'll go get ready."

Felipe gave her an edgy look and went to sit on the hammock. He put himself at ease there, yet with his eyes fixed on the sack of weapons. Selene went to splash water on her face in the bathroom. Sombra – who had nervously witnessed the whole scene with her tail between her legs – followed her pal and, as she washed, sat looking up while rocking her head from side to side as if asking, what is happening? She moved on to the bedroom and put on the dress that had buttons down the front, the one she always chose when unsure of what to wear. Once in Puerto, she could buy an outfit for the trip, and a change of clothes for Ariel. Her passport, she put that in the handbag with an automaton's gesture – even if by now it wasn't certain what her next move would be. The coin purse, a small case with basic necessities, comb, sunscreen, tooth brush – those were always ready in that handbag. Out of the drawer she pulled two headkerchiefs that had never been used, dropped one and kept the other, bigger one, stamped in shades of copper. She gathered her hair and rolled that scarf around her head. The smaller one, with bright blues and pinks, ended up in the handbag. She then checked herself in the mirror; her face looked stern, felt alien to her. Her eyes moved towards the bed and, while imagining what was hidden underneath, the black satchel, she got goosebumps and the acrid taste of coke blanketed her throat.

"Later," she told Felipe with a barely audible voice.

"*Aha*, Selene," he answered, absent, his eyes fixed on the floor, lost in his own thoughts.

A Little Death

When Selene made her way across the bridge, limping, she remembered the sentence Horacio had once shot her way: "Mark my words, woman – you'll leave this place one day with nothing but the clothes on your back."

Sombra had not followed her this time around; the little dog just lay down on the concrete slab by the well and, with ears drooping, watched her friend walking away. As she moved on along the trail, Selene heard the soft crackling of silk folds in the scarf that she'd wrapped around her head, and recalled how Hati had once given her a stern warning because she wasn't in the habit of covering her head:

"You gotta wear a headkerchief when stepping out, *mujer*, protect yo self. You see, 'round here there is an evil wind, *numa*, it blows right into women's ears, it does; and if they're not protected in their heads, evil wind does drive them women mad – all the more so when they've just given birth or gotten sick, true that. Then, when the woman's done lost her wits – the Lord look after us – no one around is safe no mo': not the men, not the children, or the animals and crops, or the women themselves, oh no; them winds, they just as mean as hurricanes. You pay attention now: it's only *la Llorona* that can wonder 'round with her hair loose on her shoulders on stormy nights."

Hati, *Laruni Hati*, Light of the moon – she

remembered that the day before the old wise woman had asked her to go visit. Then, as Selene couldn't possibly tell her anything about the things she'd just gone through, she would just go in and sit quietly in the cane-rod and palm-leaf kitchen, helping Hati peel the yuccas. She would find peace in the simple act of repeatedly digging the tip of the knife into the thick rind of the roots and drawing a line across to reveal the moist white flesh inside. But she didn't dare do it, felt too weak. Besides, just as usual, Hati would see through her and realize that something wasn't right. It would be best for her, perhaps, to take the other path, by way of the beach, where her presence wouldn't be noticed by anyone. Selene looked back over her shoulder: no one was following her. She took off her sandals and put them inside her bag; as she did that, her swollen foot felt better for a moment. She walked all the way to the sandbar dragging her right leg, which felt like nothing but a sore lump.

"*Ah-diósn!*" called out Jeremiah the Indian from his watchman's arbor by the gates of the abandoned luxury-house compound.

"*Adiós,*" Selene responded – such brief greetings being the routine obligation when meeting others in one's path.

She went around the river, passed through the vegetal junkyard that had once been a pristine beach: water-hewn tree trunks and logs stood all along the shoreline like prehistoric skeletons, and everywhere a mix of algae and rubbish pinned down vestiges of red foam that looked like coagulated blood. Now at rest, and oblivious to its whimsical-child's disarray, the sea mirrored a clear, crisp sky. As the sun climbed towards its zenith in a rush, its scalding-white light turned the shadow-less landscape into a desolate scene devoid of shelter.

"Who the hell said that the Caribbean is a paradise? Curse me if I ever come back to such a scene again. Come on, virgin beaches in postcards? In relaxing videos on transatlantic flights? – Never again, no frigging way," Selene told herself, and she fancied that beach as the stage for all tragedies: Medea – *Speak to me, sun; earth, talk to me!* – Tosca's betrayal, la Llorona endlessly searching for her dead children.

There was an almond tree not too far away; she walked towards it, leaned on its trunk and let herself slide down till she could sit on the sand. Her right foot had become a dark-red lump. On the wound, which had gone from purple to black, the pus was starting to take on a greenish tone. A searing pain climbed up her leg and ended up blended with the knife stab in her knee; and those two pains competed in unison with the most piercing of all pains, the one in her heart. Selene broke down crying; gushing torrents of merciful salty clear water instantly drenched her face and chest. All she could hope for was to die away becoming one with the tree, with the sand.

She thought of the gliders that – abandoning themselves to the whims of the wind, with nothing but a pair of cloth wings, and with their bearings lost – mistake the waters for the sky and end up crashing into the sea just as they believe themselves to be soaring towards the clouds above. That image brought echoes from a poem by Rafael Alberti to her memory:

> She was mistaken, the dove. She was so wrong.
> Believed the sea was the sky, the night the dawn
> She was so wrong.

Selene couldn't stop weeping, blissful tears that reanimated her, cooled her spirit. Then she heard unexpected voices approaching: it was two young guys going towards The Bush, each one clutching an empty sack with one hand – must have been on their way to salvage yucca roots from the flood in their plot. She muffled her sobbing and pressed her back against the trunk of the almond tree, pleading for it to swallow her. Unaware of her presence, the men went around the river and kept walking. Then again, perhaps they did see her, but ignored her, since folk in the hamlet were by now used to the drama scenes between her and Felipe. It was even rumored that she had lost her mind; there were few people left that would go near Selene, and even the kids in town were afraid of the white woman, with her character and her looks so clearly off kilter. "For all they care now, I could be lying face down in the middle of the street bleeding to death, and no one would come lend a hand," Selene thought. She'd have to move away from that spot before the sun's heat started building up – walk along the shore letting the seawater wash her wounded foot, and go on to finally reach the house of Felipe's parents. As well, and just for Ariel's sake, she had to regain at least a semblance of tranquility. She hadn't thought about the child for a while, and as she did so, her sorrows and her ailments were instantly put aside.

When she was just about to get back on her feet, Selene froze upon hearing the familiar squeaks of Patatiesa's horse cart approaching. The man was coming from the village, following the path that ran parallel to the beach, and he wasn't riding alone: there was an Indian guy seated next to him. They took a turn toward the beach and passed very close to the almond tree. The Indian man was middle-aged, thickset, had black hair greased back and wore a white *guayabera* shirt, black pants, well polished black leather shoes. Come to think of it, he pretty much looked like a politician on the campaign trail, a figure that seemed way out of place there, with those spotless shoes in a hamlet that was nothing but raw roads and dust.

The two men kept silent as they went by, with their eyes fixed straight ahead and looking as serious as a funeral. In no way did that attitude fit Pata, who was always fooling around and telling off-color jokes, but now looked downright timid, shrunken. They were surely headed for the farmstead and the reason for their visit was more than obvious to Selene. She couldn't help but feel distressed, in fear of what Felipe might be up to. The blood started rushing wild through her veins and her tears went dry along with her mouth. She wanted nothing more than to run back to the house, but there was no energy left in her body, she just couldn't. At that point in time nothing could be done, so Selene remained where she was, on the alert, keeping guard under the almond tree. Then Horacio appeared in her mind; right away she reached into her bag for the cell phone but the thing was not in service. So then, she'd just have to go

217

looking for him as soon as she reached the village.

It wasn't long before she saw the two young fellows coming back with the now loaded sacks on their backs. When they got closer, Selene started making out something like branches for firewood jutting above their shoulders. "That's strange," she thought. "Guys going to gather firewood in The Bush when there's more than enough of it on the beach." Once they went by and she could see them from behind, Selene could have sworn that, amidst the firewood in each sack, there was the muzzle of a submachine gun sticking out. She turned her eyes into slits to better focus and then saw a thicker pipe in there too, was it the bazooka? Then again, she was still feverish, so it could have been just a vision, hallucinations, but when she saw the two of them going for the path along the beach – the one that people took for furtive errands – there was no doubt left in her mind that they were carrying Felipe's weapons.

When those two figures became just two dots in the distance, the creaking of Pata's cart was heard again as it came back from the farm. Selene saw it approaching and then going around the river with the same two men riding on it. As they passed by not too far from her, and before the cart moved away on the path that led to the hamlet, as clear as daylight she saw Felipe's black satchel resting on the Indian's lap and half-hidden by his hands.

As soon as the cart disappeared from her sight, she got on all fours and, holding on to the tree, rose to her feet ever so slowly. Her immediate instinct was to get herself back to the farm, but she stopped on her tracks in the knowledge that the relationship with Felipe was over, rotten at the core – it was in fact nothing short of buried. There was no sadness in her, though, only the endless emptiness of mourning. And to top it all off, her right foot was useless. She tried to stand, but setting the sole of her foot on the hot sand was torture. Placing the strap of the bag across her chest, she went on all fours again, threw the bag over her shoulder and crawled till she found a stick that could be used as a walking cane to help her get back on her feet. And so it was that, with minute starts and leaps, Selene made her way towards the water's edge.

When she at last reached the end ripples of the waves, the sea washed her wounded foot and allayed the swelling. The water was cool liquid rust that bore swaying leaves, algae, boughs and a host of nebulous shapes. Selene's gaze rested on the cosmos at her feet and at that moment the only thing she could wish for was to become one with it, to turn herself into another one of those formless bodies. She pulled the bag up from her back, swung it over her head and – with hand firmly on the walking stick – reached as far as she could to drop it over a tree stump. Her dress, too, ended up on top of the bag like a discarded skin.

It was miracle-like, how remarkably the pain let up when the water touched her knee. Right away Selene uncoiled the scarf from her head and threw it into the sea as a present for its trophy collection. Then she untwined her braid before letting the water take control over her body. Her hair became sea tangle between the fingers of the river that sneaked its way into the sea: dark, sweet and cool water set apart from the warm and salty one beyond, as if an illusive crystal wall stood between the two. She dived in with eyes wide open as though entering the cellar that all of her dead called home. Leaves like ragged hearts floated about taking the place of fish. Coming from the depths, an animal figure bounced her reflection back to the woman, framed in a light halo; and now she sensed a shadow at her back. If she swam toward the left, there it was; and if she swam to the right, the shadow stayed behind her. "My death, that's what it is," she thought without the least dismay. She rose to the surface for air and found nothing out there, apart from the churning river water that dragged the uprooted jungle on its way into the sea. Perched on a log, a coral snake navigated the flow right in front of her; deep black and bright red rings, it didn't take much space, that deadly wanderer. In awe of its beauty and free of fear, Selene watched it ride the log on its way toward the beach.

She dived in again, thinking, "Nothing keeps me from staying down here forever. I could rest and stop breathing for good then." All the air left inside her came out through her mouth in a deep exhalation – and along with it, bubbles, tatters of memories, organic matter turning liquid. She let herself sink effortlessly, her woman-whale body rippling till it crossed the impalpable border between river and sea; all the way into deep waters that looked like translucent sapphire – so embracingly warm that you could hardly feel it as it grazed your skin. The crown of her head struggled to probe the thickness of the salt-loaded water that made her body buoyant as it pressed her upwards. As she dove deeper, Selene started hearing her heartbeat sipping out of her ears – a weary pulse growing slower by the second. Then she felt her lungs burning and for a minute tried to ignore the throbbing stings, that is, until a sudden, violent blow to the core of her body impelled her to the surface with a blast and she hurtled into open air with a howl:

"Maamaaaa-maaaaaá!"

She remained suspended face up on the surface for a good long while: a minuscule particle, a bundle of molecules floating within a blue sphere. Her whole body turned to water welled up and burst through her eyes, flowing back into the sea until she was empty of tears, empty of Felipe, empty of herself even – empty inside the emptiness of her own womb. Having been once tinted red and stabbed by shadows through Selene's eyelids, the sky turned black out there now and a sparkling star shone at its center. At that very moment she remembered Ariel once again. Her muscles became taut and she began to swim, without making much of an effort yet making sure she was heading in the right direction; it was her good fortune that the tidal flow had not pushed her too far away from the shore. Logs, algae and leaves displayed their wrinkles, twists, textures and colors in a leisurely parade all around her. It felt as though she could sense all of her surroundings, what was near and what was afar. The gas exhaled by plankton had permeated her nose and cleared her brain. She felt it was possible for her to sniff out any risk or danger, and the coral serpent came back to her mind.

When she reached the shore, the stump with her things wasn't far away and she went for it; that's when she realized that walking was no longer causing her any pain. She sat down for a while, letting the sunrays dry her body. "It's taken time, but now I understand: it was up to hurricanes to mark my fate," she thought. "This whole thing, maybe it has been a plot to let Ariel come into my life." ... Ariel, Lion of God – that was how he had been mentioned in a Kabbalah workshop she once attended in Antigua, Guatemala. Could it be that Felipe had given his son that name in honor of the Lion of Zion? Had he chosen the name urged by that tremendous intuitive power of his, or was his knowledge deeper than he let on? Selene had never given any thought to that notion. Her man was, of course, a devoted Rastafarian, and he'd been involved in a biblical studies group years before. But well, however that might be, Ariel – Lion of God, patron spirit of oceans and rivers, nature's guardian, light of her life, cherished little one – Ariel was waiting for her in the village. And yes, spurred by outright self-centeredness, Selene and Felipe had abandoned the child. That revelation hit her like a whip of lightning, and a thundering cry arose from way deep in her throat:

"Please Ariel, forgive me!"

She got her comb out of her bag: Ariel liked to see Selene with her mane well arranged. The kid had always shown a deep sensibility for all manners of beauty, and for a woman's allure most of all. Selene remembered how one day she stood by the school's entrance, as usual, waiting for him to come out, and they went off walking hand in hand. On their way they came across an Indian woman with long, flowing black hair, voluptuous bosom and swinging hips. So the barely six-years old *Arielito* had all but shouted, "Now, that's one pretty woman right there!" Then, still holding his stepmother's hand, he kept walking with his head turned back, eyes fixed on the object of his admiration until the woman went around a corner. At home that night, Ariel woke up all flustered, said something was hurting and he needed to go pee. Selene went with him to the bathroom, where Arielito's erect penis sprinkled the wall with a soaring golden stream.

Children are men and men are children in Redención. The living and the dead share their every single day: the deceased talk to the survivors in their dreams, demanding celebrations, sacrifices. "Yes, that's how things are: everything here is a continuum, everything is circular, things have neither a beginning nor an end," Selene told herself, and wondered: "Am I perchance chained to a wheel and can't break free from it – unable to leave Felipe, to ever find my way out of this place?"

For a long time she'd held on to a plane ticket to leave Redención, but when the time came, Selene missed that flight – missed it because on the way to the airport she and Felipe stopped to see Horacio, and the healer insisted that she had to be cleansed and protected with tobacco smoke before leaving – something that got Felipe into a jealous fit. Afterwards on the highway, he started acting like a madman and hurling insults at Selene: "You nothin' but waste, Selene, you a piece a trash ..." to the point that, when the car got stuck in a traffic jam, she managed to get out and break into a run, even if that meant further grinding on her clapped-out knee. She went into an alleyway that led to the highway and let herself collapse on a garbage dump at the end of that passage, hollering:

"If you really mean it when you say that I'm a piece of trash, Felipe, well, here I am where I belong, you happy now?" as the man kept going after her and the people in the neighborhood peeled their eyes when he tried to get his lady back into the car, now pleading: "Please stop it, *mujer*, can you please stop? You gonna get the cops on us any minute now, come on," he went on, till finally Selene got in the car. And, by then it was too late for them to reach the airport in time – not that she felt like leaving anymore, after they'd gone through such insane scene... so, they ended up back in the farmstead, delighted at having escaped the breakup.

When Selene called her mother: "*Mami*, I missed my flight," Mother started yelling, "Voodoo, voodoo!" now fully certain that her daughter had fallen victim to some horrid spell. And then, as if on cue, the horses started neighing, the hens clucking, the roosters crowing and the dogs barking. "For Christsake, what kind of life is this you're leading, Selene! You're grown up woman; I'd have to say it's about time for you to settle down, huh?"

The following day, when her mum called to once again try to convince her that it was best to leave that place without further delay, it was Felipe who picked up the call on the cell phone, and he hung up as soon as the mother in law's voice came through the line.

"Why in hell did you hang up on my mother?" Selene grumbled. "Man, you're crazy."

"Wasn't me that hung up, the line went dead," he answered.

When the phone rang again, she picked it up. And Mother: "I can't believe it: that good-for-nothing hung up on me!"

All of those moments filled Selene's mind as she

was braiding her hair with the almond tree still standing guard not far behind her. When there wasn't a single drop of water left on her skin and her underwear was fully dry, she saw that the sun was almost halfway up the sky; must have been around eleven in the morning. She got up, pushed one arm and then the other into the dress, fastened the buttons on the front, then pulled a small tube of cream from her bag and rubbed the stuff on her face, her hands, and finally checked her hairdo with groping fingers. Once again, with the bag hanging across her shoulder, she took the stick that had served her as a walking cane and, with a barely perceptible limp, started making her way into the hamlet. "I'll get there before noon if I make haste," she told herself, and went on walking at water's edge, where the sand was more compact, avoiding the rubble that stood as the only telling sign left from the storm of one week ago. Her mind held no thoughts as she moved along, seeing how the sea was erasing the footprints left by the young guys with weapon-filled sacks. Their load was heavy, she reckoned, looking at how deep in the sand their footprints had gone. Interesting, that her years of sharing life with Felipe had led her to learn quite a bit about forensic investigation.

Paloma Zozaya Gorostiza

Redención

She could tell her hike was coming to an end when drumbeats flooded her ears; it wasn't the Punta's triple meter, but a syncopated, restless and chaotic rhythm – not the sort of cadence that stirs up one's hips, but a beat that makes you feel like breaking into a run and taking over the streets. So then, recognizing the rhythmic pattern behind the hamlet's rite of the Warrior Dancers, Selene remembered it was December the twelfth – the date when the villagers perform rites showing their devotion to the Black Madonna: Our Lady of Guadalupe, patron mother of La Raza. "I got here around these days, five years ago," she thought, sensing the cyclic passing of time, as if she could actually see it: an immeasurable arc drawn on the sky, a circular path very much like that of the beach, which, as children well know, you can walk upon till reaching the place where the journey began.

Ariel would be turning eight in less than a month. What had been done could not be undone, and predicting the future was a fool's errand. Selene noticed how the footprints left on the sand by the two weapon-loaded young guys were growing faint and, looking back, saw her own footprints. Now a ruckus of shouting kids and a rush of bodies like birds on a stampede tore through the veil of melancholy that had come over her. She had finally reached the hamlet. A frightful figure wielding a bow and arrow – its body turned red with *achiote* paste and wearing nothing but a loincloth and a skull mask – was running after a group of children. The Barbaric Indian, that was; and fleeing from that spooky grotesquery, the kids abandoned the beach and took refuge in the hamlet's alleyways. When, still on the beach, she could make out the tin roof on the house of Felipe's parents, Selene took a turn, leaving the coolness of the shore. She started on her way up, treading on the sand that seared her feet, and doing her best to ignore the right one – all red, smarting and once again swollen. Good that her knee didn't hurt but, still, the inflammation girded it like a wringing hand. She walked around the garbage dump that separated the beach from the yard in Doña Chola and Don Joaquin's place; it was one of those pits that the furious onslaught of the Ramona storm had gouged as it passed by on their way to the sea. Selene remembered the words she'd heard Doña Chola say one day: "Wherever people see a hole, they just gotta hurl their junk in it. Ain't nothin' you can do 'bout things like that." And, as she entered the hamlet, the alien woman thought in turn, "Every void has a magnetic pull, demands to be filled, and it's up to us to be mindful of the things we fill that void with." A group of women went down the street singing; it was a river of headscarves and skirts in pink and blue. All the women had palm leaves in their hands, and at the head of the procession was an image of the Virgin drawn on a banner.

All the while, dancing wild around the village – which has no other laws than those imposed by the dead and where fences are the only things forbidden – there was the Barbaric Indian invading the open yards of every house, diligently carrying out his mission: to spook the children silly, and to stain with his *achiote* varnish anyone who wouldn't give him a coin. The far-reaching cadences of the ritual *yancunu* percussions permeated the air; and Selene, who was always brought alive by the sound of drums – so much that there were times when she'd get out of bed at midnight to go follow the beat – let herself be led by the sound until she reached the corner where the crowd was gathered.

A group of Warrior Dancers – *Wanarawas*, they're called – awaited their turn to join in the dancing circle. Colorful masks made of metal mesh, as well as long-sleeved blouses and skirts flashing animal and floral prints left not a single spot of a dancer's bare skin in view. This because, from as far back as colonial times, the purpose of donning those costumes had been to hide the fact that there was a man running around under such paraphernalia: thing is, in dressing that way, the ancestral children of Yurumein-Saint Vincent were attempting to stave off the threat of castration, or even death, at the hands of the white man.

Large headdresses crafted with tinplate and ribbons crowned the splendid costumes. One by one, young boys and teenagers took turns in the circle, some of them dancing barefoot, others wearing sneakers that made it easier to go into the leaps and skips that the dance calls for. Selene was deeply taken by that fusion between traditional and modern customs; she reckoned it was those blending details that kept folkways alive, making the communal lore current and relevant as it was yanked off museum displays. Some of the women would join the circle now and then, defying the tradition that makes it a males-only dance. Selene recalled how long ago she'd wanted to learn the moves of that dance but Felipe had objected: "That's not something women do," he'd said, and she had given up on the idea.

Now her ever-fleeing attention was captured by a boy that entered the circle wearing a dress printed with blue flowers. Skipping swiftly on bare feet, the kid took centre stage and started jumping in rapid beats, seemingly floating on little clouds of red dust that his dance moves were unleashing. He swung his arms from side to side, counterpointing the rotations of his torso. Under the metallic-mesh mask – its surface painted to highlight cheeks smeared with rouge and eyebrows joined together over enormous eye-sockets – his head kept leaning in the opposite direction to his arms. The boy danced with graceful and well-controlled moves, while his feet stomped the ground furiously as if wanting to awaken the powers that live deep inside the earth. Dazed as she still was by the pain in her foot, Selene didn't recognize at first the telling, square-shaped toes of the child: it was Ariel dancing there.

It was much more difficult to dance to the *yancunu* beats than it was to do the Punta; but Ariel loved to dance with the *Wanarawas* just because the Warrior Dancer's mask and attire rendered him anonymous. When he finished off his dance round with the prescribed swirls in front of the drum line, his friend Pichín jumped in, sporting a dress with green-yellow-red African designs on it. The sneakers he wore made his dancing light and easy: the kid's every leap bounced off the ground with an aerial feel; his energetic dancing was unique: it couldn't be any other but Pichín. Standing along with the onlookers, Omar and Chuy took in the ritual event. Enthused, and as always wide-eyed, Omar followed each and every move, while Chuy appeared distracted yet solemn in his attitude. Having her attention once again fixed on Ariel, Selene saw her boy taking off his mask and his headdress. With the gesture of a knight having just waged battle, he put them both under his arm while walking towards her, straight as an arrow, his head still wrapped in a red bandana. His nose was covered in shiny sweat drops, he took measured steps and his gaze was earnest. Just as Pichín was finishing his dance, Ariel and Selene hugged each other tight for a good while.

"You coming with me to grandma's house?" Ariel asked.

"Yes, let's go," she said, "but just give me a moment, I need to talk to Chuy." She went then around the circled audience to the spot where the other boy stood.

"What's up, Chuy?"

"Huh, just hanging out, Selenita, keeping cool and all," he answered, with his eyes sweeping the floor just to end up staring at a girl nearby, and then fleetingly returning to Selene's face. The kid seemed rather anxious.

"Listen, Chuy, I need you to be a good guy and give me a hand, but it's got to be right now, you hear? I need you to go see Horacio and tell him there's something I have to talk about with him, something urgent." She could have said very urgent but held back, to bring her urge down a notch and keep the boy from suspecting something wasn't quite right.

"A'right, I can do that okay, 'n right away as you say, just lemme ask Omar to go do the thing with me."

"No, you better go alone, Chuy, and try not to share this with anyone. I'll be over at Felipe's parents. You bring Horacio with you and wait for me by the beach. When you two get there, whistle long and hard so I can go meet him. Got it?"

Selene went back to where Ariel was waiting for her. Seeing him empty-handed now: "Hey Ariel, where's your headdress, where's the mask?" she asked.

"Oh, I gave those to Omar," he said. "He'll take 'em back to school for me."

Then they held hands and took off walking against the current of the human river that flooded the street. With every few steps they took, some new voice was heard: "*Ayo*, Selene! So, where's Felipe?" And she waved a hand to return the greeting with the warmest smile her lips could sketch.

Turning her attention to Ariel, she asked now, "Ah, but what about your costume, didn't you have to take it back to school too?"

"No, tomorrow will be fine," the boy answered, letting go of his stepmother's hand so he could put his arm around her waist; and she placed hers over his shoulders. Ariel then covered that hand of Selene's with his, and she brought her free one down to her hip to cover the kid's in turn. Thus tightly bonded, they went on walking unhurriedly towards his grandparents' home. But Ariel was quick to notice how difficult it had become for Selene to walk: "Oh, look how swollen your foot's gotten, *eihaba*! It don't look good, you're even limping, Selene."

"Yes, sweetheart, it's kind of swollen, but only because I've done a lot of walking. Tell the truth, though, it does hurt a bit." Good thing was they'd reached the house by then.

As soon as they climbed the steps to the porch, "You sit down right here," the child commanded while pushing a bench towards her, and walked away concluding: "I'll go get some *ail*."

Selene did as she was told and lifted her foot over the bench. The boy rushed into the kitchen – a thatched roof cabin made out of wild canes that stood in the middle of the yard – and ran back out holding a garlic bulb in one hand and a knife in the other. He pulled off a clove, peeled it and then paused, thinking. "... We're gonna need a rag," he mumbled now and walked into the house, only to come back a moment later bringing a piece of cloth, out of which he proceeded to cut a strip with the knife. He let the rest of the rag fall on the floor, placed the garlic clove on top and used the knife handle to crush it, ending up with a thick poultice that he placed over the crescent moon that framed Selene's ankle bone. To keep the thing in place, he bandaged the foot with the strip he'd cut off the rag. Mutely watching the child as he so attentively looked after her, Selene felt furtive tears rolling down her cheeks – rivulets of warm water that fell on Ariel's arm.

"What is it, Selene, does it hurt so much?" he wondered, with his eyes two black cherries floating on blue-white orbs looking up at her.

"Just a little, love, but it will pass."

"You go rest in my room, Selene," said the boy while folding what was left of the rag.

"But what about Gramps, and Doña Chola?" she asked him.

"The old man is asleep. He left home early this morning to get his drinks," Ariel put her at ease, "and Grandma must be still out there with the Virgin; I saw her in the street a while ago." Then he got up and offered Selene his shoulder to lean on.

The heat was bottled up in Ariel's room. At that time, with noon just past, not even a whiff of breeze came through the window that faced the beach. Selene laid down on one of the twin beds and was about to fall asleep when the boy came in, stepping gingerly. He was doing his best not to rattle her while hanging the flower-printed dress he'd just taken off on the wood post that served as a coat rack, when his step-mom opened her eyes.

"Stay here with me, Ariel, if you feel like it, dear. I don't think I'm going to sleep right now." Selene didn't want to be away from the boy, now that they'd just gotten back together again; besides, she had to be ready for Horacio and Chuy who could be showing up any moment now. Pleased to be invited, Ariel pulled out of his backpack the CD player that she had given him for his latest birthday; he turned it on and went to snuggle by her side like a kitten looking to be fondled; Selene started caressing his hair. The first violin chords of Biber's Passacaglia began flowing through the speaker: spiralling progressions traveling upwards and downwards in circular motions, reaching out in search of untold extremes and overflowing the score to the point of dissonance. Heinrich Franz von Biber, which was a name Ariel had always found amusing. And yet Selene could see how the peach fuzz on the boy's cheeks stood on end during those moments when the chords got teared up almost as they would with a mariachi's violin.

"You know something, Selene? I don't know why, but that music always makes me feel like I have a lump in my throat," the boy confessed. She pressed his shoulder to let him know it was a feeling they both shared. Choked with emotion into silent tears, they kept listening as the violin soared beyond reason. Music had been a big part of Selene's campaign to expand Ariel's horizons. They also watched films and read books in their laptop computer. She had read to him, among many tales, a novella written by some gringo that once lived in Cuba, a story about an old fisherman who, alone on the high seas, did battle with a giant fish.

She had endeavored to instil a sense of respect for every living thing in her boy and his friends, and never stopped confiscating slingshots.

There was, too, the day Ariel and Selene visited a church where a crucified Jesus hung over the altar. "Oh boy, what happened to him, did he get shot?" Ariel asked, in awe. So she told him all about the crucifixion, and how it was that, just as it had been with Jesus, many others have been crucified just because they defended the rights of the poor; till she ended up letting herself go and telling him the story of Che Guevara – something that blew the boy's mind and got him dreaming about going to Cuba to visit the Museo de la Revolución and checking out the tank that first entered Havana carrying a gleeful bunch of rebels at the end of their March to Victory; the legendary ship Granma; the weapons and the life-size plaster figures of the battle-proven *compañeros* Che, Fidel and Camilo, just as he had seen them in Selene's photo album.

Biber's violin was still weaving and unraveling sound garlands that crowded the room before fleeing through the window to placate the afternoon's sweltering heat with their refreshing mantle. But then, as if coming from nowhere, new dissonant notes started breaking through in a crescendo. Somehow it felt like the violin chords were melting and turning into shrieks. It took a few seconds for Selene and Ariel to become aware of a hullabaloo going on out on the patio.

The Fifth Sacrifice

Selene lifted her head from the pillow and Ariel detached his ear from her ribs, where he had made his haven. The two of them jumped off the bed at the same time, and it took just a second for both to go join a noisy crowd that had gathered by their doorstep. Everyone's gaze was fearfully fixed on the branches of the orange tree that stood next to the doorway. As they stepped out, the woman and the boy could see nothing at first. It was Ariel who eventually saw it. One could hardly recognize the brown and black markings of a slithery body through the tree branches – until the animal's head came into view when its forked tongue darted out with a long hiss. That's when Selene finally saw it, froze on the spot and thoughts suddenly stopped flowing through her mind. The Fer-de-lance viper wrapped around a branch of the orange tree had hypnotized her, just as snakes always did.

"We gotta chop off all the bushes 'round here, get rid a them all right away, I say: these damn critters is never alone, always roam around in couples," sentenced Felipe's father Don Joaquín, who'd been awakened from his nap by the crowd's noise, and was now trying to make himself heard over the racket right outside his home.

"True that, but we gotta kill this one first," another voice chimed in.

Some among the women just stood still and

stared agape, mesmerized as did Selene; others were crying along with their spooked children. Ariel's grandma, Doña Chola, who'd caught wind of the news as she was having coffee with a neighbor, rushed back home once she got the full report. The old lady pushed her way through the crowd and, wielding a long stick she'd picked up on her way, came to stand by her doorway like a sentry, on account of the deadly animal but also out of mistrust for folk in the neighborhood.

When the outcry brought on by the alarm started quieting down, several young guys armed with canes surrounded the orange tree while figuring their chances, but couldn't agree on how to handle the threat. Then, sending warm waves through Selene's body, a firm voice rang out prevailing over the whimpers and the murmurs:

"What's going on?" Felipe spoke out as he broke through the circle already unsheathing his machete, as right behind him Ángel came holding his in hand.

"Not with the machete, my son, don't do it with your machete!" his father shouted from the doorway of the house where he was still standing. "If you cut that mean old critter's head, it's gonna jump at you, Felipe," he went on, and ordered: "Use a stick – wooden stick will do it, son."

"Yah mon, a stick, you kill da fucker with a stick," someone echoed the command from somewhere in the crowd.

"No way you can do that with just a stick – you kiddin', bro? Gotta be done with a sharp machete, that's how you do it!" another voice broke in. And right away as if on cue, all the men got to screaming and shouting, many of them with blood-shot eyes and voices muddled by the hooch they were drinking, as they had already started celebrating Christmas, something that's done in Redención beginning with the Day of the Black Virgin, December the twelfth.

Then again, since the Fer-de-lance was floating in mid-air, so to speak, there was no way you could approach the poison-laden serpent and smash its head with a stick. So, with machete raised, and Angel covering his back, Felipe leapt into the air with a mountain lion's sharp spring and in a single blow chopped off the viper's head, just as it was about to once again wrap itself around a tree branch.

Seeing how a thick, garnet colored blob popped from the animal's neck and fell down heavily on the sand at the foot of the orange tree, everyone went silent for just an instant. But it didn't take long for the chitchat, the anecdotes and relieved laughter to get going. Don Joaquín, skipping along on his crutches because he hadn't had the time to put on his pegleg, went and sat on the porch next to his wife, still insisting that it was urgent to chop down the bushes in every corner of the hamlet; but nobody paid any mind to his entreaties.

Ángel and Felipe started pulling the serpent's limp body off the tree. Stunned at seeing those two together now, Selene was watching their moves when something made her turn her eyes to the opposite side of the street. Side by side with Chuy, Horacio was perched on the balustrade of the porch in the house across from her: from that higher position he could take in everything that was happening, and in full detail. Just as everybody else, Chuy still looked startled; but you could glimpse a half-smile floating in Horacio's face: it looked as though what he was witnessing stood as clear proof of something he had been expecting all along. Sharply focused now on Ángel and Felipe, the healer's eyes kept following their every move, as they finished untangling the snake from the branches.

The beast must have been two meters long and as thick as a man's forearm. Once done bringing it down, the two men took off for the beach holding the corpse. Pichín, who was still wearing his Warrior Dancer dress, followed in their wake along with a bunch of pumped kids that kept jumping and bouncing off each other, trying to get a better, closer look at the critter. Ariel left Selene's side and took off running, while Chuy, driven by the urge to check out the carcass, also joined his friends on the beach, putting aside his curious need to find out what it was that Selene had to tell Horacio.

As the crowd grew thin, Selene went across the street and approached the healer. While covering the short distance that separated them, she decided that, after all, there was no point in telling the man anything about the scene that had transpired in The Bush not that long ago – the reason why she'd asked Chuy to bring him over.

Horacio, holding a black book in his hand, was the first to speak: "You don't know how glad I am, Selene, that you called for me to come and see the whole thing go down; if not for you, I would have missed it."

"Horacio, really," she cried out, surprised, "how could I have known that this was going to happen when I sent Chuy to look for you?"

At that, the healer responded with a simple nod, followed by a hand gesture inviting her to go join the now small gathering of people that stood under a palm tree around the body of the deceased Fer-de-lance. It was mostly men, as the women had come together in their own group a few steps away, where, all at once and out-shouting each other, they shared hair-raising anecdotes of their encounters with such deadly reptiles.

"We better bury the head, otherwise the cursed thing's gonna come back alive," said one of the men.

"No no, we burn the body, that works best," another one volunteered.

"Good Lord, for as long as I've been alive, none of these beasts ever came around so close," moaned a woman in her eighties.

"I'll go get the shovel," Felipe told Ángel, and sliced his way through the gathering. That's when he saw Selene with Horacio standing next to her. He joined them and put his arm around her shoulders, acting as if nothing of consequence had happened between them that day. After exchanging greetings with Horacio, he dove deep into Selene's eyes with his proverbial X-Ray gaze.

"Are you okay?" he asked.

"*Aha*," she answered, not wanting to let him see how much warmth his closeness brought into her soul; how he still made her feel safe, no matter what; how much she loved him, after all was said and done.

"It'll be good if you bury the viper in The Bush, not on the beach," Horacio said, and then, with the clear authority he always projected in spite of his gentle, twangy voice: "When you're done with that job, Felipe, I need you to get the family together; I've got to talk to you all."

"Aright, consider it done. Right now I hafta go get the shovel, though," Felipe said as he started on his way toward his parents' house. He was just about to reach the porch and say hello to Doña Chola when Horacio called out to him again: "Ángel's gotta be present there too, you hear?"

The human swarm that had re-grouped lined up now in a procession behind Felipe, Ángel and the serpent they were carrying in a sack. The crowd crossed the street and disappeared in an alleyway that led to The Bush. Selene, Horacio and Doña Chola stayed on the porch listening to don Joaquín's stories of run-ins he'd had with serpents throughout his life. He even shared a yarn about a viper that, according to those in the know, made its home in The Bush and turned into a woman that bewitched men when the red moon arose in the sky at year's end.

Once the group that had been at the serpent's burial came back, people started gradually disbanding. The men – all of them and one by one – came over to say good bye to Felipe: a good handshake followed by a fist on the chest, right over the heart, all of which meant *you're my brother*. The women, keeping their distance, waved bye-bye to him openly blushing. Then, as they went by, the children shouted, "Adiós, uncle!"

Following the sun as it fell into the sea, the bustle in the Flinns' yard slowly died away. Only then did the family retreat into the house, spotless as per usual. "Anywhere people see garbage, that's where they go throw their own," the mistress of the house used to say. "That be the reason why I keep me home always real clean, so they show respect." Well, that is, even if by then her house lacked a ceiling, and one could see the rafters that supported the tin plates above, along with all the power lines, whereas some time ago only a handful of electric wires peeked through little holes in the ceiling's pressed cardboard. Felipe had told his mum he could patch it up, but Doña Chola would have none of that: "What you do just for the time being stays the same forever; I want me a ceiling that's done good 'n proper." That was her reasoning, and so she'd chosen a life lived face to face with decay rather than one surrounded by things not well done. So then, proud as he was, her son had given up on trying.

Taking up the whole sofa were: Selene, with her dress for daily errands, her bandaged foot and her face as pale as a phantom's; next to her Ariel, chasing away mosquitoes with the red bandana he'd worn on his head for the warrior dance; and Doña Chola with her Sundays' best outfit and her fine, carefully braided hair, because the commotion had occurred right in the middle of the day's celebration for the Virgen de Guadalupe. She was the spitting image of her mother, Amada, just as Selene had imagined that woman while listening to Hati's narration the day before. Felipe – his eyes sunken, wearing the same clothes he'd put on two days ago, and with mud-covered feet because he'd walked barefoot from The Bush to the hamlet – went to sit atop a barrel with his legs crossed yogi-like. The vehemence of his gaze was at odds with the exhaustion that oozed through the furrows on his face, making him look much older than he was. Selene even noticed a couple of new white hairs standing out on his beard.

Now wearing his fresh-pressed white shirt, just for the fiesta, Ángel sat on one of the two armchairs, unable to hide his excitement as the blood rushed to his cheeks. Don Joaquín took the other armchair, which by then was missing one of its arms. Horacio – surprisingly so – had come in with a two-day beard and shirt untucked, only because he was working his garden when Chuy went looking for him. He leaned against the wooden table that had replaced the mahogany dining set. And then, having arrived in her master's footsteps, Sombra took advantage of the reigning confusion to sneak into the house – made off-limits to her by Doña Chola – and was curled up at Selene and Ariel's feet.

It wasn't long before the house turned into a steam bath, even though it was spacious, with its royal-palm walls and tinplate roof; and the silence got to be so thick that not even the tip of a knife could cut through it.

"My brothers, sisters," Horacio brought the gathering to attention without further ado: "I've had you all come here because it's done happen that the fifth sacrifice got carried out today. The spell that had been haunting our brother Felipe got broken today."

Whoever had a handkerchief pulled it out to wipe the sweat away. There was a bit of throat clearing somewhere. Then the healer opened the black book he'd been carrying all along – a book without any inscriptions on its cover, nothing but a tiny golden cross engraved on its spine – and he read from it out loud:

"... Then I saw in the right hand of him that sat on the throne a book with writing on both sides and sealed with seven seals. And I saw a mighty angel proclaiming with a loud voice: 'Who is worthy to break the seals and open the scroll?' But no one in heaven or on earth or under the earth could open the scroll or look inside it. I wept much because no one was found to be worthy to open the scroll or look inside. Then one of the elders said to me, 'Weep not! See, the Lion of the Tribe of Judah, the root of David, has triumphed: he is able to open the scroll and its seven seals.' Then I saw a Lamb, looking as if it had been slain, resting in the centre of the throne, encircled by the four living creatures and the twenty-four elders. He had seven horns and seven eyes, which are the seven Spirits of God sent into the earth. He came and took the scroll from the right hand of him that sat upon the throne. And when he had taken it, the four living creatures and the elders fell down before the Lamb. Each one had a harp and they were holding golden vials full of incense, which are the prayers of the saints. And they sang a new song, saying: 'You are worthy to take the scroll and to open its seals, because you were slain, and with your blood you redeemed men for God from every tribe and language and people and nation.' "

He started talking then about many-colored horses and dragons running across burning skies at full gallop, plagues and furies too.

Petrified by Horacio's conjuration – the visions of Saint John, a hallucination-ridden prisoner in Patmos, according to some, and a holy man according to others – Ariel slid his hand from Selene's forearm down to her fingers and latched on to her. Felipe and his mother kept their eyes fixed on the healer. Shining with the glare borne of someone who has just fought a battle – or of a madman or an enlightened being – Felipe's gaze seemed to suffuse Horacio's words with understanding. Much unlike her son – with her eyes crouched deep in their sockets and filled to the bone with mistrust – Doña Chola kept staring darkly at the medicine man. Just like most people in town, the old lady had never felt at ease around that man Horacio. She had never embraced the Christian faith either. "There's no way you gonna make me believe in one single God," she'd say. "How is it possible for a single God to declare that he loves his children to no end, and at the same time he's capable of allowing so much evil?" Doña Chola would never turn her back on the faith of her ancestors, and she protested that all those pastors with flashy, brand-new cars and dubious morals had brought the Bible to the hamlet only to bamboozle the people, to rob them and take their land. Not that Horacio could be mixed up with any of those, far from it. The healer practiced his own blend of Christian beliefs and the ancestral cult.

Ángel listened from his own corner, eyes closed, his gaze turned inwards and his placid forehead beaming glimpses of devotion. Then, concerned and severe, with his eyes fixed on the absent foot, there was Don Joaquín listening intently to the portents that presaged the end of the world, wondering what did all of that have to do with his son, and expecting to hear some word that would solve the mystery for him. All this time, the spooked eyes of the child Ariel kept jumping from face to face and always returning to plunge into Selene's, over and over replicating that journey as though playing the notes on a stave that marked a recurring beat: quaver, quaver, quaver, quaver, quaver, semibreve.

Selene sensed herself afloat, with her head somehow suspended amidst cotton clouds; her mind was blurred; it all felt as though she'd just been on a very long journey. The scene with Felipe and the contraband in the farm showed up abruptly in her head, and yet it seemed so distant. At the moment she felt nothing but tenderness for that man who was now shedding an almost mystical light. She wished she could rinse the mud off his feet and then wrap him in clean sheets. But at the same time she realized something had changed in her love for the man: Selene didn't need him anymore. She saw herself at peace, whole, a self-contained being: it was a feeling she hadn't experienced since the time she fell in love with him.

Closing the black book now, Horacio continued with his thread: "Starting from this day, Felipe – and you too, brothers, sisters – you all got nothing to fear no more, and that's because God has taken us in his hands, so everything will be as it should be and whatever falls will do so under its own weight. Just keep the faith, you all." He put the book aside and went on: "With this fifth sacrifice the circle has been broken. All things remain, endure and last until they stand resolved. Any place where blood has been shed, there's a spirit left imprisoned there; that place can be a house, a street corner, a bend in the river or the shoulders of one man. And so likewise, it's with a shedding of blood that we have undone the spell, the hex which led Felipe to replicate deeds that had been trapped in this space and this time, events that were destined to be repeated till the moment when someone came in to break the cycle."

At this stage Don Joaquín was already looking

downcast, because the more he heard Horacio speaking, the less he understood. Doña Chola, on the contrary, had picked up everything down to a tee, because she was always keeping watch over her son's affairs. The woman could tell when her Felipe was lying, she knew when he was in trouble, what he felt and everything he was capable of doing. So, when the scandal on account of Ángel getting shot spread all over town, right away she could make out what was true and what was not with the many versions of the story that were going around.

There was no place for Felipe to hide when facing his mother, who loved him with the same sort of savage love that she showed with all her brood, be it by beatings or with caresses. And being her only male child, Felipe was the one most often at the receiving end of Doña Chola's iron-fisted crackdowns: "That's so they learn what it takes to live and survive in this world," she'd argue when her husband disapproved her caning the kids even when they were asleep. "You wait and see," she'd yell at Felipe and his sisters when they went into hiding after making mischief: "if I can't catch you now, I'll get you just as well when you be sleeping."

And so it was that the day a neighbor came to tell her how Ángel had been taken to hospital with a gun wound in his gut, Doña Chola had the whole thing figured out in seconds, just as if she'd seen it herself. Then all those weeks that Felipe went unseen after the incident, and through Selene's diligent comings and goings, she prayed nonstop for her mother's spirit to protect her grandchild. In a cosy corner of the house, she set up an altar in honor of Amada, and served her favorite dishes on it every single day. She filled two pipes with tobacco when afternoons came, placed one on the altar before her mother's portrait and lit the other to smoke it herself, then remained puffing away till nightfall, pleading for her son. But she never spoke about it with Don Joaquín, who kept saying that the people blaming his boy for the shooting were just a bunch of slanderers driven by envy. "If the guy who got hurt says it wasn't Felipe who done it, then gentlemen, it wasn't my Felipe, period," he argued over and over.

Then out of the blue, Ángel joined the conversation, anxious: "There's something I need to say, y'all. ... So today, when all of us who've come together here, we have nothing but love for this man Felipe, me brother ..." And now his words started running over each other as though in a hurry to reach their destination: "Jesus, everything that happened, it was all my fault, it was. Let me tell you, see? When I got to Redención a couple years ago, I was just looking for a place to hide because I'd killed a man, an innocent soul that owed me nothing, really – because, at the end a the day, nobody owes nobody nothing." At that point, his usually cheerful eyes started glimmering like fishbowls with the tears that had built up inside but still refused to burst out. Then his voice took a turn, as if he'd gotten something stuck in his gully: "That night, when Felipe came looking for me with his nine millimeter, he didn't know it was me he was going after. In his mind he was looking for an Indian guy who had these chickens that were ruining his crops, and all he wanted was to give 'im a scare. But when he went to the bar with that gun, the Indian had left already, so it was then that his wiring went weird and he came over to my place. So he finds me talking to the deceased, and that killed man is telling me my time is soon approaching, that a bullet with my name on it is coming soon: 'It's gonna catch you unawares, you somabitch, just like you done caught me.' That's what he was telling me, the man I killed, when I heard Felipe's voice at the door." And now tears finally started flowing. He went for the end of his confession as fast as he could and before his throat got closed all the way. "From then on the only thing I can remember is how I saw the dead man's face looking at me over Felipe's shoulder at the very moment when the first shot rang out."

Felipe had never heard any of that, and neither had Selene and Horacio. In their eyes, Ángel had never been anything but a sweet man. Selene tried to imagine a killer Ángel but found it impossible.

Horacio jumped in, forceful: "Brothers, sisters, we're seeing here how it is that the fates of two men came together just because they had to; there was no need for an appointment or a plan, no sir. And then it's fate again that brought them together this afternoon, so the two of them together could behead the viper on the orange tree out there. And it was through Selene that the guardian spirits of both these men were called to action. That's because, you see, spirits take command over those touched by love whose hearts are open while their intellects grow weak. It's only when an infatuation reaches the point when it becomes Love that heart and intellect start working in harmony and the will is made strong; yet through it all the lovers can't help but go about as if possessed, because they are. Today peace has returned to us and with it the superior will that is called Love, which is in truth the fate that rules us humans ..."

The healer cleared his throat, now flooded with emotion, and kept going: "I feel so honored today for having had the chance to be witness and servant in the ways of Love, those paths that – even as they turn intricate at times – are there to lead us to fulfil our destinies."

He pressed his nose bone between thumb and index finger and retreated into his own thoughts for a moment, then said, "This session is over. Let's just remember that our fates are circular and have no end; they may run parallel for a while, or cross each other now and then as roads do, only to keep going on their spiral and perpetual journey. My sisters, my brothers, let us find our way in freedom."

The first breeze of the day arrived in darkness and entered the house through the window facing the patio. As the gathering stirred now, it sounded like a rustling of leaves. Felipe jumped off the barrel where he'd been sitting and helped his father prop himself up on the crutches. Everybody got on their feet, stretching and smoothing clothes, loosening stiff joints, and started sharing farewells; they kept their words to a minimum and their voices down. Selene stayed on the sofa, playing with Ariel's curls as he slept peacefully on her lap. Felipe kissed the foreheads of both his parents before they moved on into their bedroom. It was time to say good bye to Ángel then: a quick embrace followed by the ritual of touching each other's fists and then thumping one's chest; he turned next to Horacio, stretched his hand and expressed his gratitude feelingly: "*Seremein, seremein, teinki*, me brother."

With all visitors gone now, he closed the main door which, being a big and heavy wooden thing with its hinges all beat up, let out a long groaning sigh as it got dragged across the floor. Then he went and sat next to Selene, telling her, "All that load we had stashed in the farm, it's no longer there, aright?"

"Yeah right, actually, I saw it passing by the beach," she responded, covering his lips with her hand. Ah, the woman that used to drive him crazy questioning all he did and requiring explanations, she no longer needed any of that. Felipe kissed the palm of her hand and she returned his kiss with a caress of her own. He got up then and lifted Ariel into his arms to take him to his bedroom.

Selene fell asleep the moment she stretched herself over the sofa. In her dreams she saw a gigantic serpent slithering its way down the beach and, as the monster moved forward, it left behind a dried out and wrinkled skin laying on the sand. The novel creature that emerged from that animal's jaws had a smooth, pearly skin that radiated iridescent colors – the same tones and shades that now flowed over Selene's skin, along with an exquisitely pleasurable sensation. When the early morning coolness awoke her fully, she had already spent time arranging and rearranging words between her conscious and her dream states. She then tried to snatch a verse that had been taking shape between her dreams, but it vanished when her foot started throbbing and her knee was stabbed with pain. She limped her way into Ariel's room.

Set on the table, there was a votive candle that cast a dim little light. You could barely make out in semi-darkness the ebb and flow of Ariel and Felipe's breathing under the covers. Felipe had hung his necklace from the lamp on the ceiling: the seashell nestled in its net was a talisman protecting them. Selene stepped out of the room and opened the main door making sure she lifted the thing while pulling on it to make as little noise as possible. Once outside, through the kitchen's cane walls she saw the flickering light of a candle moving around. She found Doña Chola laying firewood on the mud stove.

"Good day, Selene," said Felipe's mother without turning to watch her come in. "We're gonna make some *adulu* here to chase away the cold, seeing as to how there's bad weather coming once again."

Selene had already suffered the effects of the changed weather in her bones: the pulsations on the wound in her foot and in her knee had come together into one single, unceasing and pigheaded torment. She dragged her feet back and forth across the kitchen to bring to the table the coconut oil, the cinnamon, the flour, the other ingredients and utensils needed to prepare the thin porridge called *adulu*. Doña Chola got the fire going and turned to Selene: "You sit down now, I'll take care of the rest. And that foot of yours, soon we'll get it healed, I have the thing for it. But right now there's something I need to tell you."

Heeding the old lady's command, Selene went and sat on the bench closest to the stove. Sombra, who had not left her side since the day before, let herself down by her feet. With her attention hanging on the silent pause that followed, the harutu woman held her breath until Doña Chola spoke at last: "Got a letter from Ariel's mother in New York."

Selene instantly knew what that meant, and right

away a thick gloom took over the kitchen as the old lady continued: "The papers are ready for the boy to go up there." She kept silent for a moment then to examine Selene's face, which was now twitching as if she had sucked on a lemon. As soon as she could finally swallow the knot that had gotten stuck in her throat, the white woman said:

"Oh, that's really curious, Doña Chola: you see now, I was just about to take Ariel to his aunt's house because, well, I'm leaving too."

Selene took a pause, expecting some reaction from Ariel's grandma, but the woman didn't flinch: it was as if she already knew everything the outsider was telling her. Nonetheless, Selene went on: "But oh God, now that letting go of him is no longer something for me to decide, it hurts so much that it's like my guts are being torn right out of me." That final phrase was all but choked in her throat.

"Yes, I can imagine," said Felipe's mother, "but it's all for the better."

"Yes, of course, I know that too," Selene was quick to respond, lest the old lady think that she could make it hard for Ariel to leave.

"You know something, Selene?" the Doña chipped in: "Ariel is really lucky that he can go legal, bless his soul. Just look at those other kids getting ready to take the trip by land right about now..."

Selene peeled her eyes, in shock: she knew nothing about any boys in town planning to go north as wetbacks. "Who are they?" she asked.

"Well girl, I would of thought you'd heard about it; everyone in town knows what they're up to; it's a group from right here in our barrio, and they've already found a coyote to get them across the border. That kid Chuy is one of them taking off."

"What's that you're saying?" Selene jumped off the bench like a spring set loose, and wincing as a sharp sting shot up her leg like an electric shock. "How can that be?" she protested again, wishing her ears were betraying her and yet knowing all too well that the old lady was being truthful. "But that's dangerous as hell, Doña Chola!" she cried out, at her wit's end. "Do you know how many people die on the road to go cross the border into the United States without a visa?" Her heart was pumping wild as she limped this way and that while Doña Chola was busy at the table mixing milk and cinnamon and measuring the flour for the *adulu*.

Selene insisted: "If those boys don't end up falling off the roof of a train named the beast that goes through Mexico loaded with hopeless souls, they take to the highway on foot only to get kidnapped for ransom or massacred by the drug cartels. Then if they get lucky and make it to the border, there's just a few that get to sneak across the río Bravo into the other side. Far too many get busted by the migra, held in cages, separated from their families, humiliated and put down till they're finally sent back in chains to their homelands with their meagre belongings in a plastic bag, and poorer than they were on departing because the coyotes took the whole family's life savings. And what for in the end? There's just one or two that make it through and get to send a few dollars back home…"

Selene wasn't even aware of how loud her voice had gotten, but there was no way she could stop. "I just can't accept it, Doña Chola, that migrating should be the only option left for this village that's going to end up downright deserted! What do you think is going to happen when all the young people have left home and the future's gone with them?"

She had an urge to rush over to Chuy's house and talk to that boy, to convince him not to leave. It dawned on her then why it was that the teenager had appeared so nervous when she saw him the day before, so much that he couldn't look her in the eye. But she knew as well that there was nothing she could offer him in exchange for that mad dream of his.

Doña Chola talked Selene off her plan: "Them boys are already under the coyote's wings; you can't see them no more. So listen here, Selene, what you gotta do right now is stop putting your leg through calvary, settle down, sit quiet for a moment," she ordered now and kept going: "There's nothing for those kids in this village, if they can find a way to get out, they do it. They don't mind risking death when all they need and want is to find a better life for themselves," she concluded with a final tone, like someone plainly stating a fact of life.

"But that's just the thing that gets my blood boiling, Doña Chola. It makes me so mad that I see red." Selene shot back, with that passionate drive that seemed so amusing to the folk in Redención, where no one lost sleep over things that were unavoidable in this world. "Consider this, Doña" she kept going, "if one day the *gringos* decided to open their border, this whole continent would be left empty of people. It doesn't seem fair to me that the only option these boys have for improving their lives is migrating *al Norte*."

And now Selene's imagination came up with an even darker notion: "And the ones that make it in through legal means, like Ariel – because their parents left before them and after many a year became *gringos* with the right to have their children join them and get their green card or become citizens – well, those kids are the first to be sent to fight the wars that the United States keep starting everywhere. Those black boys, strong, in their youthful prime, they're cannon fodder, that's all they are ..."

When she saw that Doña Chola was no longer listening, Selene stopped her rant: the old lady had been focused all along on the mud stove while mixing coconut oil with the flour; now, as she started slowly adding milk to the mix, the Doña said: "It's getting lumpy now, this *adulu* better come out right..." she took a sip and laughed, pleased. "We got us some tasty *blanket lifter* here, girl!" Her *adulu* had gotten that name because of its power to spur passion. Doña Chola poured the drink in two cups with a ladle and pulled a chair close to the stove. With cups nested in their hands, the two women let their eyes rest on the fire, their souls and bodies warming up.

Selene had her first taste: dense and sweet; and as she kept drinking, the blended aromas of coconut and cinnamon allayed her anxiety. She closed her eyes and her thoughts went to Ariel and Felipe, sleeping lulled by that cool breeze that keeps eyelids and bed-sheets tight together. Ariel, oblivious to the fact that his life was about to undergo an absolute transformation, that in a matter of days he would be living amidst concrete and bricks in the Bronx, New York City, surrounded by people who spoke an alien language and drilled through by a coldness the likes of which he had never imagined could exist. Then Felipe: with his know-it-all character he had most likely recognized that the time for change couldn't be avoided, and so let sleep take over, exhausted, bowing down to his destiny, to the life that had found ways to keep him tied to Redención. There was no use: even when he'd tried to leave – on the occasion that the mother of his kids migrated and he took a chance at joining them – the man got caught at the border and was sent back home. It was his good fortune that Felipe was able to learn how to love his fisherman and land-tiller life, and he never stopped zealously loving his people. Him and The Bush were one single body; his blood ran through his veins in sync with the river waters and the sea tides. Leaving Redención would have been much like dying for him.

From the kitchen, the women heard Don Joaquín's uneven walking, with its long pauses in between steps, as he started moving things around in the bedroom. His wife got up and poured some *adulu* for her man. Then just as she was putting his cup on the table, the old man appeared on the threshold of the door.

Selene got up and let him take the bench. "Good morning, don Joaquín. I'll just go see if those two are still sleeping," she said and left the Flinns crouching in front of the fire, sipping their *adulu*.

It must have been seven in the morning and the sun was already shining bright, but Ariel's room was still dark, its blinds all closed still. Laying in bed, Felipe and Ariel were both motionless. When her eyes got used to the dimness, Selene noticed the absence of the seashell necklace that Felipe had left hanging from the ceiling lamp before going to sleep. She moved closer to the bed where Felipe should be, stretched her hand to stir him, and her heart sank as she realized that no one was there: the bed where he had gone to sleep was empty now. She felt as though the floor was being pulled from under her feet and her body went limp.

She hurried to the kitchen in spite of her hobble, and interrupted the conversation that the old couple had kept going since she left them: "Pardon, Doña Chola, have you seen Felipe?"

No, she had not seen him. Selene picked up the first stick she found on the yard ground, to use as a walking cane, and went out to the beach. Once there, she cast her sight far into the distance, looked in every direction, most of all toward the farmstead. On the beach – bookended by the twin mountains – there wasn't a single soul to be seen, not one single footprint. It was as if nothing had existed before that moment, only the sea and the sky, united by one grey tone alone: an infinite space like a blank page.

*

At the very moment her horizon faded and Selene fainted, falling softly on the sand, I knew I had to let go of her body. I was her soul and I was not ready to leave Redención. Not yet.

Paloma Zozaya Gorostiza

Finale

Wearing clothes that looked too big on her emaciated body and hung from her shoulders as though from a wire hanger, Selene crossed the great marble hall like an apparition. The weight of the small rucksack she carried on her back made her walk hunched over and with her head pointing forward as if urging her to move on. Her leg's condition had improved thanks to the days of forced rest she spent in the Flinns' house after losing consciousness on the beach, and her limp was barely noticeable now. Driven by a willpower that wasn't her own, and not really sure if everything around her was real or just a dream, she reached a check-in lane where airline clerks were beginning to settle down behind their counters without much of a hurry. Selene was the first passenger to arrive. She released the pack off her back, dropped it on the yellow line and, wary lest her bones be in no shape to keep her upright, she looked for something to prop herself up, to no avail. The scrawny and haggard woman about to take a plane was a very different Selene from the one who had arrived five years earlier, self-confident, full of spunk, and believing in a better world.

The airline agents were busy turning on computer terminals and chitchatting. No one acknowledged her presence. Some time went by before a young couple came to stand in line behind her. The woman – with rather thin blond hair and sporting Chanel flat shoes, fresh-pressed jeans – held a starched-up little girl in her arms. Not a single roundness in her being softened the apparent rigidity of that mother. Her haughty mien and dismissive demeanor marked the woman as one who could well be an heiress of one of the ten families that had turned the country into their private property. She used a close-to-perfect English when addressing her husband, no matter that the man didn't look foreign either. When the counters finally opened, the couple rushed over, ignoring the fact that Selene had been standing before them all along.

"Excuse me, Sir," Selene called the clerk's attention, trying to make herself heard even as her voice came out in a soft trickle. "I was the first to arrive, got here before them long ago, and Sir … I'm not feeling well." Looking embarrassed, the man behind the counter mumbled something incomprehensible and looked down. The woman with the Chanel shoes stuck her nose further up as if to fend off a foul smell and studied Selene from head to toes while pressing her lips which, being thin of their own, drew a cruel slash across her face.

"Look, I'm really sorry but, as you can see, we are first in line," she said, cocksure, stressing the phrase *we are first* as if that were an incontestable privilege of theirs.

Selene felt downright exposed under the scrutinizing gaze of that woman: yes, her clothes looked to be twice the size that would fit her; stains covered her fingernails, even after she had brushed and tried to get the dirt off them with a thorn from the orange tree; her hair and her skin were sunburnt, and dried out too, as a result of the chain smoking she'd fallen into; something like a threadbare aura seemed to be swaddling her.

In an attempt to appeal for something at least resembling human contact: "I'm a bit under the weather, *Señora*," said Selene; then, unwittingly perhaps, she extended a friendly hand.

"Stay away, don't you come near me, back off right now before I call the cops," the woman shot back. Her voice carried the tones that come naturally to those who are used to giving orders, it exuded the contempt that's only meant for the indigent, for the demented and the fallen: an amalgam of horror and disdain. She stretched her arm out to mark a halt, and as she did so the diamonds in her fingers stabbed the air like minute lightning bolts.

Having been schooled in the arts of survival, Selene could be as cunning as only the wretched of the earth can be, so she didn't respond, even as her insides were boiling with wrath and her immediate urge was to fight back, because she knew on whose side the authorities stand.

Seeing herself unarmed and defenceless at that moment, she realized that her compulsion to see the reverse of things had led her to fall into the underside, into that subterranean world where everything is seen from afar, from underneath, from the bottom up, from that abyss into which one can so easily fall when hungry, when spurred by anger, or emptied out – all things that can happen any time to anyone anywhere.

*

Not a single cloud broke into the blue of the sky. With one of its wings just about skimming the foothills of jungle-covered mountains, the airplane flew over a valley strewn with banana plots, cane fields and rusty huts; then it took a turn and, leaning left, offered one last look at the Caribbean sea with its sapphire-blue and light green patches to Selene, now curled up in her seat with her forehead pressed to the windowpane. Then one of her usual obsessive compulsive thoughts hijacked her mind: "If this plane were to fall into the sea right now, the children of Redención would find my body on the beach one day – something flung there by a wave – and my destiny would then come to its completion. Times without number I've ended up going back, without rhyme or reason, to that fate-bound place, to the circle wherefrom one cannot escape."

The aircraft circled the valley once again, casting its cross-shaped shadow over the mineral carpet. Selene pressed her head on the backrest of the seat and closed her eyes. She thought of Ariel, who would by then be in the frigid *Nueva York*. Her imagination flew to the little paper note folded underneath the insole of his shoe, in which Selene had written a phone number: "This will be just in case, you hear? Any time you want to, any time you need to, give me a call," she had told the kid before he got on his uncle's red car with blacked-out windows, which had arrived to drive him to the airport. Ariel took off his shoe and put in it the little paper scrap that Selene had pulled from her cleavage (a habit she'd learned from Coral).

"When my feet outgrow these shoes, I'll put

your number in the new ones," the boy said, and those words were the only farewell they needed. It was like they weren't saying "Adiós." No, it was not farewell in upper case, not a final good bye.

Selene's mind went then to Chuy – wherever that other kid might be roaming that day. A chill whipped her spine as she imagined him riding atop a train roof in the open, crushed in the midst of a hundred other migrants, or trekking across the same sierra she was flying over now. "Felipe is right," she thought, "we're all free to choose our destinies, but some have more freedom than others, and that's what makes people different: the options they have to choose from."

The airplane started gaining altitude as it approached recurring mountain strips: jungle-green over here, then sepia and lilac over where they'd been deforested. When the silhouettes of the Fire volcano and the Water volcano appeared on the horizon, Selene felt a knot in her throat and got goosebumps: "There, the guardians of my childhood, my grandparents who saw me grow up," she thought. "What have I got to show for myself before them now? What have I done?"

It dawned on her that her shoulders, her thighs, her arms were all hurting – felt as if her once slumbering body was beginning to wake up after a great exertion. "This is how newborns must feel," she thought now, "or fighters returning from war, or those who wander the earth in need of refuge." A sensation came over her that, thanks to the pain in each of its limbs, her body – lying on the seat as though disjointed, like a bag full of bones, a sack full of rusted metal – was becoming a unit again, whole again; and, for the first time since she left Redención, the shadow that had been haunting her like a shroud of guilt was lifted from her chest. Then she began to cry for herself as though crying for some other person: unfettered, with neither fanfare nor grimaces, her face free of contortions. Selene cried and cried until the dark, clinging sensation of defeat she'd been carrying till now started to finally let go of her.

"I come from the depths, las honduras. I have uncovered the dismembered bodies left in halls long forbidden. I reconstitute myself. There is a treasure that's mine: the soul of all the souls within me; a woman still unknown inside me, unique – with one leg white, the other black, one arm short and the other long, the head of a duck like the toys made by the children of Redención; this person who can say *I see, I feel, I am, this is as far as it goes, yes to this, no to that*: a figure that instils fear.

"Within me I carry all of Redención; Coral and Viola inside me; and Hati, and Doña Chola and her mother Amada; Ariel and Felipe I hold within me; everything I have lived since before I was born; my mother, my grandmothers. I am the final link and here the chain gets broken."

Now she remembers the lines that she'd put together while lost in a reverie one morning in the Flinns' house. Her eyelids closed like stage curtains coming down, and with her mind's eye Selene writes on the sand:

"Strands, we are strands running through the tapestry of encounters, reckonings and dilemmas that is life."

Once done, she fixes her gaze on the greedy sea as it licks the words and dissolves them with its effervescent liquid tongue.

Paloma Zozaya Gorostiza

Acknowledgements

I would like to express my deepest gratitude to Juan Julian Caicedo. The eleven months during which he worked on this translation, exploring the submerged landscapes and the lit up peaks of the story, were for me a wondrous journey.

To Julian Mackenzie, my husband, not only for his loving patience and support, but for accompanying Juan Julian and me, with his generous comments and invaluable editorial notes, through each step of the way during the time it took to realize this translation.

To Consuelo Rivera Fuentes, founder and director of Victorina Press, for her constant patience and her faith in me. For her passion about Bibliodiversity which has created the environment for us authors to thrive.

To Sophie Lloyd-Owen and Jorge Vasquez, who run the machinery of Victorina Press and without whom our books would not make it out into the world.

To Marco Varela for his kindness and invaluable help in locating the illustration for the book cover.

To Cultural Affairs of the Mexican Embassy in Great Britain, for their kind support and encouragement, for their open doors.